THE BOND

From somewhere, probably on the chair beside the bed, he produces his belt – black like a snake – and seizes my wrists. Without a fight, I let him draw my hands together and bind them. While he makes these preparations, he slows the fucking down, until I'm only getting short, quick pumps. When my arms are tied behind my back, something passes over my head and slides down my face. As it drops over my nose, I realise it's one of my stockings. It goes taut and pulls the side of my mouth back. Now I can only produce moans. Hank ties it around the back of my head and then grips my shoulders. He slips his cock out of my pussy and I feel it nudging upward.

THE BOND

Lindsay Gordon

This book is a work of fiction.
In real life, make sure you practise safe sex.

First published in 2000 by
Nexus
Thames Wharf Studios
Rainville Road
London W6 9HA

Typeset by TW Typesetting, Plymouth, Devon

Printed and bound by
Cox & Wyman Ltd, Reading, Berks

ISBN 0 352 33480 0

Part One
Mama's Little Monster

One

'You can love me if you don't look at me.'

'I do love you.'

'Yes, but keep your eyes closed when I'm this close. Please, don't look.' Hank's voice comes from a cold place inside him, travelling up his windpipe like a breeze chilled by stone. Some of Hank is still inside the voice, but only a sliver. His love has transformed too. When we love each other I tremble for the pain when he twists my limbs like a wrestler, and plumbs the depths inside me with the part of him I worship.

In the beginning, he was gentle.

When I was seventeen he used to read to me. After a day at high school, I'd crash at his place and he'd read to me. Reading his journals, he'd sit on a wooden chair, wearing a white vest that made his shoulders look brown as treacle sugar. Around his fine neck there was a silver chain made from little balls – a plug chain with his dog tags clinking at the end. Braces would hang from his waist like the straps on a guitar when idle. Loose black trousers covered his legs and were turned up at the hem above his broad feet. I remember his toes. Tiny copses of golden hair would shine in the bright Texas sun by which he read to me.

In this pose, with black-framed specs perched on his bumpy nose, he told me beautiful stories with his resonant voice. Deep as a well, dry as white sand, but tobacco-smoker wheezy, it suggested wisdom to me, and sadness also. There would be a short reading when this instrument of his voice made me shiver and then relax into what felt like taking a hot bath with a sleepy head. Then there would be love.

Soft kisses and caresses from his dry-palmed hands. A flick of his lizard tongue between my buttocks before it travelled up the stepping-stones of my spine to the base of my neck, where the fireworks live. Still as the white-faced lady in the painting in my grandmother's parlour, I would lie in silence. But my skin would move; changing into a universe of tiny bumps.

'Beautiful,' he'd whisper in a voice that made me think he was going to cry. Somewhere between his reading voice and his serious voice, where the last of Hank the child lives – a blond-haired boy standing next to my father on a photograph my mother kept in the kitchen.

Then I would feel the beast in him. Tensing up and taking quicker breaths, his lips would move down the back of my legs. Freshly shaven legs from my ankle to my knee, but left wild above. He liked my thigh hair, especially when he could see it through the pale shades of my nylons. And I made sure he saw lots of thigh.

His kisses would descend to my pink heels, where he would part his lips and place them on either side of my Achilles' tendon. Tracing his tongue across the soles of my feet, he'd taste what my nylons, socks, shoes and teenage sweat had left for him. His breathing would become ragged, following his tasting of my spicy feet, smooth leg skin, and the beef taste of my arse. Up the outside of my legs and body, the feathery touch of his fingers and thumbs would

4

sweep. Inhaling my hair, licking my neck, biting my shoulders, he grew into the beast. Rolling me over, he'd get busy with my nips and I'd tell him to be hard with them.

Once he'd brought tears to my eyes, his face would roam down to my belly, to scratch my tummy with his whiskers before it travelled to my thatch; nuzzle, lap, tickle, suck, tease, pull out the lips, lick them back into brown folds, circle the best bit with the tip of his tongue, then lap, lap, lap on the same spot until my sphincter went tight.

I'd close my eyes. Hank was always more vigorous when I didn't watch. My young startled eyes used to make him feel guilty because my dad was his best friend before and after the war with the Germans. I knew my eyes made him feel bad so I kept them shut tight. Then I'd hear the unzipping sound and know it wouldn't be long. Not long before the fucking. That's what I called it when he was up inside me and really going, because the sound of that word made him go faster and he would push my legs back and suck my toes.

It was madness through the afternoon until I ran home, grinning, to my supper. Lunacy on crumpled sheets. Sweating, spitting craziness with Uncle Hank in his plain room where the sunlight lit up the dust falling through the air. But now it's different. We're both older and love has to adapt to survive.

Now we do things differently. This morning, before we leave the motel and go further down the highway, I want my fill. Making sure my face is turned to one side, I grin with satisfaction, like I used to when just a girl and I had done something wrong. After all these years I can still manipulate him. I've never lost my magic.

'I'm not looking, Hank,' I say. 'And anyway, I think you're looking more distinguished these days.'

5

And he does; with a lean body gone all white, and his eyes looking like they've seen way too much, good and bad. Besides, for someone who's been alive for 73 years and has the looks and dexterity of a 30-year-old man, why is he complaining?

With a grip like handcuffs, he seizes my wrists and presses them into the mattress. Looming above me, his shadow covers my body and from the corner of my eye I can see his pale face and black eyes surveying the girl who will always be three things: seventeen, his damnation, and his own. Balancing his weight on the balls of his feet, he assumes the press-up position. Opening my legs, I form a five-pointed star with my feet, outstretched hands and tousled head forming the points. Slowly, he lowers himself to my body and I feel his hot breath on my neck. He sniffs around my throat and then tickles the outside of my ear with his tongue. 'Hard?' he asks.

'Mmm. But no bruises until tonight,' I instruct.

Leaning into one elbow he drops his face to my left breast and takes my nipple between his lips. Sucking hard, he draws the softness into his mouth, grating my skin across the tips of his front teeth. Saliva gathers around my nipple when his mouth moistens at the prospect of breakfast. Noisily, he pulls more of my breast into his mouth until his jaw is locked wide. Then, gently, he lets me slither from his mouth until my breast falls back to my chest where it quivers. I bite the sheets when his incisors clamp on my right nipple. Chewing it like a soft jelly, Hank breathes heavily through his nose and I cry out from the sting. Kicking out with my hot feet, I shove the white sheets down the bed until they tangle around my ankles.

Pushing himself up and away with his hands, his entire body rises into the air so only his toes still touch the mattress. In mid-air, he claps his hands and

I turn my head to see his teeth shine in the gloom above the bed. Falling down to me, he breaks his fall with his hands and comes to rest with his lips touching mine. I close my eyes and he says, 'Tongue.' Before my tongue is fully extended, he takes it and sucks it through his lips, pulling the muscle until I expect it to snap from out of my head. Moaning, he moves his face up and down, devouring my tongue, before his attentions move down to my musky pussy. All night she's been baking under the sheets and recovering from the hard time she had the day before. But Hank wakes her with his tongue. What a tongue he has. Longest tongue I've ever seen and it slides inside me, making me dewy in expectation of something bigger.

Lapping like a big hungry cat, he works me hard down there. Under my buttocks the sheets become damp from the pussy-honey I weep. Clenching my tummy muscles, I arch my back off the bed until the top of my head supports the weight of my upper body. First I bend my knees, then I kick my feet into the mattress, and finally I wrap them around his neck in case he thinks his mouth can leave without permission. Easing back on to my shoulders, I then lash my head from side to side and spit hair from out the side of my mouth. The end of his tongue beats my clit from side to side, as if it's slapping a prisoner silly. Then it flicks up and down and I know my chest has gone red from the turn-on, because I can feel hot patches burning like coals around my nips. Tiny lights flash on and off under my eyelids and I think I could faint. I can't feel my body any more – just the lightning he's put into my pussy.

As I come, he lifts my bottom off the bed and bends forward so the thick strawberry of his cock is touching my heat. Dipping it through my salty dew, he shimmies his hips from left to right and opens me with his meat. Thick meat on a bone that I want to die on.

'Fuck me!' I cry.

He slips the fat head inside and pauses.

'Fuck me!' I shriek, and outside our motel room I hear footsteps stop in the parking lot.

Another inch and he stops again.

'Bastard,' I whimper. 'You bastard,' I say, and dig my heels into his back to try and tug him all the way up.

But all he gives me is another inch.

'Son of a bitch,' I swear, and hit his face with a pillow.

'Just fuck –' but that's all I get out. Seizing my hips, he pushes into me. A long moan warbles at the back of my throat. I slap one of my feet on to his face, but he moves his head and clamps his teeth on the side of the foot. Banging his crotch forward, while yanking me on and off him at the same time, as the bed smashes into the wall, creaking and screaming like it's on fire.

Lifting one of my legs, he grips my calf and switches it from one side of his head to the other and I turn, instinctively, rolling on to my tummy. Doing me like a doggy, he thrusts in and out so hard that we make a noise like a big steak being slapped on a marble chopping block, over and over again. Grunting, I push myself to my knees so my weight will form a shock absorber for his pummelling. Even then, I'm shunted up the bed until I'm tasting motel wallpaper.

From somewhere, probably on the chair beside the bed, he produces his belt – black like a snake – and seizes my wrists. Without a fight, I let him draw my hands together and bind them. While he makes these

8

preparations, he slows the fucking down, until I'm only getting short, quick pumps. When my arms are tied behind my back, something passes over my head and slides down my face. As it drops over my nose, I realise it's one of my stockings. It goes taut and pulls the side of my mouth back. Now I can only produce moans. Hank ties it around the back of my head and then grips my shoulders. He slips his cock out of my pussy and I feel it nudging upward.

'No,' I try and shout, but he ignores me.

I thrash my head about and try to bite through the nylon in my mouth. If he goes in there real hard, I'll have to keep swapping from butt cheek to butt cheek in the car when we hit the road, and it could be a long journey. Hank laughs and I make a mental note to punish him later. Still, it's good. I love it in the ass. Especially when I can hear him greasing his pole with spit, but can't see him oiling up.

Ah, there it is. Screwing up my eyes and feeling my legs go weak, as he pushes inside me. On and on until I think I'm on the can, but this is passing motion in reverse. When his crispy floss tickles my cheeks, I know I have eight fat inches lodged inside me. He leaves it there and prolongs my joy at the splitting sensation. Clenching and unclenching the steel muscles of his fat cock, he works me subtly like he's massaging me from inside. I clench too, as much as I'm able to go tighter around him. Slowly, without moving in or out of my hot tunnel, he leans across my back and kisses my left cheek, which is wet with tears. 'Good?' he asks.

'Mmm,' I moan, and wiggle just a bit to renew the sensation that he's nailed into me. For a long time we sit there, squeezing each other with muscles we've trained like athletes; trained to pulse and ripple together when we're joined. One of his hands slips over my hips, disappears under me, and finds my pussy. Dipping my head, I open my eyes and watch his long fingers find my clit-pip.

As he rubs my puss with his fingertips, he thumps his cock softly through me and I start to croak. Soon, I have to close my eyes because it feels so good. When he rubs me to a climax, I start snuffling and sobbing into the pillow and I drum the top of my feet against the bed. As I lie waiting for the surf to stop rising and crashing in my head, he slips out of me and lets his fountain pitter patter over my bottom and back. One drop lands between my shoulder blades and goes cold after a glorious moment of warmth.

Sticky, and breathing like we've run a hundred metres and leaped over hurdles too, Hank and I lie against each other in bed. As my heart slows down, he unties my wrists and removes the stocking from my head. We smoke Winston reds from a crumpled packet by the bedside lamp. Sunlight has made the curtains orange. Outside someone walks away across the parking lot and then everything is quiet again.

'Clean yourself up, honey,' Hank says. 'Long drive today.'

'How close is he?' I ask.

Hank turns his head and stares at the inferno of the sun scorching the curtains. 'Hard to say.'

Two

'Where we going?' I ask.

'You'll see,' he answers.

'Why can't you tell me?'

'Surprise, darlin'.'

With a sigh, I sweep the cigarette packet off the dashboard and tap another smoke out. Beside me, I see Hank raise his eyebrow over the dark glasses he wears. I tap another smoke out. Both cigarettes hang from my lips, which I've just covered in red gloss, and I light them with his brass Zippo, rubbing the little US Marines inscription on the side with my thumb. For what feels like the zillionth time, I wonder why he won't talk about his work, but know that pushing him will result in a deeper silence.

I take his cigarette from my mouth and see the filter is stained red by my lips. As I lean across to put the smoke on Hank's bottom lip, he takes it from my fingertips with his front teeth and then rolls it around the front of his mouth, tasting my lipstick on the filter. Smiling, I turn away and continue to fix my hair. By the afternoon we should reach New Mexico, so I've dressed nice, looking forward to a sit-down meal and a few bars. Although I'm blonde I still keep it like Jackie O. Bit dated for '98, but Hank likes me to stay the way I looked when the magic began between us. My appearance makes me unusual and I like that. Pistachio coloured, cut just above the knee, and complemented by suede slingbacks and a white silk blouse, my suit makes me look like a movie star. Or at least Hank thinks so.

After we made love that morning, he watched me dress while he exercised on the floor. Sweating, he punched himself on and off the rough carpet tiles, doing press-ups on his knuckles. Not once did he take his eyes off me and I never even saw him blink. Although the blinds were still drawn, a band of light lit up the end of the bed where I perched to slip into my clothes. When I squeezed into my bra his exercising sped up. It's a long-line design and made from satin the colour of skin. Matching the bra, I used the girdle a nightclub owner bought me in Vegas. I like the way it feels firm on my tummy. Pinching my buttocks together, the girdle makes me aware of the pleasing tenderness inside my rear. Then I opened my last pair of nylons. The colour is called Sahara which has a kinship with my underwear, so I'm all co-ordinated under my suit. As I drew them up my legs, careful not to make a snag or ladder, I told Hank I needed more stockings. Slowing down with his press-ups, he nodded, and through his white shorts I could see he was excited again. From the shadows on the floor, I could feel him smiling at me, but I ignored him, remembering how he took my arse. Though I loved it, I wanted him to ache today, and he wasn't to spoil me now I was beginning to look so fine.

Two hours into our journey, we enter a small town and the car seems to brighten. Opening my window a little, I can see the place's promise. Wide, swept streets are bordered by colonial houses and big trees are rich with pink blossom. White fences gleam and the grass looks so green. Here and there sprinklers wet flowers. Reminded of home, I wind my window down further to take in the colours. The light is blinding. I squint behind my sunglasses and Hank shifts about on his seat. When we travel, the windows stay shut and the air conditioning keeps us cool, but occasionally I can't resist the outside. Sometimes the long wait for nightfall makes me impatient.

Hank pulls over by a grocery and asks me if I want anything.

'Cherry Coke, twinkies, and Marlboro menthol.'

Shaking his head in disapproval of my sweet tooth, he leaves the car and walks to the store. As he crosses the sidewalk, he pulls the collar of his overcoat up around his chin and dips his head. 'Flu,' he'll tell the store owner or anyone who gives him a funny look. Then they'll move away from his white face and hidden eyes. Works every time.

With my window open, I relax in my seat, close my eyes and enjoy the warmth of sunlight on my face. Won't do me much good, but my mama used to say a little bit of everything won't hurt anybody. Sensing a presence, I open my eyes and see a young man hanging around the front of the liquor store, two down from the grocery. Shuffling his feet, he takes quick peeks at my pretty blonde head and then looks away. There are times when a small-town Romeo is good for me; they keep me young, but their impatience and fumbling can irritate me. I always have to take control and end up feeling like a school marm. Sweet to the taste, though; they can be clean like fresh milk before they start getting liquored and smoking Camels or something. What I taste in a man is important to me; I can taste everything in them. This kid looks sweet, but when Hank comes out the store he's sure to go red and take off. Careful not to smile at him, because I don't want him coming over to spoil my sunshine and thoughts, I see a far more interesting citizen. For a moment I think I know her but when she gets closer, passing the slouching youth and heading for the grocery, I see it's just a passing resemblance to someone who left their mark on me, and I mine on them.

Late 30s, I'd say, with her glasses, sensible haircut that's brown and shoulder length, and smart black suit on her slim body, completed by low heels because she's conscious of her height. Divorcee, I guess, though it's possible she never married. What's important to me is her long, elegant nose and her thin mouth. Those features stimulate my recall of Mrs Hustvedt, the librarian in my home town. Like Mrs Hustvedt, this woman is preoccupied with something more important than what's going on around her. Bet she never smiles too. Men think she's haughty, kids think her a witch, and teenage boys stare but soon dip their eyes when she raises hers.

As she passes the car, she notices me looking and for a moment we hold a stare. When I smile by just moving my lips a little, like I do with a stranger in a bar when I want them to know I'm interested, she looks away, startled. Uncomfortable, but curious, she keeps walking but turns around for another peek before she enters the grocery. The windscreen and driver's window are tinted so she can only see my silhouette. From the position of my head she knows I'm still stalking her with my eyes, and I slip one hand out of the window to tap my lacquered fingernails on the roof of the car. Catching her attention with my long white fingers and blood-red nails, I then begin to rub my fingertips on the shiny roof. I do it slow, like I'm caressing the car; loving it and wanting it. For a moment the woman is mesmerised, but because the kid is still there, catching every subtle communication

14

between us, she slips inside the store. Too bad. Now my head is full of Mrs Hustvedt.

In '66, Hank came home from overseas with a tan like burned leather and a stare that went through everything and carried on for ever. Where he'd been no one knew, but he and my dad would talk for hours in the kitchen, drinking the sour mash Bourbon my mom hated to see in the house. It was at this time that Hank began to read to me in secret; it was helping him come to terms with wherever he'd just been, what he'd seen and what he'd done. When I wasn't with Hank, I spent a lot of time in the library because my finals were gunning down on me. To sweeten revision, I checked out some of the books Hank recommended. Although the library had few in stock, and the titles of many I requested made Mrs Hustvedt blush, I managed to read all kinds of things about people and their hearts. That's when I took an interest in the librarian and she in me. For a long time, though, Mrs Hustvedt stayed away from me; in those days, in a small southern town, we'd have been finished if word seeped out about the kind of love we had in mind.

I chose my moment well.

Just after closing on a Monday evening, as she tidied up and closed doors, I stayed behind, upstairs on the first floor. Nervous like a cat burglar, with my heart beating in my throat, I waited for her to climb the stairs and shut the top floor down. When I heard her heels on the linoleum, I slunk back into my chair and arranged myself. Stretched across a low table, I positioned my legs so they were straight but slightly parted. Pulled back to just below the welt of my nylons, my ruffled skirt no longer concealed my best feature. Tight as a corset, my red sweater compacted my breasts and completed my offering.

Making it look like I'd fallen asleep after putting in another late night, I tousled my hair a bit and rested my head against the padded leather of the reading chair. Breathing through my nose I made the whistling sound of deep sleep. Outside my darkness I heard her heels stop. She cleared her throat but I didn't stir. Silence followed and I knew her unmarried eyes were moving from my legs to my breasts to my peaceful face.

It was getting hard to keep from peeking, because it felt like an hour had rolled by. She must have been drinking me in with her eyes, which was different to the way men's eyes burn for me. Caught between two minds – self-restraint warning her that the end of the world was asleep in her chair, while desire begged her to look a little longer – I knew her thoughts were frantic. Just in case her better self won the fight, I bent one knee just a touch to let a little more electric light slip up the inside of my thigh. Now she could see my black panties; bought that day in readiness for the evening.

I loved every slow second of my game; smelling her confusion while my beauty stole the night. I didn't know it then, but this was my vocation. Although curious about so many things back then, and despite the fact that I was always fighting a conviction that I was bad to the bone, it was only when Hank opened my eyes that I understood who and what I was.

To create a thin slit, I opened one eye a fraction and was surprised to see how close Mrs Hustvedt stood beside me. With a whisper, she slipped to her knees and I felt her fingers, gentle and unsure, stroke my hair. Moaning softly, I encouraged those fingers. She whispered my name, not wanting to shock me from sleep, but I refused to respond. I wanted more of that hand touching me.

16

Enjoying her caresses on the side of my face, I eventually stirred from sleep with a pretty smile.

She beamed.

'I could sleep in here for ever,' I said. 'Surrounded by all my favourite books, while someone strokes my hair.'

Suddenly uncomfortable, she rose to her feet. 'Best be getting home.'

'Guess so,' I replied. I shook my hair loose and turned my head away to tie a pony-tail. Removing a leg from the table, I prodded my foot around, seeking a shoe, making sure the leg brushed against her. I felt her go stiff. Leaving my other leg on the table, so my skirt remained hiked up, I presented her with another view between my thighs from a different angle. Pale skin, brushed by shadow, between stockings and panties, confronted her discreet eyes. From above me, I heard her inhale and her body trembled against my leg. Standing up and smiling sweetly, I put my hand on her elbow to steady myself. For a moment longer than decorum advised, I left my long fingers on her arm and held her stare with my almond-shaped eyes.

'Mrs Hustvedt, I do love my evenings here. You know, the other day I tried a perfume sample in Masons which turned out to be your fragrance. All of a sudden, I remembered being safe and warm in the library and I wanted to run here straight away.'

Blushing, she smiled, but took a step away from me.

Had I been too quick? For weeks I'd made sure she caught me eyeing her at every opportunity and thought she was ready to fill me up.

Walking away, between the shelves, she turned off the strip lights in each aisle. As I watched the sodium tubes splutter out, I slipped my shoes on, frustrated. I wanted her mouth, desperately. Pressed against me,

17

with her lips a moment from mine, I wanted to stare into her lapis-lazuli eyes and feel her bosom squash into me. And by the time she'd doused all the lights, my fantasy became a need. More than once I'd rolled in a meadow with a curious girlfriend, but I'd learned to crave maturity. I needed a woman who took her pleasure swiftly. Someone with experience to tutor me; someone delighted by the opportunity to love a willing pup.

Baffled, I followed her out of the dark to the top of the stairs and said, 'Sorry, ma'am.'

'What have you got to be sorry for?' she asked, her voice stronger now, getting away from me.

'Well . . .' I paused. She turned, reluctantly, and dared to look into my big eyes. 'I like to spend time here because . . . because I like you.' Then I went silent and dipped my head.

Mrs Hustvedt closed the door, sealing us upstairs, with only the glow from the stairwell light for illumination, shining through a pane of frosted glass to make a pattern on the side of her face. 'Do you realise what would happen if people thought we were having an inappropriate relationship?'

I nodded.

'Well, then,' she said, struggling to keep her voice straight. 'You're seventeen. You don't know what you want.'

'Don't say that,' I said. 'I'm sick of people saying that.' It was true. I frightened people, even my parents. Only Hank accepted me. 'I know exactly what I want,' I added, raising my chin.

'Even now, you talk like a teenager.'

She was tougher than I thought, but her barriers just lit fires in my tummy. 'Depends how you look at it,' I said, coy. 'I'm a young woman too.'

This stalled her. She swallowed and her hand had

gone white on the door handle. 'Have you done this before?' Her voice was so quiet, I barely heard it.

Nodding my head, I let my lips part and rubbed my bright incisors with just the tip of my tongue. Slowly, I moved closer to her. She stiffened again.

Leaning forward, I planted a little kiss on her neck. The skin was soft and her perfume hit me. A lump formed in my throat. Everything went real still and I couldn't hear anything beside my heart until she whispered, 'Please don't. I don't know what I'd do.'

In my mind, I saw her back in her room, alone in bed, biting the knuckles of one hand while the other moved under the sheets, between her legs. On her cheeks there were tears. This passion should be mine. No one had the right to take my quarry away. 'Lose yourself in me,' I invited.

For a moment she looked right into my eyes. Since then, I've learned that if you do that you're all mine. Then she looked at my lips, hard. 'Let me lock up,' she said, and disappeared down the stairs to close the library.

Leaning back against the cool plaster of the wall, I smiled at the ceiling and then into the gloom of an unlit library. Outside, cool air settled under the stars and I understood more about the night; so much can be done in the dark.

When Mrs Hustvedt returned I was gone from where she left me. 'Where are you?' she whispered from the doorway. From where I sat on the table in the reading area, I could smell the fresh perfume she'd applied just for me and I could see the new paint on her lips.

'Over here, ma'am.'

Deciding against a light, she moved in the direction of my voice. 'Call me Eva.'

'Eva,' I said, enjoying the sound of her name as it left my lips.

I wasn't sure whether it was rage or passion that forced a gasp from her when she found me in just my underwear. For a while her hands trembled on my knees, but became firm once they found my thighs. Stroking the slippery nylon on my legs, she kissed me hard and I knew there would be no more barriers. Loving the mint and lipstick taste of her mouth, I sought her tongue. And it was given, eagerly.

Once restrained and now free, our desire overwhelmed everything. From the table, she took me to the floor and shed my bra. Clasping my breasts, she tweaked and stretched both of my nipples until I bit my hand to keep from crying out. 'Like it rough here, eh?' she said in a hissy voice before devouring my breasts. Clawing her dark hair, I slid my shin between her legs and rubbed her sex. Through her skirt and panties, I could feel the softness squash against bone. Breathing hard, she rocked back on her ankles to strip her blouse and bra free from her body. With a little pressure from my shin, I intimated she should stand, and with my eyes I encouraged her to continue undressing. Standing tall, she stepped from her shoes and unzipped her skirt. When her skirt and slip were ruffled around her feet, she clambered upon me to bite my neck. This made me smile.

Through her silk shorts – black and lace trimmed to surprise me – my fingers slithered and found moisture. Whipping my fingertips in quick flurries, the same way I touched my own puss at night, I was amazed at how wet Eva had become. Coating my fingers down to the first joint, her honey was especially sticky and the scent of it made me feel aggressive.

Sliding beneath her, I found her naked breasts: ample, soft, bigger than mine and a delight to suckle. Lashing them with my tongue and eating at them, I thought of myself as a boy at the prom with access to his date's chest, and the thought fanned my heat. Repositioning herself, Eva allowed me to prod three fingers deep in her sex while I chewed her nips at the same time, and she began to made hard sounds from deep in her chest. Slithering further beneath her, almost weeping now with the joy of my longing becoming conquest, I found her sex with my glossy lips.

Perhaps it was a mistake to flaunt my lust so quickly. Maybe she wanted a shy girl who could be manoeuvred, because when I sucked at her damp lips she pushed her weight across my face and trapped my head between her thighs. Rasps from her nylons against my earrings and hair deafened me. For a moment I struggled to breathe through the hot fumes of her sex and thought the weight of her on my face was too much, but once I regulated my breathing through my nose, while dipping my tongue deep like Hank does in me, my panic fled and I relaxed into sucking this juicy steak. Yes, it was like a rare fillet; wet enough to cover my chin with fluid, and big enough to fill my mouth with warm satisfaction.

Blood entered my thoughts.

Shudders passed through her thighs and I heard her sob. When I craned my head back and looked up and along her body, I could see the shape of her head, pressed into the floor. Her hair formed a black pool around her weeping face, and I stroked her broad ass to ease her through the shocks a pretty girl had created inside her. Slipping from under Eva, I lay beside her and held her shoulders. It had been some time, she told me. Years, she confessed. There had been trouble back east and she came to our town to escape herself. All in the past, I said, to comfort her, with a voice beyond my experience. This made her go quiet and she stared at me. Through the darkness, I could see the pale oval of her handsome face watching me. Nervous, I moved closer to her, to ease my anxiety of her pouncing through the dark at me.

Did I have a girlfriend? she asked. No, I said. This pleased her and she began to stroke me again, kissing my neck with such a hunger that I began to think maybe she was like Hank. Cupping my breasts, she said I had good tits. Not the kind of word I'd expected to hear from Mrs Hustvedt the librarian, and when I heard the word my instincts told me something unusual was about to occur.

My instincts can be trusted.

Eva called me her 'little bitch', gripped my thighs until my nylons were ruined by her nails, and then pulled me close. In the heat and dark I could feel her ferocity building, so I bared my throat to her, like I did with Hank in the beginning before my change. Going soft in her hands, I let her think I had given myself to her, completely. 'Do you want to be my bitch?' she asked, and her voice had changed; it had gone deeper and become more exciting.

'Yes,' I said.

'What if I'm rough?' she asked.

'I'll be a slut to make you tougher,' I teased, knowing this worked with Hank.

Before I knew what was happening we were fighting. First she slapped my face, then she kissed me hard, and when I asked her what was wrong she wrestled me to the ground. Alarmed, I fought back, but she was quick and had obviously fought like a cat before. In my mind I saw her as a younger woman beating up on a well-dressed lady in a dark club; a married lady who shouldn't have been in the club, but who had strayed below rainy streets to mess with her bitch. This vision excited me and I fought back enough to get her really riled. Yes, this was good, feeling her claws in my blonde hair and her slippery legs fighting with my own long limbs in the struggle to pin each other down. Rolling across the floor, we scratched and bit each other, but not too deeply – that would come later. It was hard to keep our balance because the silks and satins of our underwear made us slide all over the linoleum tiles. But this thrilled me, especially when her slippery legs, still coated in nylon, rubbed against my naked parts. That was heaven and it made my puss and bottom tingle. When we ended up wrapped tightly together with our arms around each other's necks and our feet kicking at the air, our thighs rubbed together so hard I saw a blue spark from the friction.

After a while, she won the spat. Even though I liked being her bitch, she'd hurt my wrist and I relaxed my body and began to sulk. But sulking didn't make her apologetic and she taunted me instead. Perhaps it was a mistake to have spat in her face because I had trouble sitting down for several days on account of the sweet pain she then gave me.

Put across her knee, my hair in disarray, my skin marked by her claws, I peeked over my shoulder to see the madness in her eyes. Years of denial had frozen her visage into something stiff and without warmth, but now the chill had thawed from her face. For weeks, I'd prowled around her, dropping hints with my tight breasts at the counter, or making suggestions with my long legs in the aisles where she tried to reshelve books. Now, my education was benefiting from the results. Months of painting my face the moment I left the high-school gates had finally paid off. Wearing nylons and heels to enhance my dancer's legs made her succumb. Turning my eyelashes into sharp black curls earned me another lover, another feed. No one was safe from me, man or woman. And this filled me with so much power I trembled in her lap, but not from fear. Terrible words left my pouty lips as she struck my silky buttocks. Harder, I wanted it harder, so I drove her to slapping me with such a force she hurt her hand. Pain was something Hank had already taught me to appreciate. Hearing her hand whoosh through the air, just before the moment of contact, was wonderful. Feeling the long bones of her fingers and the broad pan of her hand impact and then indent my soft buttocks and thighs made me squeal and struggle, but that only turns a lover on, making them determined to punish you further. There are ways to push a tough lover until their blows are so hard and the pain so glorious, I nearly faint.

After the spanking, we used our stinging bodies with more care and made love a second time, both wondering who had vanquished who. And it was then I fed, as she went drowsy before my keen eyes, with my purring pouring down her ears. I drank just a little, as Hank instructed, so they would enjoy the pain and not be washed out for weeks; just left weakened and haunted in sleep, but nothing more. Her taste was good; sharp and hot, rich with the opium of secrets, and salted by the poison of denial. Down my throat she slipped and then I left her alone in her dark world of books and exile.

'Who's the bitch now?' I whispered, as I ran into the delicious night, clutching my dancehall high-heels against my unfettered breasts.

That was my first time with Eva, but with my appetite growing and Hank's tuition feeding my curiosity, our liaisons continued through the summer, long after finals. We met in the library and when that became too risky we visited motels out on the highway that smelled of neglect; soon changing the scent in these sad rooms to the aroma of our heat. Eva educated me about the ways of women who were weak for other women; how to interpret their silence and indifference, how to catch their looks of interest without turning your head, and how to hold innocent conversations coded with intentions that no one else could decode. She taught me how and where to find their hidden niches in any town.

Learning quickly, I began telling Hank my own stories in a hushed voice and it became a joy to study his face in the half-light. At times his eyes would widen, then he would smoke cigarette after cigarette, hiding his lips and fingers with a screen of smoke, until he could take no more and took me instead, hurriedly, on the floor before his wooden chair.

But Mrs Hustvedt had to spoil things with her suspicions and tenacity. It was beyond her to delight in a sharing arrangement like Hank does. Soon, there were fights between Eva and me. Not the slippery wrestling we used to enjoy on the cold tiles of the library floor, but nasty hair-pulling tussles when she accused me of betrayal. Crying on the phone, waiting for me outside stores, bringing books to my home, and spying on my movements around town, she led herself to Hank.

One afternoon, just after he finished a reading, I took a peek through the blinds in his room to make sure the hot sun had slid away, and I saw my librarian watching our window from across the street. Something about her face, maybe the way it was so tight around the mouth, made me angry and I cursed her.

The following evening, ten minutes before closing, Hank drove me to the library. In his black '45 Mercury, we cruised through town to where it all began between me and Mrs Hustvedt. Frightened by the look in Hank's eyes, I begged him not to interfere. In time, I swore, she would forget me and come to her senses about her indiscretion, but he wouldn't listen. 'Never waste time when love goes bad,' was all he said, before leaving me in the car with my fear.

Alone, I sat for an hour, unable to listen to the radio, smoking myself sick. At times I wanted to get out of the car and see what had happened, but stopped myself because he'd insisted I stay put. Eventually Hank emerged from one of the side doors of the library. Calm as ever, he walked across the lawn, and even paused to admire the apricot sunset, spread behind the silhouette of the town hall.

'What did you do? What did she say?' I bombarded him with questions the moment the driver's door was open, but he just smiled, climbed in and started the car. It was then I knew there had been love. His gums were stained with claret and when he feeds there is always love. I challenged him by asking him what I already knew.

'There was love,' he replied, as if he were confessing nothing and merely answering a simple query.

With my face in my hands and the tears already starting to shine on my cheeks, Hank laughed and rubbed my head. When I pulled away, he stopped laughing. 'We talked about books, honey. And we talked about you –' I stopped my fuss. 'While we talked, I understood a part of her liked men. So I fed from it and then I fed it, real deep. Sometimes this happens. Get used to it.'

And that was all he said. Take me home, I told him. Feeling like I'd been betrayed by two people, I said I was done with him and never wanted to lay eyes on his no-good self again. 'Sure,' he replied, and took a turn towards my neighbourhood.

As I sat in silence in his '45 Mercury, I had another of my visions. This time, it was clearer than the others and I learned to control it and let it run its course. In my mind, I saw Mrs Eva Hustvedt pressed into the bookshelves in the reference section, where the heavy tomes with leather spines are kept. Hank held her buttocks and lifted her feet clean off the floor. Without even taking his pants off, he threw himself into Eva, who barked every time she juddered from his stroke. From the wall, he took her to a reading cubicle and bent her over the small table. Putting her skirt up to her shoulders and ripping her panties off her waist, he took her like a savage. In the place where people are supposed to be quiet as they read, he did something to her that turned her face into a red, wet, maniac thing, screaming lines no one has ever heard in the library before or since that night. And then they kissed and he soothed her by whispering something in her ear, until her head rested on his shoulder. When he fed from a place near her pussy, she came. Then the librarian slept where he laid her on a rug, real gentle.

'Your place,' I remember saying, after a few more tears just to let him know it would take me time to get used to his strange ways.

'Love you, baby,' he said, and turned the car around before heading back to the boarding house. On the way, I saw sun-browned cheerleaders putting in late practice on the athletics field and understood the future was full of so much promise, for both of us.

Breaking my happy recall of that summery time so long ago, I see Hank emerge from the grocery with a paper bag full of my goodies. The slouching youth disappears. By the time Hank's seated in the car, the woman who reminds me of Eva Hustvedt leaves the store too and passes the car, self-consciously.

'Something happen between you two?' Hank asks, never missing a shot.

'Something,' I say, smiling.

'Half an hour, no more,' he says, and opens *Sports Illustrated*.

Filling my lungs with clean southern air, I follow the nervous woman into her boutique. Making sure I flip the sign, hanging inside the front door, to read CLOSED instead of OPEN, I turn to her and nod towards the storeroom. Patting her hair, she leaves the counter and I follow her into the dark.

Three

From the crimson warmth I rest in, a crash wakes me. Hank blasts through the motel door; it swings open and bangs against the wall. I think my heart is about to stop beating. Fat chance of that happening to a girl like me, though.

'Baby,' I say, relieved it's only Hank, and I slink back into the soft bed. 'Come to me.'

'Preacher,' he says, short of breath and even paler than usual. Beside me in bed my companion for the evening groans but can't wake up.

'Get your shit together, baby,' Hank snaps. 'He's real close.'

Shaking my head I try to clear the fog from my brain. After feeding long, deep, and right up to the critical point when your lover might expire, you want to lie around for hours afterwards, lost to a sense of well-being. Hank told me it's a high like morphine and he's had plenty of that working for the military. Drugged up on the delicious juice I'd taken into my body, from this guy Charlie I met earlier, I see Hank as a blur throwing things on to the bed.

'Come on!' he cries out, and grabs my wrists to haul me from the warm bed. Even if he dropped me in snow, I'd want to curl up and sleep.

'Where?' I mutter, still dreamy, even though he's managed to get me standing up.

'Near where we ate, baby. I knew he was close.'

'You had the dream, honey,' I say, and try to take Hank's face in my floppy hands, but he pushes me away and I fall back on to the bed. Seizing me by the shoulders he picks me off the bed and backhands my cheek, but I've already wrapped my legs around him and want him to love me. Dropped over his shoulder, he carries me into the bathroom and puts me in the tub. Then he turns the shower on, letting a thick stream of cold water batter me.

This revives me and I start to scream at him, but I remember he said something about the Preacher so I stop yelling and reach for a towel. Cursing myself for overindulging on Charlie, I run from the bathroom, skidding on the way, and find Hank throwing my clothes in a trunk. On the bed, beside my pink suitcase, is his gun and a box of shells.

'No shooting, baby,' I say in a frightened voice, and he stops packing. For a moment he stares at me, his face impassive, but then his eyes soften and he crosses the room. As I stand there, all wet, bewildered and frightened, Hank hugs me against his chest and kisses the side of my damp head. 'Gonna be OK, honey,' he whispers. Times like this make him regret taking me along on the ride that never ends. Sniffing into his shoulder, I wake up fully and he dries my eyes with a clean white handkerchief. We kiss and then he turns away and carries on packing.

Just the thought of the Preacher being in the same state as us makes me go cold inside. Knowing he's in the same town, less than a mile away, makes me do all I can to stop from going hysterical. Keeping my mind occupied, I rummage through a case to find clothes. After throwing on jeans, boots and a leather jacket, I tell Hank I'm ready to split. Standing over by the window Hank is looking through a crack in the blinds and he holds the gun at his side. Guns frighten me. It would take a few well-placed shots to take us down but the wounds hurt like hell and they leave scars. If I was scarred I reckon I'd just give myself to the Preacher. Hank has so many scars and he's discovered they won't vanish, even on our clock.

'What's going on?' a sleepy voice moans, and we both turn around to stare at the bed. My lover, Charlie, puts his hands over his face and starts to whimper. Hank and I exchange looks and both of us fight to keep from laughing. In all the excitement we'd forgotten about my food, who has woken up in the bed to find chaos all around him.

'Go back to sleep, Chuck,' I say in a sweet voice, but he's in no mood to sleep. His eyes flick down to the gun in Hank's hand. 'Look, mister,' he says in a slow voice as if his tongue is swollen. 'She said it was OK for us to party. She said you wouldn't mind.'

I can see Hank is trying to keep his face straight. 'Well, son, you'll learn that everything pretty girls say to you in bars ain't always the truth.'

'Yes, sir,' the guy says, his face as white as the sheets he's cowering under.

'Now, listen up, son, if you don't want to get hurt.' The guy nods. 'Once we're gone, you count to a hundred and get your ass out of here. Understand?'

The guy nods again and Hank disappears through the door to check out the lot and start the car. When he comes back and tells me everything is cool, we grab our bags and flee to the car, watched all the time by Charlie in the bed.

Typically, I've forgotten my earrings, which I put beside the bed, so Hank darts back in to get them. Even from the car I hear Charlie yelp because he must have jumped out of bed the minute we vanished. With Hank thundering back through the door to get my earrings, the guy must have thought he was about to die. Even when we're running for our lives we can still see the funny side of things – one of the reasons we're still close after so many years. There's no laughing, though, when Hank gets back in the car and throws my earrings into my lap. All we care about is putting distance between us and the Preacher.

Driving out through the deserted streets makes us both tense and we pass out of town in silence, trying to cover every angle with our quick night-time eyes, secretly dreading the sight of the tall figure, dressed in black, who wears leather gloves in every kind of weather. That's the Preacher.

Our luck is in; we don't see him and once we're on the highway I light up a pair of smokes to help us relax. 'Better change the car again,' Hank says, and puts the radio on real quiet. He hates changing the car, but we can't risk exposure if the Preacher tracks us through a number plate or false name.

Outside, the night becomes a series of shapes, shadows and blurred lines as we pass desert, lonely houses and water tanks wet by the dark. With my heart slowing down and the juice of my one-night stand thickening in my every artery and vein, I feel sleepy. Bothering Hank at this point would be a mistake – he has planning to do, with the Preacher close again – so I slink deeper into my seat and open the window a touch, allowing a slipstream of cold air to pass across my face and stop me from passing out. I'll sleep when we're over the county line.

My thoughts travel back to Charlie and I curse the Preacher; once again, he has tarnished a thoroughly successful hunt. Charlie tasted great too. Minerals and vitamins stung my tongue when I drank his strength. He worked out every other day and watched what he ate; I wish more young men did. The better they taste the longer I stay with them, and any guy who's spent quality time with me can never get enough of what I have to offer. They will even look for me in every other woman they meet, which is a good thing, because I'm tough and independent and girls should be encouraged to stand up for themselves.

There was a lot of talent in the bar where I met Charlie, but I know he was the right choice. I needed some vigorous loving after the long journey to La Posada.

'May I sit down?' were his first words.

Narrowing my eyes and blowing a plume of smoke across my table, I wore my best look of disinterest. Dressed in a black suit and silk shirt with no tie, he stood before my table, smiling. His self-assurance made me suspect a cocky side if he became too comfortable in my company. I liked his smile, though, and I dug the retro style to his clothes; it reminded me of happier times. I did suspect Charlie of being vain, but knew I could work that to my advantage – vain men make me aggressive and I was in the mood for something hard.

'Sure,' I said, curious about him. If he was a fool I could easily get rid of him.

He pulled up alongside me in my booth, but didn't get too close.

'What's your name?' he asked.

'Bonny,' I answered, still looking straight ahead, already having decided that I'd like to be Bonny for the night. My real name is Missy, but Bonny suited the place I was drinking in. It had a swing band, red leather bar, dim lights and layers of smoke drifting above people's heads.

'Can I get you another drink?'

'Thanks. Bourbon, straight.'

He signalled for the waiter and introduced himself as Charlie. While he messed around opening a packet of smokes and cracking small talk, I stretched my mind to take a closer look at him. Late twenties, I guessed, gym freak, was probably self-employed, and had no worries about being single because he needed plenty of time to stand before a full-length mirror admiring his body, and although girls came easy few were that patient. Although he enjoyed a good run with the ladies in his small and knowable town, he loved to see a new face in one of his haunts. Especially mine, with a beauty spot and cherry-red lips, like a vision sent from the past.

Across the lounge, Hank sat in shadow, watching us from his booth. Through the dark I could see the end of his cigarette and could feel his eyes on my bare shoulders and cleavage, framed by the black dress I had on. He'd been to this bar before and had brought me down here after we ate steak in a diner. Once I'd finished my second dessert of ice cream and lemon pie, I told him I was hungry and he said he knew a place.

Light from the lamp on my table, shielded behind green glass, allowed my date to check me out; the way guys do when they think they're being discreet. But for a guy who was so self-assured, his speech broke up when he took a good look down my dress and at my shiny thighs crossed beneath the table. Saying little, I nodded at his comments and occasionally answered a question. Around the room I saw another four guys who had waited too long to come over and ask if I wanted company. On each of their faces something had dropped; the hope had disappeared from their eyes and been replaced by longing. Still, I

34

was happy with this Charlie character and my appetite increased every time I got a whiff of his scent under all that aftershave. Wondering if Charlie's muscle cut was deep and tanned, I gave him a little more attention. As I turned my eyes upon him, he stared at me like he would do anything not to blow it with me.

'Bet you're all of eighteen,' he said.

'Close,' I replied, smiling at last.

'You studying up at the college?'

'No, I never took that route. Fell in love instead.'

'I know that story,' he said, nodding. 'Did he turn into a louse?'

'No, he turned into my husband.'

'You're married?'

'Afraid so.'

'Sorry. I didn't see anyone with you.'

'No harm done,' I said, enjoying the smell of his anxiety.

Confused, he gave me more space in the booth. 'Want me to beat it?'

'You'd know by now if I did.'

'What you doing out, then?'

'Playing a game.'

'Don't see any cards,' he said, and then laughed nervously.

'There are other ways to gamble.'

'Like?'

'Maybe I'll show you.'

He looked uneasy.

'See all those people out there?' I said.

He nodded.

'One of them is my husband.'

Charlie started to look around.

'Don't look. That's one of the rules. Look at me instead. Why change the habit of your entire evening?'

Picking up his drink, he knocked it straight back and looked like he was ready to split. Only he couldn't; despite the alarms screaming inside his head he was unable to leave my side.

'Thought you were the type who liked a game,' I said.

'You might be the prettiest thing I've seen outside of a magazine, miss, but losing teeth is another matter.'

'He'll thank you for it.'

Charlie exhaled. 'You're shitting me.'

I shook my head and giggled. 'My husband's older than me. A lot older, and he likes his young wife to be happy.' With that I gave him a wink and he relaxed a little. 'Interested?' I added, and uncrossed my legs. He said nothing, but began to rub his mouth. In his lap, I could see the rise I had made out of this lounge Romeo.

'Want to dance with me?' I invited, when the band began a good slow Red Simpson tune.

He swallowed and I watched his Adam's apple move up and down his clean-shaven throat. 'More than anything,' he whispered.

For some reason that story gets most guys horny. I use it often when I hunt younger guys because it keeps Hank sharp too, on account of him liking the sweet pain of my betrayal. You see, later on, after my thirst is slaked, I'll tease Hank with the story and if I'm lucky his love will leave bruises. Hank seemed distracted for a few days and I lacked the energy to try levering details from him. In hindsight, I guess he'd been dreaming about the Preacher and that is never a good sign. As we drove in the late afternoon, when the sun turned red, Hank's hand was near my puss as he steered the car with the other, and my need

36

to play began to boil beneath my skin. Uncomfortable, I became sassy and snapped at him in the car. Being preoccupied with his dreams about the Preacher, it was probable he deliberately whisked me into feeling restless, not only because he liked to watch me hunt, but because he wanted to be punished in this passive way for being unable to shake that bastard from out of our lives for good. Tonight, he wanted to twist and burn over me while I took another man. And after he'd taken my bottom without permission that morning, Hank deserved to ache for me. If I was lucky, maybe he'd weep over my digression too; reassurance a girl can never get enough of.

As we danced, Charlie held me close and let me sample an impression of his thick pipe, hard as wood, and waiting for me down there. Pressing through my thin dress, I could even feel the shape of the big head. Raising myself on to my toes, it rested against my puss and I decided I loved the feel of it. Wondering about his fit inside me, I imagined it passing through the slit in my sheer panties. I let him hold me closer.

'Do you have a place?' he asked, and a shudder passed through him.

'Mmm,' I moaned, close to his smooth cheek. 'A motel room. My husband rents it for me, just out of town, so our neighbours never get wise.'

Charlie pressed his pipe against my belly, made firm by a white corselette. 'Girl, you're too much.'

'Want to see my fuck pad?' I asked.

Charlie couldn't speak but his hands clenched on my buttocks.

'But let me be honest, I want to fuck, nothing else,' I said.

His breathing became hoarse, but there were no

words, and his exhalations began to hang like low clouds over my bare neck. Feeling his energy build up was exciting. In anticipation of having him splashed all over and up inside me, I decided to make things worse for him and better for me. 'I'm real tight, though, so don't rip anything.'

With a dry hand, he pulled my face before his lips and I could see the devil in his eyes. 'Now,' he whispered.

I kissed him long and deep, giving him tongue and leaving smears of red across his mouth. 'My husband is watching, so kiss me good.'

Charlie raped my mouth right there on the dance floor. Among all those dancing couples and under the hot lights, I explored his body through his thin shirt. When my claws found his back he broke from the kiss to gasp. Lining his skin, I let him know our love would be hard. 'Maybe I can't wait,' he said.

'Then maybe you should take me outside.'

Whisked from the dance floor, Charlie pulled me through the tables and out into the parking lot. As we left I looked over my shoulder at Hank, who was slouching against a pillar by the dance floor. Through the murk of smoke and the lightning of strobe, I caught sight of simmering eyes in a drawn face. I smiled and blew a kiss. Charlie held my hand and led me from the bar.

Behind the kitchens, in long shadows, I enjoyed Charlie's fury. Panting his desperation all over my upturned face and white shoulders, his hands became busy below. He slapped his belt from the buckle and flopped his stiff meat into the night. When my cool fingers entwined around his length to massage the veins and ridges of his girth, Charlie raised my dress up to my navel. Cold air washed across my thighs, taut with suspenders, and lapped around my waist, braceleted by a corselette. Squinting through the dark, and trying not to whoop with joy, he surveyed the treasures he never expected to glimpse when preparing himself earlier in the evening.

As I squeezed his fat pipe and pushed my hand, vigorously, up and down his length, Charlie's breathing found a rhythm. 'I'm damp,' I said. 'And my panties are slit under the corset, so get this inside me, quick.' Gripping the rear of my thighs and spreading his feet, he measured my weight and then lifted. His biceps swelled and his face trembled. Passing my hands over my shoulders, I grasped a window sill. My heels left the tarmac as Charlie raised me to the right height. 'Fuck me,' I whispered to his wild eyes.

Inside my head, waves slammed and broke apart on a cliff face. Thick as a python, Charlie's fat cock stretched me so wide I thought I heard something tear. Resting my head against the rough bricks of the wall, and stiffening my shoulders to form a solid base into which he could smash, I readied myself. When he came through me I squealed like a feeding piglet. Long strokes to the very back of me made me feel as light as a feather. At the pit of my womb, where all the velvet waited to slurp his milk, the head of his cock felt like an apple. Hard and round, it slipped down to pack my box, then withdrew to the squeeze of my lips, before rifling back through me to push the air from my body. Grinding himself in hard, the flat muscles on his pelvis squashed my clit-pip and I started to croak.

Across the lot, two girls climbed from a Pontiac Firebird and stopped dead in their tracks. Over Charlie's shoulder I could read the shock and delight on their pretty faces. Staring at our bouncing silhouettes, they giggled silly, excited things to each

39

other. Deep down, I knew both of them envied the strange girl the local tough thrust up and down the wall.

Spiking the back of his thighs with my heels, that glinted like shiv blades in a street fight, I spat right into Charlie's face. My spit dripped from the black arch of his brows and in his eyes I could see a murderer's glee. 'Want to play hard?' he said in a hissy, pissy voice and his mouth went all fierce; not ugly, but savage and snarly. When I'm fucking I like to see that, and it makes me push my luck to find a man's limit. Afterwards, they always weep like babies and hold me like they're sorry, but I only smile and enjoy the bruises they leave, as if the black marks are kisses left by a movie star's lips.

'Go on,' I said to him, and widened my hips a fraction to take the blasting from his groin. Dipping his head, he groped a mouthful of brassière and the soft flesh it suspended and almost bit my breast off. After half a dozen thrusts that made me see stars, he paused and groaned. I felt two strong pulses in my womb. Pushing his floppy body away, I dropped to a crouch before him. While I made ready to collect, a thick rope of cream landed on my cheek and it felt hot. The next three ejaculations I managed to pull into my mouth and they hit my tonsils before slithering into my tummy. I suckled hard, until his brown cock waned against the inside of my clinging cheeks, and Charlie had to clutch his chest with one hand and support his weight by pressing the other into the wall.

After my own dizziness passed, I fingered the stickiness from my cheek and rubbed it over my teeth in preparation for drinking something more salty. As I pulled my stockings back up to the lips of my puss and straightened my dress, I watched the two girls

40

from the Pontiac walk past with their noses pointed at the moon. I felt their sudden disapproval and hoped they would stay quiet.

The taller blonde girl whispered 'slut' to her busty friend. Whether she intended me to hear or not, she had no idea that I could hear her thoughts if I chose. When I'm aroused I can catch a quick heartbeat in my ears from the other side of a room; I can smell a fresh slice on a finger in broken glass three blocks away; and I want to tear skin apart like pastry to lick out the filling beneath. Never fuck with me when I'm roused.

'Fuck you,' I said, real loud, and patted my hair flat where it stuck out at the back.

Busty gasped at my language but the tall bitch with the mouth said, 'Against a wall, not likely.'

They only enjoyed a few seconds of laughter before I was beside them. While Busty cried, I took Lanky back to her car, slapping her tight arse all the way to humiliate her into being my bitch. Stunned by the strength in my hands, and unsteady on her pencil-thin heels, she was manoeuvred against the rear door of the car so I could shove her over. When her long legs were stuck in the air and her head slid about on the leatherette of the back seat, I took a peek at her puss.

'Leave her alone!' her busty friend shrieked from behind. 'I'll call the cops.'

Lanky looked frightened and her fight was gone. I smiled down at the peroxide-softened beauty before me and I stroked her lean, tanned legs. Terrified, she clamped both of her hands, palm down, across her pussy; somehow understanding that was where the truth lived. Fixing her frightened doe eyes with my own, I said, 'From now on, bitch, you'll roll with every slut in boots who rides through your town.'

'Sorry,' she said, trying not to cry. 'I didn't mean it.'

41

'That's right, you didn't. You only said it to cool your own heat. It turned you on to see me against that wall and it disgusted you too. But we both know what you'll be dreaming about tonight between your safe, crisp sheets. Don't we?'

I didn't expect her to answer, but she moved her hands away from the silk and moisture between those gazelle legs.

'Stop it! What are you doing to my friend? Harriet, please get up. Don't let her hurt you,' Busty whined from behind me. But Busty's cries petered out to whispers and then nothingness, when her lanky friend, Harriet, clasped the back of my head with her athlete's thighs and began to moan. From behind, I guess the fat-chested friend could see my slim body, elegantly dressed, dipping its perfect blonde head between the rangy legs of her best friend. Enough to cut anyone's tongue out, I guess.

Charlie watched the whole thing from the shadows. Freaked out by the girl that had lured him from the dance, he seemed to be entertaining second thoughts about going home with me. But as I teetered towards him across the lot on my slingbacks, all sweet as apple pie and Marilyn wiggly, he fished a set of car keys out of a pocket and nodded in the direction of his car.

As we drove to my motel, I caught him peeking at me. Not at my legs or chest like before, but at me – the idea of me. After discharging himself so furiously, I guessed he now had the clarity of mind to think things over, and what I had done to the lanky girl worried him. Once or twice he was about to say something but stopped himself.

'Charlie,' I said, and when he looked me in the eye, I dabbed some of him from the side of my mouth. He swallowed and nearly ran a red light. 'When I'm excited,' I said, 'I sometimes go too far.'

Charlie nodded.

Crossing my legs at the thigh removed his last misgiving.

Back in the motel, I poured Red Label Scotch into the tooth glasses I found in the bathroom, while Charlie sat on the bed and eyed Hank's things that were folded on a chair.

'Relax,' I said, and stretched myself out on the bed behind his back. The clattering sound of my high heels when they hit the floor encouraged him to lie alongside me, propped up on one elbow.

'You live near here?' he asked.

Sipping my Scotch, I ignored him.

'Sure I would have seen you before.'

'Not scared are you, Chuck?' I said, and he looked away, feeling silly. 'I'm seventeen, the door is locked and no one is going to disturb us until I'm finished. No one.'

Taking quick gulps from his drink, Charlie watched the door for a while and I surveyed my prize. Fat cock and a hard body; I had chosen well. Moving closer to him, I placed a finger beneath his chin and made him look at me. Slowly, I untucked his shirt. When my red fingernails brushed against his skin, he closed his eyes. Deftly, I popped each button from its hole on his shirt and he accommodated my hands when I shed it from his body. Along each side of his spine, beneath his shoulder blades, there were welts that looked tender, like the pink gills of a fish.

Seizing me by the elbows, he held me away from his body and I could see the muscles trembling around his mouth. Lowering my eyes, I spied his cock poling his trousers out like a tent. I made a little humming sound that vibrated off the bones of my face and I smiled at him. 'You want that?' he said, and I could see the brown skin on his shoulders goosing. Stretching out my tongue, I wet my lips and made a noise like a small animal. Charlie yanked me forward and on to his chest.

Our kisses were clumsy at first because we were trying to eat too much of each other, but I withdrew a fraction and he followed my lead until we settled into an easy embrace of the lips that seemed to employ my whole body. As he sucked my tongue in and out of his mouth and I enjoyed the scratch of his stubble on my face, I slipped a hand down to his cock. With only the tips of my nails making contact, I ran my hand up and down his length and felt his thighs and buttocks tense.

Our kissing became heated again and I wished Hank had been watching; it's really hard on him when I kiss another man's mouth. Perhaps it's more intimate than penetration. This time, we could sustain the kiss without clicking our teeth together or pinching each other's lip skin. We vanished into the kiss; became absorbed from ourselves into the union of mouth. As he pressed my face down, like he wanted to swallow my head, I felt my dress start to move up my body. His hands became impatient when the hem caught under my buttocks, and he hoisted me off the bed to yank the garment up to my armpits.

'Steady,' I warned, suddenly concerned for the thousand-dollar dress, but Charlie was lost in me. He unclipped my brassière and plucked the gauzy cups from off my chest. As his mouth encircled one of my breasts and the palm of his hand rubbed the other, so my nip would tickle his skin, I peeled my dress over my head and let it fall to the rug beside the bed. His mouth and hands swapped from one breast to the other while I watched, enjoying the sight of a stranger busy with my chest. I'm lucky to have a good hard bosom – not unwieldy, but prominent naked or clothed, with sensitive nips.

Sliding my legs around the bed and raking my nails through his hair, I encouraged his feeding, and when he tried to remove his mouth from my wet skin to take a breath, I commanded 'No' and squashed his face back into my softness. Pleasure began to blind me; I closed my eyes and stared into the dark red things that swirled inside my head. Empowered by my arousal, I felt as if I could raise Charlie above my head or trample him beneath my angry feet.

When he stuck a hand under my corselette, I wondered whether my glowing puss burned his fingers. 'You're so wet,' he murmured, with a mouth full of nip and puppy-fat tit. 'Can I take a sip? Just a taste, little lady?'

Arching my back off the bed, I spread my thighs and rolled my eyes back, knowing he would pay for his goading. The bed shook as he hurried around me and the mattress dipped under my bottom as he arranged my legs over his shoulders. 'I'm going to suck you through these slut panties,' he told me, and then I felt his breath on my inner thighs, followed by his whiskers in the place where my puss meets my buttocks. Twisting my wrists so my hands would lock at a right angle to my forearms, I pressed my palms against the wall, between the brass rungs of the headboard.

Charlie licked the dew from my panties and then he whipped my lips and trimmed floss with his tongue. Soon I lost patience with his teasing and jammed my groin against his face. There was a moment of resistance from Charlie, but I strangled his neck with my slippery legs and seized the cold metal of the headboard – two-fisted – to pump his face. Fastening his jaws over my hole, he made long, measured laps at my lips with his broad tongue, slipping through my furrows, passing across my opening and meandering back to my pip.

Trying to move my bottom so I would only receive his tongue on my special spot, Charlie seized my garter straps and held me still by those harnesses so he could continue collecting my moisture with his tongue. I had to respect him for making me wait for a while, but I guessed he wouldn't be able to restrain himself for long. He would want to hear my music; my bird sounds and my baby-crying noises when my pip is under the lash of a tongue.

Holding his head fast by using my thighs like a vice, he licked me to my second peak of the evening. Only when my legs seemed to fall away from the rest of me did I allow Charlie to disentangle himself.

'That was good. So good, you bastard,' I said, between breaths. Charlie had risen to his knees, and from his nose to the cleft in his chin I could see how my honey had made his skin shiny. Raising my head off the pillow, I peeked between his legs and liked what had risen to gut me. Shuffling my bottom up and down the bed, and sliding my feet up his chest, I let him know I was ready.

'Pretty girl,' he whispered, 'you're gonna suck me first.'

Giggling, I opened my mouth and rubbed the tip of my tongue over my front teeth. Charlie clasped my ankles and then rubbed his hands, fiercely, up and down the outside of my legs, creasing my nylons. He even dipped his cock towards my puss as if he couldn't wait to skewer me. 'Thought you wanted to fuck my mouth,' I said, lost to my new lover, and my love of this game.

Throwing my legs to one side, Charlie loomed over my body. With an excited sigh, I pushed myself down the bed until his cock and balls and their meaty odour hung about my face. Gripping himself at the base of his thick stem, he jammed himself at my mouth and missed. Pinching his purple berry of a phallus between finger and thumb, I planted him in my warmth. Greeting his organ with my curling tongue, I stretched my jaw and let him pass to the back of my throat. Angling my head back and fighting the involuntary urge to gag, I took three-quarters of him inside my skull and gripped his hard buttocks to hold him there. Before allowing him to withdraw, I was content to consume him and measure his length and weight with the bones and flesh of my head. When he finally slipped back, I hugged the bumps of his meat with my lips until the salty tip was cradled between my pursed lips.

'That's the greatest,' he said, real quiet.

I flashed my eyes at him – eyes still heavy with dark paint and luxurious with false lashes. He slipped back inside. Overjoyed with my catch who played along with everything, I moulded the shape of his manhood with my fingers, squeezed its putty with my hand and sucked its briny beads into my stomach.

'I'm going to come,' Charlie said.

'No,' I commanded, holding him away from my mouth. Even though he tried to push his cock back into my mouth, I held him firm. Desperate to splash wave after wave of relief down my throat, he then tried to beat himself in and out of my fingers, but I gripped him, refusing him the friction he required. When the safety catch was back on and the moment of danger had passed, I used my tongue to cleanse him of dew. 'I don't want you shooting off and then passing out. I have a need tonight.'

'You want to be fucked good,' he said, torturing himself with the pain of anticipation.

'Mmm,' I encouraged. 'Like a pretty slut wife who picks men up in bars.'

He tried to press his cock back into my mouth

again but I would not relent. 'Let me come in your mouth, Bonny,' he pleaded, and said it so sweetly I nearly gave in. I laughed at him instead, slipped through his legs, and sat up behind him. Charlie looked angry when he turned to face me; desperation clouded his reason. I'd made him mindless – the way I needed him for what I had planned.

'You want to fuck me, tough guy, then you better do it good. Understand that. You don't want me going back to town tonight, do you?'

'How did a kid like you get such a smart mouth?' he said.

I smiled.

'Had much practice?' he said, angry and jealous, but delighted too.

My smile stiffened and, behind my back, I unthreaded the thick leather belt from his trousers. Welling up inside me came the strongest urge to both love and destroy.

'Where you going?' he asked, when I moved off the bed. Before the wide mirror on the dresser, I stood looking at myself, entwining Charlie's belt around my hands.

'Turn the main light off,' I said.

He sat in silence.

'Go on.' The certainty in my voice made him obey. Inhaling the dark like the aroma of good food, I said, 'Now switch the bedside lamps on.'

With heavy shades angled downward, the lamps covered the bed with a reddish glow. In the mirror, I watched Charlie move behind me. Understanding, he gently bent me over so my hands rested, palm down, on the top of the dresser. From my left hand he removed the strap of leather trailing from my fingers. His breathing sounded louder.

In the mirror, his reflection was obscured with

48

shadow but the cut of his physique was more defined. From his hands there was a sudden snapping sound and I realised he had flexed the leather. 'Wait,' I said, and unclipped all four garter clasps from my stocking tops. Nylon, coloured like Sahara dunes, slithered down my legs until only my feet were covered. After stepping from my corselette, I peeled both stockings off the pinky soles of my feet.

'Now,' I said.

Before the echo of the word died in my head, it was drowned out by the scream of pain in my body. When the leather roped around my buttocks it made a wet sound. *Plat!* I shuddered and held the air in my lungs.

Plat!

Moaning, I cantered from one foot to the other.

Plat!

Fisting my hands on the dresser, I lowered my head between my shoulders.

Plat!

My knees began to give way and through my tears I saw Charlie hesitate and then suspend his next stroke.

'Do it!' I cried out.

He delivered, lashing me against the dresser, and shouted, 'Why?'

'Fuck you,' I said.

Again and again, he whipped me and the blows spanked the hard walls with echoes that hurt my ears inside.

'I want you,' Charlie said. 'You're going to be mine.'

Sniffing, I smiled, glad it was dark because my reflection would have revealed what I can be. Sometimes I don't like to see my own face.

Charlie's breath laboured. 'Does your old man whip you, girl?'

'Everybody does.'

The next blow was harder than the others and I sucked my hair into my mouth and bit down on it, before laughing through gritted teeth.

'Slut,' he swore and came up behind me. I turned around and slapped my hands against his chest, making him flinch and blink. He grabbed my shoulders but I bit his wrist. When he recoiled I fell to my knees and swallowed him. With rough, kneading fingers he scruffed my hair into fuzz and strands that stuck out at all angles.

Losing his balance from the force of my suckling, he staggered away from me to keep his feet. I followed on foot, my thin body flashing white in the gloom. Charlie cupped my tender cheeks with his hands. I slipped my arms around his neck and crossed my legs around his waist, locking my ankles in the small of his back. Like Hank, he had the strength to cradle the blonde demon bound to his body. Taken to the bed, I was thrown upon the mattress and then covered by his body, raw and slicked with sweat.

He made me claw his face like that. What else could I do with him shunting me across the bed, slapping his body against mine, and crying out for salvation in this dark place I had made for us?

Like a thirsty dog, he licked my face from chin to forehead. No one had ever done that before and I knew my memory of Charlie had formed; whenever a tongue touched my skin, I would think of this boy who tried to dissolve my beauty with his broad tongue.

Squeezing my breasts until the breath had gone from me, he fucked me into the bed. A hard sound, like I was clearing my throat, came out of my mouth when he touched the back of my womb. Harder and harder he fucked, until I had moved to the other half of the bed and gone over the side, where my weight was supported by my shoulders and the back of my tousled head. With a fleshy thump, our still-grinding bodies joined our snatching mouths on the floor, where the violence of his thrusts were like flashes of murder in the dark.

'Fuck–' He slammed into me and then withdrew '– me.' My voice warbled and he threw himself back into me. 'Yes, yes, yes,' I cried with every quick pump from his hips until I came and became wordless. Pushed across the floor, the carpet burned us, but we didn't care. When my softness was jammed against the skirting board, he thumped clots of warmth against the sides of my womb and whispered, 'Love you.'

Stroking his head against my breasts, where the slowing tempo of my heart lulled him to sleep, my eyes flashed open so wide I could see a spider emptying a fly on the ceiling.

'Could you love me?' he asked.

'For ever,' I said.

'Can we be together?'

'For ever,' I replied, and he hugged me close, making me feel insignificant with his hard arms.

'Do you want me in every dream?' I asked.

'Yes,' he said, and nuzzled his head between my breasts.

A warm current of goodness pumped through my pet. He brimmed with wealth: iron-stock, rust-pepper, broth-spice. 'This won't hurt,' I whispered, lowering my gleaming smile to a part of him that was as soft as a shorn lamb.

'You liked him,' Hank says, breaking my dream, and he nods, as though he has just decided on which route to take on a map. 'You prefer them young, I know.'

With a sad sigh, I take one of his hands from the steering wheel and suck his middle finger. 'I'm yours,' I say.

'Yeah?'

'For ever,' I say.

Four

She is extraordinary and Hank understands her need.

One side of her face is pressed into the pillow; her eyes are open wide and tiny rivulets of charcoal eye-liner streak her cheekbones. Gulping at the hot air, her mouth seems ready to swallow the world and she coughs like a cat with fur stuck in its throat. From behind her comes the sound of flesh thudding into flesh; of pelvic bones slapping wetly into the cushion of her white buttocks. Reaming her pink innards, riding her still-clothed back, Hanks cuts the reins to let this beautiful animal run wild from the stables, where she has paced for too long.

Discreet liberty on the cock of stranger; the handsome mother and wife he's captured releases her zeal in a flood. Gushing from her mouth, in a torrent of self-abuse, she repeats, 'I'm a whore,' to herself. Quiet at first, her voice then rises to a crescendo as Hank digs himself inside her and loops his arms over her back to clasp her breasts with his inquisitor hands. 'I'm a whore,' she says to punish herself for abandoning the supermarket and all it stands for – the place our hunt led us to, the place we took her from.

In the anonymity of our room at the 8 Ball motel – home of transient lusts and salesman's frustration, of high-school clinches and middle-class sins –

that we've rented for two nights, she can be free of children, husband and home. With this lean white-bodied phantom clawing her, binding her, fucking her, she can reveal her truths to the night. No rules on the wrong side of our door.

She is so pretty. Pale and red-haired, tall and elegant, long-limbed and straight-necked, she glides more than she walks. Her glamour is mute and stronger for it. There are discreet glimpses of gold on her fingers and in her ears. Knee-length boots, made from supple leather, hide her long feet but frame the curve of her strong calves. Her hair was once long, but the conservatism of middle age has chased it up to her throat where it curls and shines. At a first glance, her face will tell you this woman stands for no nonsense. The green of her eyes is emerald bright, but crystal hard. The ends of her mouth have begun to turn down, as if a weight of disappointment is pulling at her chiselled, European face. But beyond the fine lines around her eyes, and the stiff pout of her lips, I sense a tenderness. She hides the richness of this other vulnerable self from the routine and drudgery of mid-town life. It's a part of her she's saved from youth; a quality that craves the sensual but has never found succour.

Stretching my intuition into her past, I know a boyfriend became a husband and this man has denied the intensity of her stare at bedtime for too long. Now, she realises it's impossible to articulate her hunger. It's too late for her to describe her appetite to the man she married; it will never become a request for the shocking and the depraved. There was no way she would find this thrill in the safety of family and home. Imprisoned within her, it would take a special stranger to lever her treasure into the light. Hank sensed these gifts from afar. From just a glimpse of her, as she strode from her car to the market, he felt himself pulled from a stupor. I observed his change; his eyes blinked to a sniper's stare, the aperture of his pupils shrank, and the target was sighted. As the tension passed from his facial muscles, his lips parted and his teeth could be seen. Awoken by her, he followed her into the store – a giant place full of food and lights that offered no satisfaction for this woman of the world who desired the underworld.

Once through the door of the motel, he must have led her straight to the bedroom and then fallen upon her, ripping at her lips and hoisting her skirts as she panted and soon shook like a doll in his quick, savage hands. When they began, I hid, listening and trembling outside the window. When the bedroom light flashed on and off, I had been given a sign and then fled up to our rooms.

In the adjoining lounge in the honeymoon suite, I send my intuition through the thin wall to spy on Hank's passion for another woman. Clairvoyant with the projections our bond provides, I am able to see his encounter in my mind. When I love, Hank is even able to pass into my body and experience my experience. But he's older and his skills are sharper. Mostly, I just get to watch him, but sometimes there are exhilarating flashes of enlightenment, when I can feel his cock sinking into a girl and smell the perfume of her hair.

As I relax into the cream sofa in the lounge of our honeymoon hell, still fully dressed, I regulate my excited breathing and concentrate my will into a stream until I see inside the bedroom. In my mind, the litter of notions and distracting thoughts blows away. For years I have endured this; I have loved this. Frightening myself with rages and trembling with the urge to join the adulterous couplings, I have adored the torment until my rubbing fingers, folded inside my puss, have either released me or coaxed me to run on swift feet to share a feed.

The woman chastises herself again. 'Am I a whore?' she says.

'You're beautiful, lady,' Hank encourages, moving her limp and surrendered body to accommodate his thrusting. From all fours, he collapses with her so they lie side by side – two shuffling spoons wet with love beneath their clothes. There was no time for them to undress and I guess, as they drove here, the mutual hunger commanded silence too. Words could have spoiled the surprise and horror of what she was about to do; of what she had dreamed every night for years, of what she had looked for and not found in ten years of marriage.

Strewn upon the bed, caught up in messy sheets, my Hank introduces her to the place in her dreams. He makes it become hard and tangible. No longer obscured by the mists of her fantasy, he shows her the truth; the initial clumsiness, the sweat, the deafening sound of a heart running ragged, the lungs that can't work fast enough, the taste of anxiety she will grow to love, and the cold shock of a new body against her own. To offer an insight into the night ahead, he has thrown her upon the bed, ruffled her skirt and slip around her slender waist, pulled her sheer knickers to the side, and then plunged himself into her anus without invite or lubricant.

She must understand there will be pain and demands made of her. There must be shame so she will be thrilled by it, so she will writhe in it, request it, and blush hot from it for years to come. Fastidious in his approach, Hank thrusts deep and dog-like. To increase the friction he yanks her hips back to meet him. Her fingernails draw blood on the palms of her own hands and Hank sucks in his cheeks when she cries out. As he prepares to empty himself in her virgin rectum, he slaps her gartered bottom and she responds by shouting, 'Yes.'

He comes. Under his white T-shirt, made damp with sweat, I see his muscles strain. His back curves and his neck ripples as if steel cables are working beneath the flushed skin. Flashing his eyes open, he stares at the ceiling and opens his mouth to draw a deep lungful of air across his teeth. Pouring from him, his hot seed scorches through his cock and throbs into her stretched passage. On her hips, his fingers sink like hooks and lift her off the bed. He shakes her, like a dog worrying a hare in its jaws, until every drop of his seed is cast inside the tatters of her fidelity and propriety. After he withdraws from her, he kisses the base of her spine and smooths his hands over the silk of her knickers to let her know he has the touch she wants and not just the power she craves.

In the post-coital silence, he crouches on the floor at the foot of the bed and catches his breath. The woman stays motionless for a while, with her bottom still thrust upward and her weight resting on her forearms. Slowly, she uncurls her fingers from the palm of her hands and shakes the hair from her face. Moving gently, she rises to her knees, pushes her skirt down, turns, and then swings her legs over the side of the bed. Without looking at Hank, she raises her chin and wipes her eyes. 'Thank you,' she says, and her voice is strong.

Hank nods and stands up. Before she can feel uncomfortable in his silence, he asks her to strip; informs her they are a long way from conclusion. I hear his gruff commands through the plaster and wallpaper. Concentrating hard, I seek the smallest details because they are a delight to me – like the way this woman's fine fingers become clumsy as they pop buttons and struggle with a zipper. Disrobing from her elegant shield of designer suit and satin slip, I catch a flash in my mind of Hank's need for this woman and wife. It is blinding. By unveiling her chic-whore underwear, she's made him giddy with impatience.

Staring fixedly at her reflection in the mirrored ceiling, his lover sees herself played like a banned movie on the sleazy screen of this run-down picture house. Splayed across the mirrors, she can see herself in full colour, filtered through the amber glow of dimmed wall lights. Stripped to her lingerie – the feminine secrets she wears beneath her working-wife suit – it's as if she's been dressing like this each morning to prepare for this moment, when a prowler with hot eyes would lead her to her undoing. Does her husband know of the black French knickers? Does he notice the dark sheen they stretch across her hips? Does he know she offers her small but sensitive breasts to imaginary mouths when she presents them in lacy half-cups? Could he guess that her pantyhose have been shed for slut-black stockings, conspiring with a thin garter belt, to be glimpsed between the slash in her long skirt, above the tops of her tight leather boots? How could he know these garments expressed his wife's yearning for foreign hands and travelling tongues? How could he know there was a man who would eventually understand and deliver the dreams?

Hank walks across to her. He kisses her lips, made fuller and younger by their love, and strokes her naked shoulders. Inside me, there is a spasm and I frown and whip my head about on the cushion where it rests. Hank smiles and guides her towards the bed. As he wishes, she sits down. He kneels before her.

Unzipping her boots first, he takes time to caress her calves, made slippery by warm nylon, and then he kisses her toes and ankle-chain. Making her shiver, his fingers creep across her inner thighs, up to the black smoke of her knickers. Teeth delight her. Hard ivory, intent on blood, brushes against the tender furrows of her sex, now shiny with sap, and she knows a tongue is ready to follow the teeth. Shuddering, she lies back under his shadow. It passes over her black and white body, suddenly pornographic with this tall man who has pursued her through the colourful aisles of a supermarket.

Widening her thighs, she lets the stranger's face inhale, taste and swallow the perfume and wine that belong to her husband. Abducted from the marital bed, she spreads her arms and claws the sheets as Hank's mouth eats through her damp to find the dynamite. Sobbing but smiling, she suddenly says, 'Yes', to encourage the tongue at play with her clit and milky dew. As her feet twist the sheets and her body twitches into the death throes of complete sacrifice, Hank moves upward to devour her thick pink nipples – the size of the top hat on the Monopoly board, I think. The brassière with the half-cups is shed down to her waist where she is already bound by a garter belt. Sucked whole between his teeth, he takes her pink top hats into his mouth and rinses them of scent and soap with his saliva.

My own nips begin to tingle.

Undoing my blouse, I unclip my long-line bra to get at these wayward bumps. Pinching them and biting my bottom lip, I moan like a sulky child and writhe on the couch. I need to hurt my own flesh and emulate the attentions of Hank's mouth on the small breasts next door, so I squash my breasts together, tug my nips out and then squeeze bruises into the skin around them, gasping at the delightful results of my punishment. It's good but not enough. Soon I will need real love in the room next door. But first, I'll wait until Hank has taken her further into a place where any disgrace can be enjoyed, where any player can partake of her, where she's mindless and sacrificial.

After undressing quickly, while the housewife's heat smoulders red, Hank strokes his long cock out beneath his hard stomach and kneels between the thighs he has opened on the bed. Daring to look, she sees a weapon that ended her life as a faithful wife and devoted mother. Thick and senseless, it seems to be peering at her sex with its one pink-rimmed eye. As if prison walls have tumbled down inside her soul, the evil inmate of her lust streaks through the gaps of her broken defences. 'Be hard, please,' she says, her voice quivering. 'You see, I . . .'

'It's OK, sweetheart,' Hank assures her, and leans forward to enter her. I nearly cry out to curse his treachery, but instead I bite my knuckle and thump cushions. Parting the flimsy curtain of labia – more like an usher of welcome – he splits her final thought of denial and squeezes through her. On and on he goes until the root of his manhood is embraced by the drapes of her sex.

'No,' she moans, and raises both legs to his shoulders. 'Don't. Please don't, mister. Whoever you are,' she mutters, closing her eyes and then her ankles behind his head.

Feeling confined, Hank unhooks her ankles from around his neck. Gripping the heels of her taut feet, he presses them down so her legs bend and her thighs squash against her breasts. Between the soles of her upturned feet, he can see the pain and joy in her expression. Delighted by the change that has arrived to her handsome features, framed by the red hair now tousled out of its neat style, he withdraws to the tip of his rigidity, and then plunges it back inside her, until his stem is buried in the mother's rich earth.

Next door, on the couch, I arch my back and then slither from my tight pink skirt. I slide my hand inside my tight Directoire knickers and find moisture. Pushing three fingers into my sticky puss, and stretching my legs out to their maximum length, I climax immediately. There is a popping sound as the heels of my stilettos puncture the armrest of the sofa. As if my snakeskin pumps have rediscovered their sting, they sink into the sofa foam while my red nails reveal a bite of their own. Deep inside me they go to work, tickling my slick pink walls, and I sustain the headless wonder of my climax.

Ramming the housewife down into the bed, so she produces yelps as if she's burned her fingers on the stove, Hank delivers the payload of his own desperation. As I mutter in the half-light of the lounge, I listen to the shrieks of the lovers and the creaks of their bed, and know we must make her suffer. I said she was extraordinary and she truly is. Unlike the flaunters and exhibitionists who offer no epiphany through discovery, she is one who hides her desire. And the part of her she conceals has not been diluted by excess or thinned by confession; it has been left to tighten like a spring until the spring must be released and the woman must be saved. Perhaps the husband was blind to her nature, but I think him a fool for not mining the gold and silver of her needs. Still, we should be grateful for his neglect, because the secrets of this ordinary woman have become ours.

Maybe she thinks it will soon be over. As Hank throws his sinews, stamina and killer's technique into her womb, she cries her every indiscretion at him. 'Tell me what I am. Hurt me there ...' It's not her fault if she thinks her night will end when the stranger ejaculates for a second time. I almost want to tell her to save her energy because dawn is a long way off and Hank will need her until the sun rises. We shall want to exhaust this one.

Not having fed for longer than is good for him, Hank's mind has been filled with the Preacher. Other than the favours of his sweet Missy, who pampers him most mornings and gave him beautiful torments with Charlie, my Hank has neglected himself. You must get nourishment, baby, I told him. He nodded and his lips went thin. How could he stand the dry mouth and the start of the cramps, I thought, when so many fine citizens stream past us in cars and bars, and offer themselves on the streets and in the booths of midnight diners? But Hank's waters run so deep, sometimes I'm unable to hear their currents. Lately, he's been adrift on a sea I've never chartered and cannot bring him back from. It worries me: he's never been this withdrawn before. I need him to be strong for me; to take me places where the prey is slow and tasty, and where the Preacher won't show. I need him to plan our routes and take me to the safe havens where his ancient friends offer us shelter in return for stories. So you can understand my delight when he finally took this lover, even if she is handsome, tall, elegant and full of so much darkness it makes my head spin. If I wasn't around, I wonder if he'd bond with this one and take her on the ride that never ends. It's hard but I stop myself thinking like that, because I'll only start to play Hank up with a row to get reassurance. It's not fair on him. Sometimes I can be such a selfish kitten – a 'madam', he says. Hank has never been tempted to take another over me. That guilt is mine. That shame I own alone, but that's another story.

Earlier in the evening, it was me who encouraged him to rouse from the chair by the open window and to go on a hunt. Waiting for the stars to wink at him, he'd just sat around from the time we arrived at the 8 Ball until about nine in the evening. Engulfed by the infinity of his thoughts, he'd smoked two packs of Marlboro to keep a grip on his mind. Watching him for hours was stifling. After I'd eaten a dozen donuts and stained the lapel of my jacket with powdered sugar, I had to go out.

'OK, baby. OK,' he finally said, and slid into his overcoat.

But crawling past the taverns and diners of Santa Fe did little to stimulate his interest. Staring through the windscreen as he drove, Hank only seemed able to look back inside his own head. 'What about her?' I said, as we stopped at a junction to let a long-haired woman in leather trousers cross the street, but he never seemed to even notice her. 'Over there, baby,' I said, as three blondes leapt from a jeep and made their way to a bar called Rodeo Nites. Hank shook his head, sighed, and carried on down the main boulevard. 'Baby, we're out of the main strip,' I said, as the neon trailed away behind the car. Folding my arms across my chest, and tugging on my cigarette with annoyance, I started to wonder if he'd ever snap out of this mood. Dressed up in my favourite suit – a pink two-piece that somehow works with snakeskin heels, flesh stockings and a headscarf – I imagined the evening descending back into a weary gloom, spent in the honeymoon suite of the 8 Ball, when Hank suddenly pulled the car into the parking lot of a supermarket.

'What –' I started to say, but he pressed one finger against my lips and said 'Ssh' real quiet.

'Over there,' was all Hank said, and he was out of the car by the time I caught sight of a tall woman in a nice suit, disappearing through the sliding doors of the supermarket.

Watching keenly, I waited in the car for no more than twenty minutes before Hank reappeared, walking by the side of the tall red-headed woman in her great suit. She looked about her and seemed unsteady on her feet. I knew she was wracked with indecision, but Hank paused, lit a cigarette, and then said something to her. She nodded, and her mouth broke into the weak but encouraging smile of relief. Right then, I knew the hunter had seized his quarry, unconditionally. I slid across to the driver's seat, turned the engine over, and then raced the car back to the 8 Ball Motel, with little shivers of glee shortening my breaths and making me giggle all the way home.

Back in the bedroom, Hank's getting busy with his belt now. With that evil black whip, he's showing her the delight of pain, and there is a noise like a handgun going off in a metal booth. There's a bumping sound too as she crawls around the floor, followed by the master's bull whip. I sink back into my thoughts and chase the shadows in my mind until they harden into real images.

Hank's being tough. I've not seen him like this for a while, with his concentration so keen and his body firm as a dancer. At first, his violence frightens me. But when I see her face, I squeeze my nips so hard, tears fill up my eyes with a salty refreshment.

'You fuck. You crazy fucking bastard,' she says, raising her buttocks to exalt in the streak lightning he bathes her pale thighs and panty-covered buttocks with. But then she's on the bed, leaping up, cat-quick, and she turns on Hank. He pauses, surprised. Slowly, she narrows her eyes, extends her tongue between her smudged mouth and taunts him by trailing it around the thickly painted, blood-red oval of her mouth.

'Oh, baby,' he whispers and moves to the bed.

'Bastard,' I whisper. That's my name. He calls me baby, and suddenly I want to laugh hysterically. That white-fleshed bastard of the endless night will suffer for that.

The wife and mother rolls on her side, slips her hands between her legs and rips the gusset of her French knickers apart. Clenching her toes, she stretches her long, stocking-sheathed legs down the bed towards Hank and calls him a 'bad man'.

'Oh, baby,' I say, and stand up in the lounge. I shake the images of them from my mind. Even if I have to fist-fight Hank, I will have this woman. She is food from the darkest gods.

In I go, through the door with no hesitation. The door swings wide open and it slams into the bedroom wall, catching their attention. Her back, thighs and buttocks are a warm red – even in the dim light I can see the fire he's put in her flesh. She's sitting astride Hank now, and working him inside her by making little rotations with her hips. She looks over her shoulder and shows me her face; clownish and slutty in smeared make-up. There is no panic at the arrival of a female intruder, only a smile so evil it takes my breath away. Honey, I think, what have you brought into our bed?

'Easy, girl,' Hank whispers to his lover, and strokes her hair. 'It's OK, she's folk.'

The woman closes her eyes and seems ready to cry with happiness. I am thrilled to the marrow of my bones because I know she has dreamed of loving a woman. She has locked this desire in the smallest and most secret place inside her. Smiling, and stripped to my stockings and white garter belt, I walk towards the tender fruit that Hank has peeled and revealed to me. 'What's your name, ma'am?'

'Barbara,' she says in a soft voice, and stares at my breasts, seeing the red marks on a soft, white surround. 'You're so young,' she says with a sigh, as if remembering her own body at seventeen.

'But old enough to hurt you,' I say sweetly, and see Hank start to smile behind her.

Barbara looks confused. I slip on to the bed behind her. I get close but don't touch. Her lips part and her eyes slit. Gently, I slip one hand into her hair and stroke her head. She angles her head into my palm and begins to rub it against my hand. She relaxes into my touch and I trace my fingers across one of her pale shoulders. 'Fuck him,' I whisper.

Smiling, she starts to move on Hank's cock, circling and nuzzling the thickness inside her.

'It's like he's so far inside me, he's holding me up,' she says. Over Hank's shoulder, I can see she's kneading his smooth chest with her fingers – the stroke of a lover, the sign of familiarity.

So they have a rhythm. This I can see.

My fingers tighten in her hair and then relax to slip around to the base of her warm skull, where her pelt grows thickest and most lush. 'Is it good, Barbara?' I whisper.

'Oh, yeah,' she says, nodding her head. 'The best.'

'Better than your husband's cock?' I ask.

She smiles like a lunatic. 'Thicker. Longer.'

I love this woman. 'Then ride it, bitch,' I say. 'Ride my man's cock.'

Before I finish speaking, she's bumping up and down on Hank. He blows air through his lips, and his nostrils flare. Our tension has invigorated him.

'Ride him,' I say, louder. 'Fuck him, bitch.'

'Oh, yeah,' she says, her voice getting thin. She bites her bottom lip, stares into my eyes and then looks at my snarling mouth. Her pumping gets faster.

'You're a whore,' I say. 'A cheap motel whore.'

Barbara snatches Hank's hands from her waist and slaps them on to her breasts. Following her lead, he mauls them, and now she's bouncing on and off his body. I fist my hand in her hair and as she goes up and down it's like I'm yanking her on and off Hank's cock.

'You give it away for free, barstool bitch.'

'Yes!' she suddenly screams, and I pull her hair so she's facing the ceiling.

'Look at your pretty slut face,' I say through clenched teeth.

'That's me, that's me,' she shouts.

'A whore who picks up strange men in supermarkets.'

'That's me, that's me,' she shrieks, but before she can make any more noise I pull her face around, press it into mine, and kiss her deep. Barbara sucks my face and I lick her runny make-up from her cheekbones. I'm blind with the need to eat her alive and I clean my delicious food.

I hold her body still, so she can't bang in and out of Hank. She whimpers with alarm because the pummelling in her sex has stopped. But Hank reads my sign and seizes her hip bones. As I pull her long tongue inside my mouth, he thrusts his hips like a jackhammer, on and off the bed, until she comes. Barbara's climax electrocutes through her. As if she's spitting poison from her mouth, she says hideous things. Such filth from Barbara surprises and delights me.

'In her mouth,' Hank begs me, and pulls his slippery stem from her sex.

I push Barbara's head down between Hank's legs and he stuffs himself in her mouth. As he beats his cream into her head, we both hear the melody of her moans to the beat of a tongue slapping against rigid flesh. In his excitement, Hank then pulls a pillow over his face and bites right through it. I pull her still-lapping mouth from his groin and move her lips to mine. As I share the salty milk on her tongue, she moans like a real lady with a mouthful of splendid cake.

'In two days we'll be with Valerie,' Hank says from somewhere close by, in the stillness of our dark room.

This concerns me, but I smile from where I lie in Barbara's hair, my lips still close to hers. Her lids are heavy, but the green of her eyes is still bright and I feel it adoring my face with its special light.

'Why couldn't you tell me before? You know I love to hang out with Valerie,' I lie.

For a moment, it seems he hasn't heard me because he stays quiet. But then he whispers, 'You like surprises, baby.' Only I'm not convinced; where his voice lacks the usual quiet decisiveness, the hollows are filled with guilt. I'm about to question him, even though I'm in a stupor from the feed, but Barbara speaks. 'Take me with you, to Valerie.'

I giggle. Hank strokes her hair. He's lying behind her and has been soothing the passage he made into her body. With his tongue he cleans and numbs the place he fed from. 'Not a place for you, sweet,' he says to Barbara.

'But I want to go,' she insists in her sleepy voice, but doesn't have the energy to prop herself up and turn to face him.

'Ssh,' I whisper, and kiss her lips which are red and swollen from our attentions. 'We'll always be with you, ma'am.'

'Will you come back?' she says, desperately.

'Yes,' I say. 'We're always going to be coming back to you.'

'I'll be watching out for you in the stores,' she says through a smile, and she seems to have worn herself out from all the talk.

'Sleep, honey,' Hank murmurs, so his deep voice vibrates through the mattress under us, under his loves.

'Rest,' I say, and kiss both of her eyelids shut.

We'd been hard with her for a long time. In an hour the sun will be up and we'll set out for Valerie's place – a farm near Big Spring, Texas. On the map in my mind, I draw straight lines from the place we started to run from to the place we're running to. A part of me is unsatisfied; unable to believe that Hank would have rushed us through the country, when we were so happy in California a week ago, just to reach Valerie's farm. It had not been more than three years since we last visited her so it seemed strange to be going back so soon.

Our life is travel – an endless voyage from state to state because of Hank's work. Sometimes we even cross the border and go to Mexico where it's easier to be ourselves. Sometimes I'm left alone for months and I guess he goes abroad on account of the beautiful things he brings back. My favourite gift is the little golden Buddha. The clothes from Paris are beautiful, but I love my Buddha most. It reminds me of Hank, because inside its tiny smooth head is all the wisdom and calm that one day I shall want for myself.

I know he used to work for the government after the war with Germany, and I know the Preacher did too. Even Valerie had connections. But I don't know what Hank does now. He told me once that

69

governments change and on his time scale he needed more security. There are agencies, he said, that suit people like him.

'What about Barbara?' I ask Hank.

'Leave her here and let her heal. We'll pay another night in case she needs it.'

Barbara is asleep now and I doubt she'll wake up until tomorrow afternoon. When she wakes up, she'll be confused and her body will be tender in parts. Her memory will trick or fail her, but at night her dreams will recount the stories our touch left behind, for ever. Our love with this woman has been good; better than so many others recently. It has been some time since we found one so needy, and although we rarely take too much time from the family types – because of the obvious complications – Barbara was special. Maybe our love saved her.

'Is he close?' I ask, as the shadow of the Preacher stoops across my mind.

'I think so,' Hank says, but I can tell by his voice that he is reluctant to worry me. 'The dreams are clearer.'

A shiver passes across my skin and I cuddle against Barbara.

'I don't want you to fret now, baby,' Hank says. 'Soon, there'll be peace for us.'

'How?'

'Just take my word. Even though I want to, there are things I can't talk about.'

'I can't do this much longer, Hank. I have to know what's been going on. My ass is on the line too.'

He reaches over Barbara and touches my head. 'You'll know soon, baby.'

'Promise?'

'Promise.'

Part Two

Somewhere Between Heaven
and Hell

Five

Leaning out of the window, I feel the sun's warmth on my face. Behind my sunglasses I keep my eyes closed but my head still fills with golden hues. Above me the Texas sky is blue and cloudless. Below me there is pasture, wood and hill, sweeping away and out of sight as if the land's green and yellow patchwork continues for ever. 'Yessum,' I say, and take a long draw on my cigarette before blowing a plume of blue smoke into the cool air of morning. This is my country.

Outside my head things aren't that tranquil. Upstairs in the attic, Valerie is rippin' Sweet Boy Denver. She'll be taking him apart and going about him with her cane on account of my indiscretion, conducted earlier. There's not much hollerin' from Sweet Boy Denver as the streak-lightning stings across his rump. He makes more of a muffled yelp and then a hiss because his teeth are clamped shut. I can hear him in my room, one floor down, where Val bid me stay after finding us out back. If I didn't know that quick-eyed scamp got a kick out of such treatment, I'd feel worse. Still, I feel bad because my mama brought me up right and when you're a guest in somebody's house you follow certain rules even if you don't care for the folk. It should be me getting that seasoned wood across my pink panties, but because of Hank I guess Val doesn't feel right about raising a hand to me.

Getting caught with both hands in Val's pantry makes me feel stupid as well as guilty. After all Hank showed me, I should have chosen a better time to go mooning after her handyman. Might not have made any difference, though, because Val is real clever. Even if she hadn't walked into the laundry room and found that sweet boy between my legs, I guess she would have read deceit in both of our eyes soon enough. Never mess with someone's food unless you get the nod. Big rule among us who have the bond and I broke it. Way I figure, though, I never had much patience with laws and such.

With Texas out there and the hot feeling of being caught red-handed easing off, I can understand why I did it. I took what was hers to take my mind off all the strain Hank is putting me under, with his strange Preacher-frighted behaviour and then his sudden vanishing act within an hour of our arrival at Val's place.

'Where you going, baby?' I asked.

'Get us some peace of mind,' was all he said, before driving off at an incautious speed.

I just needed a little taste of something sweet but manly, that's all. And spying that boy taking a pause in his chores to finger my skimpies was all the encouragement I needed. The way he sought my fragrance stirred me up. Seeing him worship those black panties with that look of wonder in his eyes, and his Adam's apple bobbing in his throat like Halloween was going on in his thoughts, made up my mind. Sure, I'd stalked him around the house for three days whenever Val's back was turned, but I was mixed up. Gave myself away by raising my snubby nose to catch his spicy hound-in-heat smell, and by

74

feeling those fine limbs with my eyes, and by letting too much show through my denim shorts, especially when he brought cold lemonade or Johnny Walker Red out to the porch, where I swung in a hammock, reading. But he played his part too. That boy was always messing in my room while I was out walking; caressing my shoes and looking for the smell of my blondeness in the pillow cases, not to mention his lifting of my cast-away delicacies up to his nose in the laundry shack. You see, that's what I caught him doing – shooting up on the new girl's opium. Familiar with Val's fragrance, which I guess is kind of sour, he needed something fresh to take into his lungs. Risk anything for my musk, that boy, and knowing Val was so tough, he had balls to go a-sneaking through linen baskets and bottom drawers. Sometimes I know a man just can't help himself.

Giving him the opportunity to wash my under-things was a mistake on Val's part. 'Boy will take care of it,' she said, and snatched up our laundry after I'd unpacked on the day we arrived. Could she have not known he had the taste for that kind of drink? Like a bum near a pint of wine, that boy didn't fool me. First day, the moment he saw my legs slink from the car, Sweet Boy Denver was eroding my outfit with his red-rock eyes. 'Better put the stud in the bottom field,' Hank said to Val, which made her go stiffer than usual when she pecked my cheeks in welcome. Hank don't miss a thing.

Well, on this fine morning, he was in the laundry shack when I found him, just leaning back against the big dryer, barefoot, long-legged in his cobalt-wash jeans, shirt off, all browned, and lean and rangy like he should have been a cowboy smoking Marlboro on the back of a magazine. Val has taste; I'll give her that. But this boy was toking on the delicate aroma drifting off my silk panties bought from Paris, France. He had them cupped in his hands in the way a thirsty rider will raise spring water to his mouth, looking at the wonder of the sparkles soon to quench the thirst that's taken over his mind.

One minute he's on his own, next minute little Missy's outline appears in the doorway. No bra in this heat, and I had my shirt tied in a knot under my bosom like a prison prostitute looking to score. Around my tummy were a pair of butt-hiking shorts; made so a girl's legs never end in a man's eyes.

For a moment he looked sick. Went kind of white to green in a heartbeat and I almost thought of playing the fear hand to my advantage. But there was no need; this game was already won. Swinging the door shut with my ankle, I went through the cool room to where Sweet Boy Denver stood shivering. I locked my eyes into his and smiled.

'Good?' I said.

There was a big swallow and then he exhaled. 'Real good.'

'Good enough to eat?' I said, moving in real close so he could see the gloss on my lips and the clear water of my eyes.

'And then some,' he said, his voice a ghost.

Picking up a stocking, I ran it between my Corvette-red nails and then ran it back and forth across the stubble on his top lip, under his nose. I felt his weighty pipe rest against my tummy button, so I left the stocking around his neck, held his stare, and then unzipped him to give the boy a shake-up.

'Baby,' he moaned, when my cool fingers circled muscle.

'Ooh, that's a real fine piece. Can Missy go to work?'

'Got to be real careful,' he breathed, but his eyes were long gone.

Down to the cold stone of the floor I slipped, wetting my lips and lining the rock muscle of his stomach with my claws, knowing they would slide to a handhold – a thick root sticking from the sheer face of this boy's washboard. A man tastes fine after a shower, and Sweet Boy Denver must have just pine-soaped himself out of his keeper's bed, via the washroom, before getting busy with his chores. On my knees, I stared at his thick pear-headed cock and its fat stem and just had to savour that trace of salt on the brown satin skin, on account of his blood being up with my panties recently in the neighbourhood of his face. Closing my eyes, opening my nose for air, I took that boy's trunk to the back door of my skull. By lowering my jaw, I was able to scoop his sweet-potato balls inside too. Kept him there as well until I'd dissolved the very taste from the pores of his skin. A little shiny fingernail up his ass and my other hand pressing his body against the machine behind prevented him from curling into the knot his spine begged for. Ideally, a man needs to lie down when Missy clears his plate with one mouthful, but we were being opportunists out there in the laundry and when the need is mutual and burns under the skin even a gun rack can feel like an emperor's bed.

Pulling back when my sucking bleached his skin, I chopped him through my white fingers with a tight grip until his wood looked too thick to get up inside me.

'Baby, baby, baby,' was all he kept saying, while he ran his long fingers through my kitten locks, which I like, because it's as if a guy is suddenly going to grip my head and force a mouth fuck through my strawberry lips.

'Take my heat away,' I whispered. Denver moaned and shook his head to make sure this was no country-boy dream.

For a wiry guy he was strong. Lifting me high and clean from my knees, he swung me up and then placed my bottom on the cold lid of the enamel clothes dryer. After whipping my shorts down, which was not easy because of their clinging nature, he paused to admire the sheer pink wispies beneath. Made from sheer nylon, with a pinkish tint that coloured my puss, I wore the panties because I like to feel something sliding around under denim when I walk. These little girls were damp at the front and Sweet Boy could see the heavier fabric sopping with high-school musk. Raising my bottom to slip them over my thighs, he then drew them down my calves before pinching them off my pretty red toes. His tawny hand stuffed them under his nose and he made this big huffing sound. I watched his chest inflate to a triangular shape which I found pleasing. The panties were there for only one breath before he turned to the business in hand. After stuffing my flimsies in his back pocket (I guessed I'd seen the last of those slippery friends), he slipped between my thighs, raised my chin with a bent finger and then shaped his mouth into my cherry lips. While we kissed so finely, rocking our heads side to side and only losing each other's lips when we pulled back on a long tongue suck, I wondered if Hank, wherever he was, felt a pang.

Lost to this smooth-chinned boy, I only stopped purring when I felt the head of his round wood pushing away at my puss. There was a moment of resistance, which made me squeal, and he was inside, slipping in, going down, stretching me white with his fat pole. Raised to his tippy toes, with his steel fingers locked into the cleft of my bottom, he hauled me towards him and planted himself at the back of me, staking me to his body as if nothing would shake that rivet lose. What was left of my legs I wrapped around his waist and then lay back, sucking three fingers into a mouth that looked like it had been busy about a pot of red jam.

'Oh, baby,' he said, which surprised me none, so I decided to give this tousle-haired country boy some big-city hooker talk. 'Fuck me, honey. Give me that sweet cock. Put it between my white thighs. I want to lose my mind.'

'Baby,' he cried out, his voice a few octaves lower, and started to yank me on and off his meat. Gripping my thighs, where the soft gold fur grows and shines, he made me grunt in the most unladylike manner. I suddenly wished we were under trees and lying on stream mud, because I had a need to be wild.

That boy growled and switched my legs from shoulder to shoulder, poking me from every angle. Gone were my fancy city airs; this was the kind of boy I wanted to lie naked with. No need for slapping or restraining and the other things I enjoy whenever I'm sleeping under neon; in that Texan wash house, I just wanted to be raw and nude and wet with a clean-smiling farm boy.

'Want to put it all inside you, miss,' he said, still humble, out of respect for the lady and her fine fancy things that smelled so good.

'Fuck it in me. Throw it inside, baby.'

'So pretty. You're so pretty, girl,' he panted, and banged up against that dryer, so his knees made the sounds you hear thundering from a kettle drum and the whole place seemed to be shaking and rattling down around our ears.

Screwing up my face, I felt it come over me. Sparks ricocheted inside my skull, making my ears hot, and under the strawberry blossoms that appeared around my pinky nips, my heart seemed to have grown to twice its size just to thump and thump until I was deaf.

Making a sound, like he was pushing something from his body that could both hurt and delight a man, Sweet Boy Denver squeezed three days' worth of his longing and admiring and lusting and sinning inside my tight, sucking puss-puss. For a while I sobbed but then I found myself laughing.

After his head had settled on my damp tummy, so his mouth could gape and gulp like a fish on a river bank, I clawed his hair and felt so close to him that, if I'd been twenty years younger, I swear it would have been love. For a moment that I never wanted to see the back of, there was the warmth of paradise on our skin and the blood of the devil pounding through our heads. But when I caught sight of Val at the door, the layer of sweat all over our bodies – trickling between our legs, running around my breasts, and dripping off Sweet Boy's chin – turned to ice.

Caught in such a way so as no amount of lying, denying or excusing would create subsidence in Val's high ground, me and Sweet Boy could only stay in the same position and blink at her hard silhouette in the doorway.

Since the moment she turned on her heel, jaw set, and was followed up into the cool darkness of the farmhouse with Denver at her heel, she's still not said anything to me besides, 'Missy, go to your room.' And that boy knew what was coming his way. I could tell by the way his love-flush thinned to a milky pink and then a starched bedsheet-white. But follow her he did: through the kitchen, up the stairs, past their room, and into the attic – which I guess Val only maintains in order to exercise what Hank calls 'her curious taste in discipline'. Sweet Boy has stopped by that place before, I imagine, when the interior of her home has not been as easy on her eyes as she would have liked, or when one of his many chores and errands was not carried out to her complete satisfaction. 'Can get anything out of a man, that girl,' Hank once said, and I presumed he was talking about her dealings for the agency. This morning, it sure sounds like she's whupped everything out of her sweet handyman – tears, confessions, apologies, and, just now, a prairie-dog cry that I know I'll be hearing a month down the road. Perhaps her thoroughness and the volume of its results are all designed to make me feel an extra weight on top of my already leaden shame. If so, and I'm prepared to take the consequences, I mean to put an end to her tormenting of Sweet Boy Denver.

For a moment I pause outside the attic door, hoping she hasn't heard my feet creaking on the wooden stairwell to the roof. There is a lull in the proceedings. Sweet Boy Denver is silent so all I can hear are her stiletto points tapping on the floor and one or two other miscellaneous sounds. Here and there, in the thickness of the loft ceasefire, I intuit the clink of a chain and the tightening of a buckle.

Real slow, I inch the handle down and push the thin door in. It's as if the dark inside the attic sucks me in. Feeling like I'm afloat, I struggle to see the walls, corners and floors as I seep into the murk of attic-night. Hoping my heart thuds won't give me up to the gun I imagine is pointing at me, I try and swallow the fat berry that seems to have lodged my throat closed. With the door pressed, ever so gently, back into place, I crouch down and stretch my sight into this pocket of night that hides from the Texan sun.

The place is full of energy; I sense that. The air molecules are jostling like they've been stirred by a ripple of electricity. Permeating the invisible activity of the air, which is too cold for this part of the world, I catch the scents. Hot perfume, chilled sweat, new leather and fresh meat smells are thickening inside my dizzy head. Palm down, my hands pad me into the gloom and my long body stretches out behind. Not knowing whether this place calls for a fight or love, I slink across the floor, eyes wide, ears pinned back, nose high, to where I hear the *phut*, suck, *phut*, suck noises. Pausing, I hear someone swallow with relish and then gulp at something I sense is sprinkling the darkness with reddy ink.

I have loved and not fed. My stomach growls. Out there, but so close, is the sustenance I crave. Corn fed and whiskey hot, some sweet country boy is giving up his goodness to puckered, cold, heart-shaped lips. My hot mouth moistens and my big eyes get heavy. I moan. The gulping sounds stop. To my right side I hear the scrape and strike of high heels passing across the varnished floorboards. Beneath the clatter of a woman's well-shod feet, I can hear the rasp of nylon-sheer thighs as they scissor together. Twisting into a crouch and ready to leap, I quiver and hear the heels run behind me and then come to a stop. I can't see much: every window must be boarded, every crack taped over. Only the infra-red of my instincts tells me there are hard shapes all around me and something dangerous breathing behind me. Val's perfume drifts across the swept floor to gather and settle around me like invisible gas.

When a red lightbulb explodes into life, I hiss and cower back to the point of tension, on all fours – a springboard to propel me at a throat.

The only attack I face is one against my senses.

Blood-light washes the attic, throwing the shapes and contours of Val's 'curious tastes' at my bewildered eyes. Never have I seen such a place. It is a place designed to weaken and make vulnerable and I can attest to it working. From neat racks, the canes, flails and weird whippy snake-things make my skin goose. Lined along the one wall, in perfect symmetry, are shoes forged with sin in mind for wicked women, who are destined for, or recently escaped from, hell. The heels are like nails, the bootlace straps are crafted to garrotte white ankles into the stiff beauty of domination, the pale leather undersides of soles are designed to squash tongues and tenderise man-flesh, and the shine on the patent leather is there to light the narrow-stepped path a punisher takes to her captive, in even the dimmest cellar.

'I bid you stay put, girl,' comes Val's voice from behind the red light. 'But such a sneak and a snake, I wager, cannot be kept from any hole, until she slithers into the wrong one.'

Can't find my voice.

'You took a fair portion of my Denver, but there's juice in that fruit enough for thief and mistress both.'

'Came to apologise, Val,' I say. 'Not to fight. And I crept up those stairs to offer amends. Seems the wrong person is doing the squealing up here. Should be me, not Denver.'

'I be best judge of what happens to what I own,' she says, with a drop of vinaigrette to her tongue. 'Boy is stupid and easily led by a clever tongue and a slut's body. Served him right if I'd ended his run right here. And real slow too, drop by sweet drop. And whose conscience would that have been heavy on, from here on out to judgement day? Not mine, girl. Not mine.'

'I'm willing to pay.'

'What price?' I don't like the hiss in her voice.

'What a wronged woman thinks is fit,' I say. 'Once

her blood goes down a notch. All this talk of finality brings my claws out.'

She laughs but not in a pretty way. 'A fighter. Just like me. Hank likes that in a woman.'

'Leave him be,' I warn.

'But you've had a slice of my pie. It's only fair I nibble yours.'

'There's a difference between food, no matter how tasty, and what amounts to a wife and her man. You know it. Denver's not bonded.'

'And if he was, you'd still have come up on him.'

'Not so,' I say, not altogether sure whether I'm telling the truth. 'I might have looked at him in the same way you eat up Hank with your pretty eyes, but bonded love is a bigger meal than a snack on the road. I'm in the wrong, Val, but can't we keep this between sisters?'

Behind that big red lamp – the kind they use on movie sets – I know she's thinking. She's breathing deep; I can hear her. Maybe there is some sense in what I say and her recent feasting upon Sweet Boy Denver has probably slowed up her calculations.

In these parts, not liking Val has always been my biggest problem. She knows me and Hank are tight but she always makes the eyes. They had a time in Chile and then another, later, in Saigon, but that was way back and she's not for Hank. More than anything I don't trust her, which may sound like a contradiction in present circumstances, but something about Val's long stares and longer silences make me aware of her calculating the odds of taking my man for keeps. We're like two rattlers sunning ourselves on the same rock. Whenever we get together – on account of Hank and Val's agency work – we can't keep from looking each other in the eye. And I don't like what I see. 'Soon me and that girl are going to have a spat, Hank. So don't lead me there,' I told him, but he just knocked me back.

'She'll bust you, girl. Make no mistake, she's real elegant and all, but she's a killer. Don't go getting her riled. I see you in her, Missy, that's how I know.'

Hank's been gone no more than three days and I've got her riled. Worried about me and her, he even asked Val if I should stay in the shack she has down by the bubbling stream in the backwoods. But Val said no. She has a tenant – some beatnik poet whom she doesn't want disturbed.

I stand up and turn to face what the floodlamp has lit up – the place where Sweet Boy Denver hangs so still and silent. Val's gallows are black and made from metal tubes that are assembled into a rectangle by brackets at each corner. Up and down the inner side of the uprights, and screwed under the crossbar, are fixtures for the attaching of chains and so forth. Along the bottom are leather straps for holding the ankles in place. Each of the cuffs shows the sign of much use.

In the middle of this frame is Sweet Boy Denver and never have I seen a man so reduced. Naked, with his wrists and ankles cuffed at the corners of the frame, his limbs stretch out so his body forms a star-shape. His head is gone. That is, his pretty face and soft hair are covered up real tight by a rubber head-piece, allowing slits for the eyes and a hole for the rigorous breathing a fella must take when affixed to such a contraption.

That muffin-gold complexion, so recently grazed by my claws, has been lined by an implement altogether straighter, thinner and less sensitive to entreaty. When Val appears beside me, I see her right hand is gloved in latex and holding a devil-black riding crop; the kind they used to favour in the South for the discipline of the uppity and the correcting of the wayward.

'Seen to him good,' Val says, and her delight lights up her perfect teeth in the dark. 'Yes, sir, tapped him too – right near the place that gave you so much pleasure.'

I look down to his still-erect manhood and glimpse a shadowy abrasion. Good rich place to feed from when a man's blood is up.

'He's walking through paradise now,' she says, which is not incorrect because once a girl has supped a man's strength, he's freed from care or the meddling of thought. He's loose the way he was when just a babe. Guess a part of us all needs supervising and some regimentation of the will too. For men like Sweet Boy Denver it's a way of life. This I know.

It seems Val and I are not about to mix it up with nails and teeth, so I move from the place where the scent of good food is thick. To take my mind off the fix, I inspect Val's wares, especially the clothes.

Up here, it seems she's fond of stowing the kind of garb that I imagine makes her cold beauty well worth the investigation of any man. Lined in a shiny metal closet is an array of rubber skirts that seem too tight for a woman's loins. They stick to my fingertips when I touch them. Dresses with the backs cut away, corsets with six metal suspender clasps for each leg, black net blouses and studded leather brassières all hang in an immaculate order from teeny silver hangers which remind me of the triangles in a high-school orchestra.

Still nervous of Val wearing that grin, I only take a quick peek at the outfit she's wearing when she glides to where I stand. Looks like discipline in this crazy household requires a uniform and a ritual. Seems she dressed especially to correct Denver too.

Maybe he even helped her to stretch those long nylons up her legs before the knee-length skirt – made from latex as thin as cotton – was fitted around her hips. Wearing that corset seems to have something to do with endurance too, but I like the way the leather holds her breasts high while keeping her waist so tight.

'Takes a team to get it hitched,' she says, and her voice has softened since she's seen my interest in her midnight wardrobe. 'And there's other stuff,' she adds, real quiet, and stops before a cupboard that is waist-high and beside the clothes rack. 'Some of Denver's toys.'

I smile, but I'm afraid it's a weak one. She watches my eyes without blinking her own and then steps aside. 'A girl may take a man,' she says, 'but it takes time to see into his heart.'

'There is truth in that,' I say, with a nod. Inside the cupboard my eyes alight on Denver's rubber hoods. From the rooster to the pig faces that hang, deflated, I can gather this boy was destined to become a lady's livestock. I look at the floor. 'He's special to you.'

'Had our times, but just having the one makes it hard to stem wayward thoughts. Guess that goes both ways.'

'Especially when you came from the wild.'

'Sure enough,' she says with her face looking dreamy. 'Grass is always greener. When I was through running for the agency, I thought this place would suit me until the sun winked out. But it's an awful long time until you reach the end of our highway.' Val goes quiet and looks uppity again, as if letting her guard down was the last thing she originally intended.

'Do you think we can heal what was done earlier?' I say, moving closer to her, anxious not to be burnt by her frost again. 'Seems like I should make a gesture. You know, I really ain't so bad and I'll stay away from the boy.'

'Should think so,' she says, but not unpleasantly. 'He won't be showing his face for a while, anyways.'

I nod, looking grave, but at least I know Sweet Boy Denver won't mind a stay in the attic. 'Being so restless and all, what with Hank's disappearing act, maybe I should take a lesson from someone who knows a thing or two.' This is either brave of me or damned foolish. 'Sometimes it's good to feel a woman's touch,' I whisper, looking down at Val's slender feet, tight in those pointy shoes.

'You should dress for the privilege,' she says, after a pause in acknowledgement of my compromise, and I can feel her cool breath on my mouth. Feeling dizzy with so much fizzing in my tummy, like there are a zillion crystals dissolving, I raise my face to the handsome woman who wants my man and hates my hold upon him. She's so close now and her eyes lower to my throat when I swallow.

We kiss. Then we hold hands.

'I'm different with girls,' Val says, brushing my blondeness with a pearl-handled brush that I bet has been across Denver's britches. 'Rare I take to a lady, and then it took some time to fall for one. But you know how it is with our clock ticking so slow, you just find things you never guessed were there.'

I smile and relax on my stool, so my weight rests against her firm belly. 'Speaking from the heart, I've always had an eye for the ladies.'

'Girl, you're too much,' she says and laughs. I'm getting used to her laugh and it's not all bad. Strange how adversity can sometimes bring people close. Almost seems too good to be right.

'Surprises me you were reticent,' I say. 'Way you

been preparing me for your supper makes this chick think her fox is often on the prowl.'

Smiling, Val leans down and kisses my cheek. 'The girls in Asia are magical. Truly magical. No one forgets a touch of magic.'

'No, ma'am,' I say, thinking back on the glorious bath she ran for me, loaded with scent and brimming with hot frothy water. Getting sponged by her cool hands, on the nips, tummy, neck, shoulders and inner thigh, made me think of the magic out in Asia. And the way she shaved my legs and trimmed my puss-floss inclines me to believe my spiritual home could lie out there in Asia.

'Come and get dressed. I have something I'd like you to try on,' she invites, and takes me by the hand to her broad bed. On both sides there are large stand-up mirrors to fit all of a vain woman inside. One large mirror is fastened to the ceiling and another big gold-edged affair hangs on the wall behind the brass struts of the headboard. Girl with a penchant for eyeing herself over could like this place. Funnily enough, I feel right at home.

'I want my own place like this in Texas,' I say. 'You're lucky.'

'And the road always seems full of promise when you're not on it,' Val says, and winks.

'Still, maybe you should ride free more. Us girls should have ourselves a time in Atlanta or Vegas.'

Val smiles but looks kind of sad. She turns away from me and raises a clothes hanger from the bed. Drifting below her hand is what I would describe as a black mist and I forget about the melancholy in her eyes. The edges of the garments are barely defined because the fabric is so sheer. The French knickers are so fine that everything you can see through them looks sexy, even a chair. And just the thought of that transparent brassière drifting like smoke across my pink nips makes me shiver. 'So pretty,' I say, and walk over to Val. While I finger the dainty fabric I notice her eyes are shiny and wet with tears. 'Why the rain, girl?' I ask.

'Because looking at a fine young thing like you makes an old girl weep.'

'One thing you're not is old-looking. Rare that I've met a woman so fine limbed and milk-white. You're how I imagine a European lady to be.'

'Silly thing,' Val says, but I'm pleased to see her blush. It's true, she's beautiful. Cold, stiff and menacing like a predatory thing in a jungle river, but also so easy on a girl's eyes, and many a man's too, I guess. Her dress tonight is Italian, cut off-the-knee, and shimmery where the candlelight catches it. The make-up on those pointed cheekbones is sparse. Her ghostly neck has green jewels around it and her spidery fingers are heavy with clots of red varnish at the ends. I liked watching those hands go through my hair and between my legs in the tub, and even now, as they raise a champagne flute to her dark lips, I feel myself give way inside to the manoeuvre. Maybe some of her class will rub off on me. Val can spit like a tomcat but, from somewhere, she picked up grace too. I try to drink my fizzy liquor in the way she does but my face goes all kind of phoney and pinched. She sees this and I go red. We both end up laughing.

Val sits down on the bed and watches me gather the flimsies to my heart. One thing I can do is dress. That came to me in the schoolroom of motel, striptease joint and lap-dancing club, and in the observation of pretty married girls, when they left me alone in the mornings after we'd done fooling through the night. There was always something sad but careful about the way they clothed themselves before going back to their husbands. I liked it and drank it down.

'Put these on first,' she says, and slides a thin box across the bed. 'But be real careful. They've been waiting for a fine pair of legs since '48, and are more delicate than a spider's web.'

'No ways,' I say.

'Yes, miss, and they belong with this.' She drops a garter belt on the bed, with the appearance of antiquity I like. 'Together they'll make you look like a movie star.'

'Wow,' I say, and slip the garter belt around my waist. After putting fine cotton gloves on her hands, Val kneels before me and raises one of my feet. I pass the hose in the box to her. Together, it's like we're defusing a bomb, as the nylon is worked up my leg. They're so slithery I can only feel something akin to a gentle breeze from their touch, but with my feet inside the fashioned heel and instep, my toes feel compact. Real slow, she slips the thinnest-heeled shoes I have ever worn on to my feet.

'Now look,' she says, standing back and pointing at a mirror beside the bed.

Dressed in this finery, with my make-up applied so carefully by Val, I want to stay looking this fine for ever. 'Take a picture,' I cry out.

Val laughs.

'Please, Val.'

'OK,' she says and leaves the room. While I'm still twisting and turning in the mirror, she returns with a camera.

'Calls for black and white,' she says, and kneels down to start snapping away at me.

For a while I walk up and down, then I look over my shoulder like a surprised Marilyn, before I end up sitting, cross-legged, on a cushioned stool. From the

91

stool, I move to the bed, where my demeanour takes on a more provocative air. And, if I'm not mistaken, Val's starting to get me holding poses for close-ups longer than was necessary before.

When she sits side-saddle on the end of the bed, something happens between us. It was an accident the way my foot landed on her lap, but it startles her. We both freeze and our eyes lock. My head feels real heavy and I can't stop trailing my leg up her body until I can rub the naked part of her breasts that rises above her dress. 'Time I made amends,' I say, in a trembly voice. Val's breathing gets speedy and I can't stop swallowing. I want to love and feed at the same time, real bad. Guess she does too.

Suddenly, we're together, side by side, then we're rolling over and over each other. In the distance I hear the camera hit the floor with a bump. Are we fighting? I can't say, because she digs her claws into my arms and I spread her legs with my knee before tumbling her off to the side. I see her teeth in the flurry of action and my claws get busy in her hair. But then we're kissing. Now we're kissing. Her mouth feels so hot and not cold like I thought. And her face is refreshingly soft; not bristly like a man's, but smooth. We seem to get a better seal with our mouths than we would with some unshaven jaw, and in the middle of that tight circle of warm flesh our tongues dart back and forth like fish dipping in to feed on something they suddenly find before them.

I open my eyes and she does too. We look right into each other's colours and whites and pupils and our eyes seem so pretty and fierce. It increases the fury of our tongues, lips and teeth. It's like we're trying to weld our faces together, to push inside each other's skull. How it's happening I don't know, but all that spleen we've been hankering on to has just exploded so the bad part is gone and only the hot, determined bits are left to take control of us.

Although she slows herself down to protect the weightless fabric wrapped about my body, Val is making a sound; quick, nervous murmurs from up near the back of her nose. I know this tune, peculiar to girls with a need for love, and I realise I'm making my own call – a kind of long 'mmm' sound that rises in pitch but stays continuous like I don't need to take a breath.

Val takes my breasts with what feels like relief; it's as if she's wanted to maul those white lambs since she first saw them. I roll my eyes back and start to squirm under the efficient administration of her hands. Pressing my pert girls down, she makes the nylon swish across my nips which begin to sing their own tune. Then she cups my breasts with the base of her hands and stretches her long fingers upward to worry my nips, pinching them and rolling the pads of her fingers across them, while her mouth moves into position above it all. I look down and see her sleek black hair falling across the shadow of my negligee. Her mouth is obscured but I can feel its close proximity to my pebbles. Shallow breaths, full of hot steam, are panted on to my breasts and warn me to prepare for teeth.

They come to the left breast first. Seizing my nip with her front teeth, she pulls it up and then rolls it back and forth, before her tongue starts to whip about and moisten the motion. Fingertips clamp my right nip and begin working her good. Sliding my legs over her back, I squash Val down into the feast and pull her on to me at the same time. Sensing my need for her hard and fine body to be put across my own, Val slithers up further between my legs so her breasts rest on my tum. Our shift in position doesn't disturb her mouth's close bond with my nips, and this natural accommodation of the new lengths and angles of each other's bodies pleases me. There's no stumbling and nothing feels awkward. We're both long and soft and entwine as a perfect pair.

By the time she's sucked my chest until my negligee clings like a new dark skin over my breasts, I have a need to taste something rare. 'Need some of you in my mouth, girl,' I say.

Immediately, Val sits up. 'Get me out of this.'

Slinking around behind her on the bed, I find the back-zip to her dress and razor it down so I can see the white-chocolate goodness beneath. When my hands find warmth she sighs and closes her eyes. Touching her pale shoulders and neck sends a current between us, a magnetism that draws my hands around to the front of her. As her dress falls away, I'm free to handle her breasts; two tight features secured with nothing but a wisp of lace.

'Oh, yeah,' I say in encouragement. Her body moves up and down with the pulling and tugging motions of my hands. Sitting behind her, I am able to look her over and see the tiny triangle of her panties disappearing to a point between her snowy buttocks. Around her waist is a garter belt and the stockings on her legs are black with thin seams that run and rise over contoured flesh from thigh to ankle. 'Mmm,' I murmur in the crook of her neck so the vibrations of my appreciation run through her. 'Lie down, baby. On your back.'

She obeys. Hold off, I tell myself. Make this last, Missy.

Sieving the air through my nose, I catch the sharp tang of her musk. Immediately, I jam my puss against her body and give my pip the little rub she's been screaming for since I peeled Val down to her ice.

Parting her legs, by gripping her own knees, Val opens herself to me, eager for my touch. Holding my stare with the dark velvet I can see between the narrow aperture of her eyelids, which now seem prettier with their long lashes curling together, she beckons me. I moan and slip my hands down her inner thighs, right to the base where her legs join her hips and the floss tickles my knuckles. 'Now?' I breathe at the woman.

'Now,' she mouths back.

'Right now,' I whisper, and then move my hips in a tiny circle.

'Right now,' she mouths again, and her eyes open a fraction more. There is fire inside them.

Rubbing my hands up and down her legs, I take a moment to enjoy the slippery surface in my hands. The swish and hiss of her stockings make my palms hot. 'Close your eyes,' I say, because I want her to be in the dark when she feels a new mouth eating its fill.

When I can see the pale brown eye-shadow on the outside of her lids, I sink down to her, parting my cherry lips in readiness for her opaque milk and slippery morsels. When I find the treasures to my liking, I suck hard and lap eagerly, wanting to swallow every drop of honey. But the more I immerse myself the damper her satin becomes.

Val squirms about and takes two fingers into her mouth. With her teeny bud getting a whirlpool from my tongue, she starts this 'ugh, ugh, ugh' sound which I like. Now I'm moving my whole head to get this lady high. Even when my jaw aches and it feels like my temples are bruised, I keep loving her sex, because this lady is screwing her face up so tight and thumping her bottom against the damp sheets.

Let it out, I want to say. Let it slip, slide away, Val, 'cus life is too short to hate and to bitch over silly sweet boys that don't know any better than to get into a girl's underthings, and before lunch at that.

I reel her in with my goodness and she starts to say, 'Missy, oh, Missy,' and then 'ugh, ugh, ugh' again. Shaking from toe to scalp, Val seems to fall into a faint, so I go to move my tired face from between these white thighs. They suddenly close to hold my head still. Smiling, I caress her buttocks and then her tummy until she releases my head.

'Better?' I ask, and slink alongside her. Feeling pleased that maybe I'm righting my wrong, I brush Val's hair off her forehead and kiss her cheek. It's wet.

'Much better,' she says, opening her eyes. Nothing but sweetness in them either. 'I can see why Hank held on to you, girl,' she adds, and rolls into me, into another kiss. This one lasts longer than the first and is so concentrated it's like we're passing a knowledge to each other, between our bodies.

From out of nowhere, her fingers find my puss. I didn't even feel her arm move, but her fingertips are sorting through my lips, looking for a sweet bean. They find her, tease her, rub her and then circle her gently until it's my turn to writhe. Arching my back, I cry out because Val is stroking me with an insistence that's driving me out of body and mind. Almost frightened by the way she excites me, it feels like my soul is being extracted. Wriggling on a pin and gasping, I'm led around the bed and made vulnerable until I feel I could give anything up for this woman. I start to see things.

It seems Hank is injured and in a hospital bed. Green vinyl curtains have been pulled around the bed he lies in. Val sits at the top of the bed and cradles him against her chest. Her blouse is open and her bra unclipped so the straps hang about her elbows. The back of Hank's fuzzy head slides into her breasts. There is a look of anguish and then the most acute pleasure on Val's face. I have seen this before; on the faces of the women Hank feeds from. He is feeding from Val, from near her heart.

I see more. Hank is lying on the floor of a hotel room in a hot country, naked and tanned. His hair is in a buzz cut and there is a bandage around his waist. On the chair above him, Val sits in a white nurse's uniform. Despite the heat, her face is still very pale, which makes her lips appear black and cold. She is doing something to his mouth with her shoe. It's hard to see but Hank is sucking furiously while she watches him with indifference and twists a tourniquet between her hands.

Shaking my head I clear the vision. Looking down my body, I see Val's little sucker-fish mouth leaving red butterflies all over my own breasts. As I try to figure out what the visions mean, Val's quick mouth moves to my sex and starts weakening my brief moment of composure and clarity of mind. I close my eyes and have a third dream.

On a bed in another hotel room lies a pretty Vietnamese girl. She's smiling and tied to the bedframe. Above her, a big ceiling fan whoops above the bed like a chopper blade. Beyond the thin curtains over the single window, scooters and taxis whiz by. Dressed in a khaki uniform, Val walks near the bed and removes her hat and then shakes her hair loose. When in just her stockings and slip, she looks so pretty but so mean too. I sense the girl on the bed is afraid of her. Hank appears, naked accept for his combat shorts and dog tags. He sneaks between the girl's legs. Right away, she relaxes and blows a kiss at him with her big red lips, so thick with paint. He enters the girl on the bed and slides through her until she begins to move up and down the mattress with him, pulling the sheets loose. When the girl's eyes close and Hank's hard buttocks thrust to a blur, I see Val, who has watched with pain and delight on her face, suddenly descend to the girl's throat. I can almost smell food and I groan as three of Val's fingers slip inside me.

Wrapped together, we search the surface of each other's body and open the secret trapdoors in each other's memory. The sheets grow damp beneath us and we go beyond words. Whether she intends it or not, I am rifling through her reflections of Hank and I soon understand that he broke her heart. She nursed him back to health and he bust her up inside.

Feeling angry at Hank at the same time as a need for him, I kiss Val harder and slip a hand between her buttocks. I want all of her; to be in every tight part, to lick every moist part, to taste every inch of her pale skin that my man explored so many years past.

Together we blend and disperse into each other's thoughts in this curious dream life. At times she becomes so excited, I think she has uncovered a glimpse of the passions Hank and I share. I'm not sure of this, but she will shake her head and say 'no' and then claw my back, or noisily sup from between my sticky thighs as if some fresh urge has overtaken her will.

'Do you see him?' I whimper, when Val kneels between my legs and raises my buttocks to put my puss on her lips. One of her hands goes down between her own thighs. 'Yes,' she says.

'He should come now and love us both,' I say, wanting Hank's strength and silence and his terrible lust to be thrown upon our soft flesh. Val begins to moan with a longing that sounds haunted. As she comes, she lashes at my sex with her tongue and spears my bottom with her cruel middle finger. I climax straight away and whisper, 'Food,' because our love has increased the fever inside me.

Val falls across me and sucks the tears from my eyes. Seizing her chin I pull her mouth to mine and we kiss hard, before breaking away from each other's teeth to fight for air. 'Let us feed,' she says, with a smile that is without deceit. It is a generous and flushed face that looks down at me – the face of a beautiful woman who is willing to share her bounty.

Holding hands, we climb the stairs to the attic. Tousle-headed and wild-eyed, we walk through the dark dressed in nothing but our black underthings, to the young man who worships them.

'Sweet Boy,' Val says, in a voice that makes me think her throat is raspy and dry.

'Sweet Boy Denver,' I call through the attic gloom.

Ahead of us, we hear chains rattle and we smell the exhilaration of cornered prey.

When I awoke, late the next day, Val was sitting beside me in bed, watching me. There was something in her face I couldn't read and it never left her fine features when I smiled. 'Val, what's wrong?'

'Nothing,' she said with a sigh, and then forced her face into life, but it was a struggle for her to do so. Waking up with a girl you hated only yesterday morning takes some comprehending, I guess.

Cleaning my mouth with the back of my hand, I sat up and then shook my tangled hair loose. 'What's the time?' I asked, and was about to reach for Val but she slipped from the bed. 'Time we were up and about, girl. I'll fix us some coffee,' was all she said.

After she had padded out of the room I stared about the bed, confused. Around the floor our clothes and underthings were tangled and discarded where we dropped them after peeling them from each other.

All of last night seemed dreamy and I could hardly remember descending from the attic after saying a long goodnight to Sweet Boy Denver. My head had a little thickness to it, but the good long sleep had rid me of most of that. Hank has never been one for lying in and I often stay hungover until noon.

I showered and then Val and I ate Texan toast, eggs and streaky bacon out on the porch just before the sun got fierce.

'What you planning to do today?' Val asked, looking at the floor through her glasses.

'Don't feel up to much on account of troubling you,' I said.

Val held my hand and smiled. 'You stirred me up, girl. That's all. There is no bad blood between us now.'

'Sure?' I asked, feeling warmer inside.

'Sure,' she said, and kissed my cheek. 'Why don't you look about the farm?'

'I'd like to. Will you come?'

'No. I have things to do.'

'Agency stuff?' I asked, chomping on an apple at the same time.

'That's right. Been a while since I retired from field operations, but I keep my hand in as a consultant. Always been good with plans, I guess.'

'Last night was real special, Val,' I said, squeezing her fingers.

Val looked at the sky. 'Was that, girl. Been a while since I had such a time –' She paused to sigh and looked uncomfortable. 'I know you could get hungry, Missy –'

'Val, I won't touch that boy again,' I interrupted.

'I wasn't referring to Denver. Down by the creek is a cottage with a young man inside who writes poetry. All I'm saying is that should you meet him, be gentle.'

'Had my fill of country boys, Val,' I said. 'And it's about time I learned to curb my appetite.'

'Well, whatever you think is best,' she replied. Looking happier, she finished her coffee. 'About time I got down to work.'

'You and Hank are so smart,' I said, looking across the yard to the dusty road that runs by the front of Val's big old white house. 'Working for the agency and the military and all. Sometimes I wish I had a job.'

Val looked real sad after I said that. Her next smile was a long time coming. 'And you, Missy, have something that the rest of us would kill for.'

I giggled, but wasn't sure what she meant.

'Being complicated and making life more difficult than it should be is something you never want to do, girl. But the way you took the bond from Hank and the way you put it to use, it made you special. Precious, I believe. A light like yours should never go out.'

I chewed this over and thought I understood what she said. It was a compliment, I think, but I wish she hadn't looked so sad when she said it.

Eager to be on my own and feeling that Val needed space, I left the house right after breakfast. Val stood on the porch and watched me walk away. 'Oh, Missy,' she called.

'Yes?' I said, and turned to her.

Leaning against the porch rail, she didn't seem too steady on her feet.

'What's up?' I cried.

'Oh, nothing. You just take care now. What with this sun and all, pay a mind to your skin.'

I waved and set off to the little wood that faces south on her land. There is a stream that bubbles through it and a swimming hole too.

101

Six

Three days after I left Val sitting on the porch, I find myself naked and in chains. Undisturbed for two nights and a day, I have had the time to move from a rage that felt bad for my health, to a sobbing that brought my eyes out like mumps, to a silence that finally comes to the desperate. There is no escape. Banging on the door and picking at the window latch is futile. Too many of them have sided against me and tricked me with ease.

Now stop that, Missy, I tell myself, trapped in my own head as much as this room. That will make you angry and you hurt yourself last time by pulling on those tight cuffs and stamping your feet that cannot part more than a foot from each other, on account of the hobbling chain strung from ankle to ankle.

Face the truth, girl – greed and vanity brought you down. Guess I always knew they would too. Serves you right, girl. And through your stupidity Hank could take a final tumble too. Could it be over? After so long, it's hard to comprehend that our run nears its end. And in the same state as where it all started.

Thinking back, I must have been blind not to see the thin wires of the snare I skipped into. Baited by the firm textures and scents of pretty boys, I carried on like I was sixteen and had never been kissed. Two days back, I blithely took another step up a scaffold that had been prepared exactingly for my undoing. Constructed with some sophistication too, I might suggest to ease my conscience. All the same, a fundamental lack of discipline, which Hank has chided me over for so long, finally put this kitten in a box she can't sneak out of.

All started down by the swimming hole.

Just couldn't take my eyes off the boy. So I stayed put for a time. It was just that, for a moment, I had to watch him. The way he cut into the water, after leaping from the small waterfall, was beautiful; he barely made a splash. Chin up, arms spread wide, body straight and tapering, he seemed to hang in the air like a swallow before disappearing into the dark water. For a second I could see his pale shape beneath the flat and still surface, but then he was gone into the depths, unafraid.

Rising from the deep, he threw his black fringe off his square face and grinned, like he was pleased with himself. After clambering up the rocks, he sought a patch of yellow sunlight, falling through the canopy of trees, as if it was sent from heaven just to dry the boy off. On the smooth, broad stones at the creek's edge, he then lay still, smiling to himself. Could this be the poet swimming in the creek? I thought. Spilling from the canvas satchel that rested beside his heavy boots and jeans, I spotted some books – two paperbacks and one hardcover – which increased the odds of this being Val's tenant. He had a guitar too and seemed to favour a cowboy hat made from straw, with the sides curling over like the melon pickers wear.

With his tight muscles still taut on his chest and stomach, even though he was at ease, and that large snake idle in his lap (the kind that could sting a girl real good), I was left wondering why Val hadn't been going to him at night. Every time that boy reclined in his crib, I was amazed Val hadn't been slipping through his window like the white phantom I knew her to be. Just didn't add up. Under all those slabs of sculpted brawn there must be the sweetest wine a bonded girl could taste.

No, poet, you fine young thing, I will not come to thee. Or so I said to myself. Seemed like there was a price to pay in these parts every time a girl took a sip. But just for a moment longer, I needed to take him in; right inside the hot part of me where the visions of so much love writhe to create the hunger.

When he stirred from drying off, I crouched behind an old oak. He stood up and ran his fingers through his sleek locks before walking across to his guitar. On the sunny rock, he took a seat and strummed a chord. Through the stillness and gloom of the hollow, the D minor chord resounded and then died to a hum among the trees. When he started to play, I recognised the melody instantly and it only took a moment for me to place it in a song. It was one of my favourites – 'Long Black Veil' by Johnny Cash. Closing my eyes, I slunk further behind the trunk and wished he'd never started. It was like he was playing just for me – making my tummy tighten and pushing all the little hairs up on the back of my neck. Not that song, I thought; it mixes me up. I grew older with the man in black and bits of me are trapped in each of his songs: tears, smiles, everything. They say Elvis was king, but Johnny Cash will always be royalty to me.

That boy down there on the rock could hold a tune too. My, how rich his voice was. Richer than dark tobacco and brandy pudding, husky-edged and angel-high if need be. Nothing like a man with a voice that resonant. Reminded me of my Hank and I found myself blinking a tear away.

Seemed like the poet had the same taste in swimming holes and cool creek smells as me. Next day, I found him crooning in the place I intended to get raw and swim deep in. Butt-naked, showing off his camel-tan skin, he was lying up on that rock again, playing 'Crazy Arms' by Ray Price. To be honest with myself, I knew it was a sense of relief I experienced after pacing through the trail between the fields to find him there two days in a row. Through the previous night, my fingers were busy and sticky while my dreams searched to find this poet in sleep. Boy was under my skin. No doubt.

Val still remained distant and we said little overnight, both before and after we ate silent meals. Sweet Boy Denver was let out that morning too, so I wanted to be away from the farmhouse on account of him. Val was hurting over something she could not or would not tell me about. Damn agency, I reckoned at the time, so it was best I stayed outdoors; I didn't want the shadows in Val's farmhouse getting inside my head any more. Seems like there had been a lot of fretting and so forth in Val's place lately. I could sense it. So I took my little picnic, my collection of Robert Frost's poems – a constant companion when I'm in the woods – and my enduring need for cold water against my skin before going back to the hollow.

Perhaps, I mused, the poet and I could share the swimming hole on this fine day. Maybe I could learn a little discipline too. You know, we could be friends without hitting on each other. Sure thing, girl.

'Do you know "Pounding Heart" by the VRoys?' I hollered, from up above his flat-rock perch.

'Jesus, girl!' he cried, and twisted to his feet like a

man who just heard the devil call. Maybe he had, I thought, as I stifled a giggle. 'You nearly stopped my heart.'

'Knoxville,' I said. 'Thought so as you sang. Tennessee boy. Then you should know the song I just mentioned.'

He collected himself, slowing his breathing down and taking me in with his eyes as I went down the gloomy slope to the hollow. He placed his guitar over his privates. 'Know the song to dance to, but not to play. Who are you, girl? And how long you been up in those woods?'

'I'm a friend of Val's, staying up at the farmhouse, and I've been hanging back from here for two days, which is long enough to need a dip in that water.'

He nodded and smiled. It was the kind of smile that stuns me a little. I don't see many of those. 'Ain't this heat something?' He stretched a hand over the guitar in greeting. 'I'm Walt, and I'd be reluctant to hand this spot over to anyone who didn't appreciate it. But as you've been back two days running, I guess that should make you a preferred guest.'

I smiled and accepted his hand, but only for a second because its width and toughness made me shiver. 'No need to blow,' I said. 'Mother nature's big enough for both of us.'

He would have tipped his hat had it been on his pretty-boy head.

'You must be the poet,' I said, stripping down to my brassière.

'And you must be someone's muse,' he replied, real quiet. When I turned to him he looked away, embarrassed. I was a little disappointed and immediately thought that he didn't care for girls. Not again, I cried to myself, as too many of these dreamy creatures are lost to kittens like me. And there's

106

nothing you can do to change their minds. But, by the furtive movements of his turquoise eyes, I soon saw that he was just being polite while sneaking a peek at the same time. He liked ladies all right.

'There was a man,' I said, feeling cold with guilt, 'but he's not here now.'

Walt screwed up his eyes. 'Go figure that.'

I wriggled my shorts down to my ankles.

Couldn't help laughing as I dived off the rock, right into the deepest part of the swimming hole where the waterfall has scooped the bottom out. But the water knocked the breath from me. Once you're through the warm surface the depths are icy. What's more, my panties just shot straight down my legs and popped off my toes. Imagine that.

I surfaced and blew a thick rope of water into the air. As my eyes cleared, I spied Walt's tanned buttocks as he struggled into his jeans. So as not to offend the lady, he was putting his britches on. I have to admit I was touched by the gesture. 'Woo! This is so fine,' I said, clapping my hands down on the water. 'Must inspire you.'

'For all the good it does,' he said, grinning and nodding towards my black briefs, bobbing beside me like some fresh creek-water jellyfish.

I swept them up and hurled them on to the shore. 'You not having any luck then?'

'Isn't much call for poetry these days. Maybe I can put them into songs. That's the plan.'

'So how do you eat?'

Walt laughed. 'Someone in New York City took my photograph and gave me a whole bunch of money. Be a while before it runs out.'

'You a model?'

'Not just any model. A soap model.'

'Soap! You crazy poet. What do you mean?' I said,

and floated on my back until I realised my puss was on display.

Walt giggled and lit a smoke – one he'd just rolled using only one hand. 'I was the 1995 Baby Soft soap boy. Maybe you saw me on a billboard, taking a shower.'

'Well, Baby Soft, why don't you roll one of those stogies for me? I'm coming out now, so turn your back.'

Walt complied and I scurried up the rocks to find the beach towel that Val had let me borrow. 'Can you do that on the back of a horse, cowboy?' I said, and nodded towards the cigarette he had just rolled for me.

'Sure, facing the wind with a leather glove on too.'

'Well, you sure have imagination,' I said, through my giggles, and took the smoke.

We ended up sitting together, cross-legged like a couple of hippy folk. Walt had whiskey, mixed with coke and ice, which is my favourite drink, and I shared my donuts, muffins and cookies with him. 'Girl, you have any teeth left?' he asked, at one point, querying the lack of savouries or fruit in my picnic. Yes, Baby Soft, I thought. So don't you go making me get them out.

Chewing the fat with Walt was exactly what I needed after Val's moods and all the complications of my stay at the farm, but it was an effort to keep my eyes on the boy's face. At least all the sugar helped to take the edge off the ache in my tum; the sweet pain of the appetite.

Walt was funny, and a little loony, I suspected, but harmless all the same. Rare I'd seen a boy so easy on the eyes, too, and this troubled me, knowing how I am. Always found it easy to bury a nagging doubt about myself, despite knowing that the problem will only dig itself up and I'll end up making the same mistake again.

After we were done eating, I asked him for a song. A big mistake, I reckon, in hindsight. With a smile, he scooped up his guitar and launched into 'Good Hearted Woman'. Once, I saw Waylon Jennings sing that song with Willie Nelson and I was so happy I cried. On this day, after a swim and so many sweetmeats, sitting in this glorious spot, a little of me fell for this pretty-boy poet. My resolve not to touch him had ebbed away during the first verse and by the time he'd reached the second chorus the foundations of my self-restraint had all tumbled down. Listening to his voice, the guitar and even the rough pads of his fingers on the brass guitar strings started to make me loosen up to the point of my issuing a growl. Unable to stop myself I caught his eye and stared deep; right through that boy until his smile died and his face softened up. Take me, I said, in this silent communication of eye-to-eye. Take me right here and now by this water. Inhale my blondeness, touch my skin, eat me. Stretch your soul inside me, pump every part of your longing and desperation, your frustration and needing into me. Come on, Baby Soft. Come on, rangy man. Take, take, take. Love me.

When the vibration of his last chord died in the air, swallowed by the silence and peace of the creek world, he leaned across to me. His breath was soft but fast like he was a little anxious. Smoothing my hand on the outside of his face, over his square and gritty jaw, along the angular bones of his cheeks and into the mop of his hair, I made Walt relax. A look of yearning that made his eyebrows dip in the middle of his forehead replaced his reticence. He came closer. Lips parted. Throats swallowed. Tongues touched. The seal was made. He was mine.

We worked the guitar from out between us and he gathered me to his chest. There was a fragrance of fresh water and woody damp on his skin. Breathing in, I consumed this smell and found the deeper meatier scent of his sweat. It was good. Gently, I placed my teeth on his cheek and tasted his face with the tip of my tongue. There was a cry inside me to bite down hard, to taste him, and then drink him dry, but I recognised the urge and knew how to control it. Teasing my own desire to feed, I nestled my soft face against his neck instead. He sighed; I smiled.

Cautiously, he stretched his hand out and cupped my left breast. Brushing his thumb up and down against my nip started the purring in me. I grasped his open mouth with my lips and dragged his tongue from safety. Taking it prisoner allowed me to convert it to the will of my mouth. Up and down my head moved, fastidious in its suckling of his tongue, as if promising a similar glide and thoroughness with another extendable part of him. With squeezy hands, he enveloped both of my breasts in rough but warm palms. By caging my breasts he was able to squash them against my body, turning them into twin suns swelling with delight. I started to make a throaty sound that passed through my mouth, along his tongue and down into his body. We moulded, squashing our warm torsos and snaking our long limbs together.

Stretched out and rolling on to the picnic blanket, I felt him go inside me. I had to pull my face away from his kisses to groan because this pillar of muscle was so fat and rock-like. Stretched wide, I parted my legs and sank beneath him. On and on it squeezed until I choked, whimpered and then pushed at his chest with the palms of my hands to slow him down. Immediately, my puss responded with her milk and yearning for girth, but at the start I needed him to go slow.

Soon, he was right at the back of my womb and I felt my neck go slack. Gently, he rose to his knees and held me, speared to his trunk, with just one slow hand. In this crouch with my body falling away from him, he pulled me to his stomach while pushing in the other direction with his hips. I was his. Trapped, rifled, and played out along the length of his meat, all I could do was moan with my eyes shut and my hair trailing over the stones.

For an age he fucked me this way; slowly with a grace and ease that come naturally to the athletic and co-ordinated. Despite his tortuous rhythm in and out of my puss, there was an intensity to these strokes equal in effect to the hardest ride. For a moment, I thought the boy was a hustler. Some pool-room gigolo who blinded tourist wives and businesswomen with his stroke-work – these men I have met and danced with. Once I saw a hustler take a woman in a strip club this way. She was throwing money at the guy and clawing at his legs, just begging the boy to take her slow and deep while he did his cowboy dance up on a small stage. And he did too, in front of all her friends, who fell real quiet around the podium. One of the strangest things I ever saw happen among regular folk, without the slightest interference from me or Hank. But then I guessed Walt was just a Baby Soft poet who preferred to take the soulful approach. Measured himself out, this one, and I liked the variety. Meant he could last all night and would fall asleep inside a girl, still hard, only to pull her from sleep before dawn to empty himself again, and then again at first light.

This tempo was wonderful, but I couldn't help imagining the pleasure his hard stud body could give

111

me at full gallop. Ummm, yessum. Give me soup, dinner, dessert and the cigar, all on the same plate. I'd have whipped it from him if the need arose.

'Harder, Walt,' I said, in encouragement, now that I was so slippery around his pole. 'Fuck me harder.'

'That how you need it, girl?' he teased, grinning with mischief.

'Do it, baby. Please –'

One thrust I never saw coming killed my words. Stricken with a pain that was a delight, I slapped a hand to my mouth and bit down on the soft outside of my palm. Breathing out as he withdrew, I felt as if he was pulling my insides out on his cock. Creating a vacuum inside me, I seemed to deflate when only the thick head of him was half inside my puss. As if to assuage my desire to be filled again, which began to feel like anger in me, Walt punched his hips forward and I took him right to the back wall.

I tried to speak, but he denied me a voice by pumping at speed. All I could do was claw out at his forearms that suspended the bridge of my body before him. Being shaken about and pummelled up and down the stones, which were warm and smooth beneath us, I began to look through my tears to see Walt's face. It was possessed.

'Coming,' he said, and his features strained to scarlet.

Just the thought of this poet's milk washing through me was all I needed to drop a thousand feet into a climax that blinded me. On and on he went, grunting and praying, riding me until the last spark of wincing pleasure was doused along his enervated length and width. When at last the rider slowed and softened, I tried to recover the pieces of my mind.

We kissed until the discomfort in his knees, from crouching on the stones for so long, forced him to

withdraw from my sex. I rolled my eyes towards the
tree tops, where the sun flashed through the dark
underside of bough and branch, and I smiled. 'Rode
hard, cowboy, put away wet.' There was no pleasure
greater.

Hot-skinned and sticky about our thighs, the poet
plucked me from the rock. Casually, with two unlit
cigarettes drooping from his mouth, he took me
down to the cold lagoon. I could have fainted with
happiness when the cold water rose between my
buttocks and lapped over my stomach. When all of
me was under the water, except for my head, I
nuzzled under Walt's jaw with appreciative lips.
While he smoked, I went into him with kitten teeth.
Pleasure needles covered with the anaesthetic of
arousal opened my path to nutrition. Under the water
and against my tummy, I felt the poet's organ go
hard.

Lamb, prepare for the tigress.

This is how it will be, I told myself on the evening
that followed my creek rendezvous. Without fear of
discovery or guilt, I would go and take my pleasure
from the poet again. Immersing myself in a pocket of
pure delight without thought of Hank, Val or the
Preacher, I would exist on this night by the laws of
my blood. Powerless and blind to the machinations of
their agency, to Hank's silent will, and the endless,
directionless night we ride through, I would seek my
own knowledge on my own journey. Extraordinary
men and women, found in ordinary worlds, would
continue to be my food. When left to my own devices
I could go wherever my spirit willed. Oh, poet, I said,
prepare yourself for an inspiration you will never
escape.

Clad in a white dress that lapped about my ankles

but left the brown of my shoulders and arms bare, I stalked across to the poet's cottage. Down a dry path I flitted. Crushed grass and hard red clay formed a trail for the gold heels of an invited dinner guest whose appetite would blow through the host like a hurricane. All day, since I sampled Walt's crimson, I had longed for more of his spicy wine and endearing nature. Greedy, libidinous and vain, I walked to my doom.

Under the big silver moon the landscape was streaked with phosphorus light. Under trees and along hedgerows, purple shadows would clot and glut. Strange creatures cried out as I cut through the electric night, painted like a leading lady, indifferent as a princess.

Only stopping here and there to drink from an innocent fountain without guide or leader to follow, could I walk through every night without Hank? I wondered. Such was my feeling of power.

Ahead of me I soon saw the slouch of a shingle roof, the light of an oil lantern and the smoke from a cobbled chimney stack. From the open door, I heard a strange but familiar song. It was 'Candyman', from my favourite record, *American Beauty*. How can this poet's soul be stirred by the same melodies as mine? I pondered.

He moved in his easy, long-limbed way on to the porch. Faded denim gripped his legs and from somewhere he had produced a linen shirt that went with his black jacket and was completed with a bootlace tie. Like an old lawman, freshly shaved, with a hidden peacemaker about him, he waited to court his belle. Overwhelmed by the romance of our encounter, I suddenly wanted every situation to be full of this moon-eerie seduction and cool-night anticipation. No more hotels, I swore, or loud clubs where leather boys move and twist around Hank's watchful eyes. This is what I want: poets and sepulchral air, strangers who communicate with smiles and heavily lidded eyes, love in the open and under stars with cowboy ghosts, and all to the music of outlaws. My, how the country gets to me.

'Hey, now, beautiful,' he said, too entranced by the way my body moved under the silk to smile.

I could feel the shine in my eyes as he took my hand to aid my careful step up to the porch. 'Not sure whether it's food or you that smells so good, Baby Soft,' I said.

For a moment he held my chin and looked to lose himself in my eyes. I dipped my headlights, wanting the preliminaries to last. We have all night to love, I told him, and popped a kiss on the little scar I had blessed his throat with earlier.

After crossing the threshold of the house, I found myself in one room that ran the length of the ground floor. Spartan and swept, there was little inside besides basic wooden furniture and the poet's books. On the kitchen table a clean white cloth had been spread and a small vase held yellow flowers. In one corner, overseen by a reading lamp on a twisty metal stem, was a desk. Against the opposite wall there was an old soft-cushioned sofa designed for one lounger, but with room for two lovers in a hurry. Oil lanterns hung from wall hooks and their yellow light soothed the interior wood and stone into softer-looking shapes. A staircase rose from the far corner of the room opposite the kitchen area. Above me I heard a floorboard creak. 'Ghosts?' I asked.

Walt gave me a smile that could have sold a reservoir of toothpaste. 'Of course.'

From the doorway he led me to the table and pulled out a chair. After clearing his throat, he said, 'Beer?' and raised one eyebrow, blushing.

'Sure,' I said with enthusiasm. 'What you cooking?'
Walt relaxed. 'My speciality.'

'Which is?'

'The finest chilli with flour tortillas. Made them myself. Should be ready too.'

'Nothing I want to eat as much as a home-cooked chilli,' I said. 'Besides the chef.'

Walt laughed as he got busy with a ladle and strainer. He served the chilli and rice in white bowls and covered the tortillas with a red check towel to keep them warm. Between us, he placed the beer and covered tortillas, and then polished two spoons. I started to giggle at the fine display of boyish resourcefulness.

Under my nose the smell of his chilli was soon rising and my mouth moistened. Dipping into the red broth with my spoon, I raised a lady's mouthful and blew across it. He watched my lips with dreamy eyes. Chilli was real good too; hot but not so as you lose a sense of taste. Under the table I uncrossed my legs and reached out with a foot to touch his shin, letting him know that all was appreciated and would be rewarded soon enough.

We ate in silence, keeping each other in our sights, and by the time I was done with the food, I placed the foot in his lap and found him to be hard. With the leather sole of my shoe, I rubbed his wood.

With a third beer in hand, we retired to the couch and turned our faces each to the other. In the slowly vanishing warmth of the room, I felt a little sleepy. Thick-headed and limp-necked, I rested against his chest and let him stroke my hair.

'Girl, I want you,' he said, in a breathy, beery voice.

'Mmm,' I moaned, and nuzzled against his shirt. Placing a hand on his inner thigh made his lap go all

116

tight. 'Be gentle to start,' I said. 'Don't roll me around with a full stomach. It's no good for the digestion.'

I heard him swallow. 'OK.'

Above us, the old shack let forth another creak as if it was preparing for a quake in the foundations. 'Miss, will you . . .'

'Go on.'

'Miss, will you bite me again, like you did before in the water?'

'Was it so good?'

'You moved me,' he said.

I knew he had more to say and I wanted to hear it. 'Go on.'

'It was like the first time I fell in love with a girl. I kind of passed from my body. I was still there but all shimmery. It was like I had a tingling in my centre too, that I knew I'd dream about and try to find the words for. Always.'

I kissed Walt and let a casual hand play between his legs, brushing his thighs and stroking his shaft. With my fingers squeezed together, I slipped a flattened hand inside the waistband of his jeans and pressed down until my fingertips found heat. Inside my open mouth his tongue moved about, impatient. 'Easy, boy,' I whispered, pulling away, knowing he'd soon be looking to throw my dress up and bang me like a prisoner with access to the governor's wife.

Going limp under his shaky hands, I let Walt ease me on to the couch until I was lying straight with my feet hanging over the armrest. Above me, he hovered and swallowed me whole with a face full of so much longing I started to glow inside. Seeing what I can do to a boy never loses its thrill.

'Walt?' I whispered. He nodded, angling his head to peer into my cleavage, which rose like sweet dough

117

over a pan that is way too small for so much cake. 'Take your clothes off. Every stitch.'

With a swallow he complied, popping his shirt buttons with anxious hands, ripping at his tie, and finally staggering about with one leg of his jeans pulled inside out and stuck around an ankle. Down went his white shorts too, and I tasted the air with my tongue, hoping to taste the garlic and salt on that meat, quivering like a diving board no more than a foot away from its rightful home.

'Clear the table,' I said. He looked puzzled so I raised an eyebrow and nodded towards the kitchen. As he proceeded to whip the cloth and dishes away to the draining board, I rose from the couch and waited for him to turn around.

My white shroud fell from my shoulders to the spotless floor in one swift torrent. In the cabin's shadows and flickers of lantern light, I stood before him, naked from the waist up save for my pearls. Around my waist were two things: a silver belly chain that glinted against my sun-browned skin, and a white garter belt with four thin suspenders. The garter belt is made from a sheer, diaphanous whiteness so you can see my hips through the material. My stockings were flesh-tone and so fine that only under strong light could they be seen to shimmer. Like rubies in all my blondeness and skin tone were my lips and nails, both finger and toe, painted fresh and red. Closing my eyes and tilting my head back, I stretched one arm out to him. He came to me on swift feet – a hard, brown streak, panting like a wolf, with something altogether prehistoric burning up his eyes.

On the table, I arranged myself to his delectation; one leg drawn up, the other leg and both arms trailing over the table sides. Watching him with one eye through my fringe, I could see his chest rising and falling and his face seemed to be filling out. This is the moment I adore – when both lovers engorge with hot blood, desperate to feast upon one another but tempted to hold back and stare a little longer, to prolong the anticipation. Stroking my slippery legs from ankle to thigh, he shook his head from side to side as if in disbelief and then peered at my puss lips, which were peeking through my blonde floss, folded and covered with a special sheen that looks grey where it gathers on pink flesh. Gently, he eased my thighs apart and slid me down the table until the lower half of my buttocks hung over the edge. A sudden feeling of vulnerability, which tingled around my anus, tempted me to close my legs. I felt so open, so ready, and almost ashamed of my eager face. Leaning on to his toes, I felt the head of his cock nuzzle against my puss. Too low down and then too high. He took a quick look below for navigation and pushed his hips forward. When my dewy hole was discovered, it looked like all his worries had just melted off his face.

Feeling it pass through me, from the rounded head to the thick stem, made me hiss like I'd put an idle hand on a hot plate. There seemed to be too much of him. A light pain, a need for more, a desire to engulf all of my tender parts with the same pleasure, led my hands to my breasts. Squeezing both of my breasts so my nipples protruded between my fingers, I started to make a throaty sound. Walt withdrew. Rubbing my legs against his chest made my calves feel slippery. Encouraged by my long limbs pressing up and against his hard body, Walt sank back into me.

At first he tried to pump me slow, but when I put my ankles beside his smooth cheeks and showed him some tongue, the boy went at me like a dog on a perfumed bitch. With no regard for the food and all the fizzy beer recently swallowed, we started to bang and smash against each other, our pelvic bones cushioned by my floss and softness. This was better than down by the water, I decided, in a mind soon cleared of distractions. Besides the effect of all the chilled alcohol and long stares across the dinner table, I had dressed to guarantee his hardest payload and my most feminine mode of sacrifice. And by telling the boy to go a little slower, I guess I made him all the more eager to thrust into the delicate girl-thing that allowed herself to adorn his kitchen table.

My cries began to warble from the vibrations passing throughout my body. My whole skin seemed to have come alive with tiny ripples of energy. I was a storm at sea with churning black depths. 'Oh, boy, fuck me,' I said in my quivery voice. 'Fuck, fuck, fuck me . . .'

And he did until the sweat gathered on his angry brow and his shoulders stiffened into hard curves and deep hollows by the bone. Holding my thighs, he then drew my botty off the table, stiffened his body and thrust in and out, hard, so my puss was in mid-air, kept aloft by his hands and stabbed at by his fat, slippery baton. Being suspended from his body allowed him maximum power and awarded me maximum pleasure. Every thrust of his groin and stomach against my buttocks and thighs sent a caress to my clit-pip.

Losing control of my mind and mouth is always a part of my coming. 'Bastard. You bastard. You fucking bastard.'

'Harder, girl?' he cried. His eyes slit, his teeth gritted and I liked the snarl that contorted his pretty face.

'Harder, bastard. Harder!'

Deeper strokes and a thick pulsing beat on his meat let me know I'd made him come. Pulled up higher off the table, like my weight was of no consequence, I had to slap my hands down to prevent myself rolling on to the floor. Walt slammed and ground into me and then shook his cock about inside. His face screwed up all red, and I knew he was going through the last moment of his pumping efforts while receiving the scolding rewards of hot cream, passing through his pipe to rush inside his lover. A starburst of white lights, with millions of sparks no bigger than a pin's head, exploded in my head and, for a moment, I went blind.

When I opened my eyes, Walt lowered my body to the table, withdrew from me and then chucked his hands up and down his own wet length to cast the last two dollops of seed on to my belly. Before he had a chance to rub both cooling lumps into my tummy, I scooped them up with my fingers and then stuffed the digits into my mouth. Hot, salty goodness around my teeth just sent me higher. Sitting up straight, I lashed my arms around his damp neck and then pulled his face into mine.

'Want to get bit?' I whispered, and then scratched the skin on his back with my claws.

His eyes went all panicky but he kissed my mouth. When he made a little whimper of delight and fright, I wrapped both legs around his tight waist, seized the back of his head, and plunged my mouth at the soft dough of his neck skin. I could feel my nostrils flaring and my scalp prickling. He struggled and shuddered but my grip held him tight. When he moved away from the table, my body went with him, attached to the front of him. We staggered to the couch and by the time he was lying down with me on top, I had filled another opening to my body with a warm flood from this boy.

Narcoleptic trances, swooning narcotic dream worlds, a catatonia of delight; I left the world for a while and would have stayed away had I not heard a disturbance. Despite the cry of whippoorwills and the chirp of crickets outside, and the heavy thump, thump of my poet's heart beneath my breasts, I could hear something. And it was close. A creaking. Buried in the red warmth and sleepy haze, relaxed and full and well loved with this rangy brute wrapped around me, I struggled to pull my thoughts together. Although they kept unravelling, I knew the ceiling was creaking. Floorboards sank and straightened above as light footfalls moved through the darkness of upstairs. My senses struggled to gather and focus on the sound. It was like being drunk. My tongue felt swollen and all the walls seemed to judder, go still, and then judder again. All I wanted was sleep but instinct told me to be alert.

'Walt?' I whispered.

He stayed silent.

'Baby,' I said again, but he could only murmur from his sleep of conquered champions.

I wanted to tell him someone was in the house, but I wasn't sure that it was not just a case of the old place shifting about. Or was I imagining it on account of having taken so much of the good sweet stuff from my poet?

Rising off Walt's body, I pointed my face towards the staircase. Along my spine a frost of fear sowed itself between each vertebra. There it was again – a creaking and a creeping sound. Something man-size was coming down those stairs. A darkness suddenly invaded my dreamy mind as the steps reached the bend in the staircase. Walt moaned again and tried to hug me back to his body. Swatting his hands away, I stood up beside the couch, wobbly on my heels that the poet liked me to keep on during our loving. Falling backwards, I ended up sitting on Walt's leg while more of the black shadow crept into my mind. This was the bond working – it sensed something. A threat.

Biting down on panic, I started to unbuckle my heels and look about for a weapon. Although Walt must have done some chopping, the knife rack beside the wall cabinet was empty. Outside the cabin and behind me, I heard a second pair of feet run across the porch. The cabin door slammed shut and I twisted about to face the noise, but my head seemed to keep spinning even though my body had stopped moving.

'Well, well, well,' a voice said from the stairs.

'No,' I whispered, unable to look.

'If you bait the hook just right and have the patience to wait, you never know what kind of catch could come your way.'

'No,' I said louder. I'd never heard the voice before, but I knew who owned it. Frozen in a crouch, I was unable to turn and see what had come down the stairs.

'Most hunters would be satisfied to just haul you out of the wild, girl. But a professional would keep you and hang on to you so as to bait a larger trap for a bigger cat.' Once the Preacher stopped laughing, I turned to look at my Nemesis.

Seven

So now I'm in chains. The more I think, the more it seems some thought has been applied to the preparation of my present predicament. No one can hear me yell for assistance, there are no neighbours, and from what I deduced earlier it wouldn't make a difference if Val heard my screams. I'm stuck in the middle of rural Texas with a crazy man as my jailer. There may have been a time when things were worse for me, but I can't remember when.

From what I have seen of the first floor of the poet's cabin, besides the master bedroom that I am currently incarcerated in, there is a bathroom and one other smaller room. My captors bathed me on the first night and I only saw one other door in the hallway when being led to and from the tub. The door to this room was bolted shut so there is no way through without making a racket. Across from the door in my room is a window, latched shut, but with my hands and ankles tied I'd make a poor show of escaping through there. Beside the big brass-framed bed only an old pine dresser, with a jug of water on top, serves as furniture. There was a pitcher of lemonade on the dresser too, but my natural sense of petulance demanded I throw something at the door when first deposited here. So now there is a stain on the rug and a lot of broken glass on the floorboards.

There has been a ghost chasing Hank since '45 and it looks like he's captured the next best thing – his heart. Hank and I have been looking out for this dark spectre of a man, known in the agency as the Preacher, since we first hit the road. We've kept watch in the rear-view mirrors of the hundred or so cars we've owned, peeked between Venetian blinds hanging in a thousand motels we watched TV in, peered up at rooftops we walked under, looked over our shoulders on the smoky dancefloors we've hunted on, glanced under the beds we've slept in, and cast a cautious eye at any place a trap could be laid. In every moment of bliss he's been with us. Even when we gave him the slip for five years, one part of us never relaxed. Preacher's out there, Hank's eyes and silence would say to me. Somewhere, he be waiting.

Even though Hank is not here, I feel like he's taught me a lesson about being careless and about not connecting the clues. This makes me especially angry. Angry at him for taking off first day at Val's and angry at myself for seducing sweet boys and swimming with poets instead of looking harder and deeper into everything around me.

Strangely, though, a part of me almost feels relief because the dark has caught up with us. A fight between two men has the opportunity to end. Even though the Preacher is holding the trump card and there is a chance that Hank could lose – the very thought makes this huge pineapple thing grow in my throat – part of me is done with running and hiding.

Two nights back, it wasn't hard for the Preacher to subdue me. Even though my claws were out the moment I heard his voice, I was all slowed up, dizzy-brained and on the brink of a two-day hibernation after loving the poet. In the tussle that followed his surprise attack, all I managed to give

125

him was a scratch on the chin when I was looking to put a set of gills in his throat, the way Hank showed me. I was pitiful. Struggling to get my second shoe off, thinking of running, putting all my fear and rage into cursing instead of fighting, he just snatched me up, one wrist after another. Silver US Marshal cuffs were slapped on my wrists and a death-row chain was strung around my ankles, until all I could manage was a heavy two-step shuffle, like an old boy I once saw doing his thing to a blue-grass band.

Humiliation sobered me quicker than ice water and black coffee. Dressed in stockings and chains and not a stitch more, with my head bowed in the room I had just eaten, loved and fed in, the Preacher did nothing but stroll around his prize for an age. Round and round he paced, talking under his breath to god knows what, sometimes referring to me without addressing me. 'I can see why Hank picked this one. Yes, sir. She's just right. Same figure too.' He would shake his head like he'd seen a miracle, amazed by something I didn't understand. 'Bet he takes his belt to her, the way she liked it. And her hair is that colour to remind him.' This made me go real cold, on account of his lunatic whispering making some sense. It was like he had intimate knowledge of Hank's preferences for me.

But the strangest thing was seeing the Preacher that close. Curiously, I've always had a strong impression of what the Preacher looks like and yet I had only ever seen him twice and then from a distance. The first time, back in the beginning when Hank and I had been on the road no more than six months, the Preacher had been twenty yards away and wearing sunglasses as he ran through the parking lot of a cinema throwing shots at Hank, who covered me with his body and returned fire until he spun the crazy

Preacher around like a big crow with a wing hit by buckshot. It's insane why Hank never put him down for good. I seen my man hit a dime cast 30 feet above his head, out in the desert where he would think and practise before an agency job. But he always maintained that he never killed the Preacher that time because of me being there; I rattled his judgement with my squirming on the tarmac beneath him and with my hollering like a baby. Always left me wondering, though. The next time, about two years back, we saw the Preacher from across a street in New York City. There was a river of yellow taxi-cabs whizzing past us in a reckless current, keeping the Preacher on the far bank. But that time the Preacher never pulled his gun – he raised his hat and smiled instead. Smiled right at me.

But I got my first good look at him the other night and it unnerved me to see a similarity to Hank. Same age, height and build – give or take twenty pounds. Same walk too. Only the Preacher's hair was streaked with more white and his face was leaner. More distinguished-looking than Hank, like a young James Mason. Could be considered handsome, I suppose.

'Hank does more than peep, that's fo' sure,' I finally said, raising my chin and eventually finding the guts to speak downstairs in the poet's trap. I'd begun to feel defiant again once the cool night air had helped to clear my head.

The Preacher stopped dead, right in front of my face, no more than a foot away, and he made me flinch just by looking me in the eye. Must have rubbed his hands together because I heard the squeak of soft leather. When he smiled at me, all the lines on his sun-baked face just creased up, giving prominence to his pale blue eyes. 'Sure he does. Hank's a regular lover boy.'

This reduced me further and my anger overflowed. 'Son of a bitch!' I cried out.

Preacher just studied my face for a while and then gave me this look like he was a headmaster intent on dispensing punishment but holding back, stunned by the pupil's innocence. 'Don't have a clue, do you, Missy Lafeyette?'

Hearing him mention my family name made me spit like a wild cat. But he never even blinked when my weak, dry-mouthed drizzle pattered on his face. His smile broadened and he laughed to himself in a soft and wheezy manner. 'No, sir, she don't know shit about him or me.'

'I know plenty,' I said, but my voice had gone all tremolo and cry-baby.

When the Preacher brushed a piece of hair off my cheek, which had been hanging and tickling my skin, my legs seemed to disappear and all the strength in my greedy body poured out all over the floor. It was fear. This man was crazy, but his craziness was contagious. I'd begun to believe him.

Still bound hand and foot, I was led upstairs by two traitors – Sweet Boy Denver, who had been lurking out on the porch while I loved and fed, and his partner, the now sleepy Walt. Preacher took up the rear, silent with triumph. The poet looked fit to fall down at any moment and he had this silly look on his face that I wanted to slap off. Even the Preacher seemed annoyed with the boys, especially Walt, who he had slapped off the sofa, yelling, 'Git boy!' right after my capture. Guess he hated having to employ minions to get his evil way.

Too afraid to remove my manacles in order to strip the remainder of my scanties off, they plunged me in the big iron tub in the washroom upstairs and scrubbed me down. All on the Preacher's directions,

128

of course. He said he wanted me cleansed of sin –
meaning the paint on my face and the traces of the
poet's lust, inside and outside my body. So into the
bath I went, still wearing creased stockings and a
satin garter belt.

'When Val gets a hold of you, boy, you may never
leave that attic you seem so fond of,' I said to
Denver, who had been finding it difficult to look me
in the eye since my capture. 'As for you–' I jerked my
head back to make the poet flinch, but was unable to
think of a suitable curse or insult. At least he was
suffering from the same mixture of fear and guilt as
Denver, but that offered little consolation; these boys
had disappointed me more than I cared to admit.

The bath water was hot. I suppose even the
Preacher has some twisted code of conduct towards
the condemned. Or maybe it was not chivalry. Maybe
after all these years of following loose ends and cold
trails, he wanted to prolong the humiliation of my
capture. Being scrubbed down by the two Romeos
that had lured me to shame, and managed to bruise
my heart along the way too, does nothing for a girl's
self-respect. 'How could you?' I hissed at Walt, as he
sponged my back.

'Pay her no mind,' the Preacher said, from the stool
he sat on over in the corner while intertwining his
gloved fingers. But Walt seemed uncomfortable and
so did Sweet Boy Denver. I sensed their anxiety
around the Preacher, who had not even raised his
voice yet. I wished he had because his apparent calm
was worse than any yelling.

'He just used you to get me and now you two are
as good as dead,' I said to the shame-faced boys. And
straight away, I felt both pairs of hands go soft
against my body until they did no more than just pad
the sponge and flannel against my skin.

'No one gets hurt, Miss,' the poet said. Then he looked at his paymaster. 'Ain't that right?'

'Sure,' the Preacher said, before winking at me. 'No one present, provided the procedure is followed.'

'You son of a –' I tried to cry, but the Preacher leaped from his stool and shoved a bar of soap in my mouth. 'Time you stopped speaking like a tramp, girl. There's no need for that talk. No need.'

I spat the vile-tasting soap from my mouth and would have continued telling him a thing or two about his parentage, but the look on his face suggested all sorts of things to me – associations of things unhinged and bent from shape, things gone off course and loose where they should be tight.

After the bath, Denver ripped the stockings from my legs, which he pocketed promptly when the Preacher's back was turned, and I was led to my cell – the master bedroom. Now all I have to clothe me are chains and a few regrets.

Third night and Val is in the room; I can smell her. Never heard the door unlock and the lights are doused. It is her perfume that wakes me.

'Better rip my throat out,' I say. 'Cus if I ever get free, I'm coming for you.'

'Be still, girl. I'm here to tell you something. An explanation of why you're here is the least I can offer.'

'Keep it to yourself, snake. I know I'm here because you betrayed me on account of your cold green heart. Gave me up to the Preacher to trap Hank when he comes looking. Guess Hank's better dead than with me.'

'Hush!' she insists. 'Time you learned the truth about your man. True he broke my heart, but this trap has been laid on agency orders. He deceived them too.'

'Lies!' I cry, and whip my head about to drown her voice out, because the cuffs prevent me from muffing my ears with my hands. Thin fingers seize my face and dig into my cheeks; fingers that caressed my softest parts only a few nights back. 'Quit your crying, girl. And hush, I said.' Her voice is close to the tone it had in the attic when I caught her feeding on Denver. I don't like it. Suddenly I think of the Asian girl from my vision and the look on her face.

With only a half-moon gleaming between the curtains, I can see little but the outline of her head. It gets closer and I feel her breath on my mouth. 'This has killed me inside, girl. Jamming you up was the first thing I wanted after you took Denver, even though I laid him on to whet your appetite, but hurting you was the last thing I wanted after the night we spent together. Looks like everything is all upside-down now and not just for you. Understand me. I had no choice but to help Preacher. We work for the same company, girl. My allegiance has to go beyond my love for Hank. Yes, we love the same man. Even after what he did to me in Asia, I love him and always will. But that's not why I tricked you into chains, girl. Believe me.'

I stay quiet.

Now she's crying, silently, save for a sniffle, and she kisses my mouth, real soft. 'No harm is going to come your way, Missy,' she whispers. 'I promise you that. No harm.'

'But you and the Preacher,' I say. 'I just can't believe you'd side with –' Tears stop my voice. I've held it in for long enough, but out it comes like a hot salty spring. Seems like I've gone without a good weep for far too long. Not resisting Val and the lies she tells, I just go soft in her arms and let her cradle my head. Once this rain has gone I'll get my fight back, I promise myself.

'Nothing is simple here, Missy,' she whispers, trying to soothe my aching mind. 'Old scores that run back to the war against the Germans have been given a chance to settle themselves. Those two boys have to meet.'

'Why?' I say, in a voice that seems croaky, and I feel a bubble burst from my lips.

'It's a story only Preacher can tell you. Way things are, I guess you'll hear it soon enough. It's older than you and me, girl. Hank has a reason for everything. Lord knows what it is, but there is a reason why he kept it from you for so long.'

Lying alongside me, with only a thin sheet between us, Val holds me and whispers shushy sounds into my hair. Maybe I should go for her throat. Maybe she left the door unlocked. But I can't. I can't feel enough hate for this woman. Through her fine clothes and porcelain skin I can feel the wound that is timeless and still seeping. The way Hank left it. And then there are my damned instincts telling me there are things I don't want to hear but these are things I just got to know.

'You say he done the agency a wrong. This I don't get. You just have to look on the scars on his body and the months I spend waiting for him to come home to know he's loyal.'

'Not just loyal, the best. But Hank had a moment of weakness with the wife of a powerful man.'

'Who?'

'Wouldn't even tell that secret to my maker.'

'But –'

'Ssh.' Her finger touches my lips. 'She was making eyes at him while he was her guard. Hank held back for so long, but she reminded him of someone who once left a mark deeper than any war wound on his body. And when Hank sees a certain quality in a girl

132

. . . a girl like you, Missy, he needs love. Can't help himself.'

My eyes flash wide, my mind stretches wider.

Val sighs. 'Only recently did this Washington wife's papers open before the wrong pair of eyes and the truth was out. Then it was hushed away so quick it was like no one ever knew. Only the husband knows the full story and it was he that ordered the hit. A hit on a great patriot.' She sighs again, but for longer this time. For a while she stays silent, trying to find the words, I guess. 'Preacher was only too pleased to accept the job. And I was asked to join him. It was never a choice for me, Missy. It was just worded that way.'

I recall a dream. A dream I had a long time back. Hank was away for months on a job and I spent my time watching the Stones stagger around the Midwest. One night, I took a Hell's Angel to my bed, who looked like a Viking, which was new to me. And as I enjoyed a particularly good night and feed, I recall dreaming about this pretty woman who wore beautiful clothes. A woman I always wanted to look like to please Hank. And in the dream Hank was loving her on a plane. I mentioned it to him when he came home, claiming it was a vision because of the bond. Hank seemed roused that I had intuited something like that with him so far away. He said he had to take a piece of an air stewardess on account of his hunger. Didn't look much like a stewardess in my dream, I told him, with her own room on a plane and all. 'First Class,' he said, reluctant to share the story. But now, I know it was no dream. His feelings were so strong for this woman the vision of them together found a way into my sleep from way up above the clouds. So it was real, him throwing himself into that woman who never even took her clothes off;

133

who hugged her pretty legs and arms around his back to keep his pumping hard and fast; who made him give her some rough trade stuff real quick, like she was expecting someone to barge into her quarters at any moment. Remembering her pleading face, runny with tears and mascara, starts to spread a warmth though me.

'You knew it,' Val says. 'You felt it. Girl, you have the bond strong as that rogue you ride with. You saw him with her.'

'Thought it was a dream.'

'Better stay a dream, because if you were to realise who that woman on the plane is and who she was married to . . . Well, it would be no good for you. No good.'

Our faces are damp and slippery on the cheeks when they meet to kiss. Don't know why I'm kissing her, but I am, deeply. Even though it's too dark to see, I know her eyes are shut like mine. Maybe I want to try and heal that wound she carries, even though a part of me is more dangerous than a sleek-furred puma and would die fighting to keep Hank as my pride. Could be I just don't want to spend a third night alone trussed up by Pennsylvania steel. Or possibly this revelation of Hank's deceit is inducing me to stray. Might be the need to feed is making me impatient. And where there is hunger there is also love.

Gasping tears of relief we embrace in that dark room, kissing and nuzzling into necks and breasts that are peeled naked like pale moon fruits. My mobility is hampered but Val makes the moves to get both our mouths wet with puss nectar. Topping and tailing each other, her wafer-thin tongue feels rough enough on my sex to make me moan and stretch that chain taut between my feet. Sensing my frustration at

134

not being able to grip her buttocks, Val presses her puss on to my mouth so I can engorge my adulterer's mouth on her silk and honey. Through the panty fabric, which feels so sheer and slippery, I sup from her narrow sex until she's forced to sob down there between my legs. Once more, I make this broken woman shiver and whimper. With my mouth I deliver her from the pain.

She has me riled too, but I haven't climaxed. Collaborating with the enemy has held part of me back. This I know even if I'm not sure whether she is all enemy. 'I brought this for you, girl,' she says, between taking air into her lungs. As the bed creaks and the mattress dips about me, Val moves into a crouch beside my waist. 'Being in chains doesn't mean you have to go without.'

Directed by Val's hand, a rounded object plays at the entrance of my sex. Prodding gently, it starts to widen me. Can I take this shaft? I wonder. Am I just going along with Val to seize an advantage? I ask myself. One thing I know in my heart to be true, Val will protect me. As our bond germinates, the Preacher's hold loosens. Maybe I could get Val to warn Hank off. The better side of her might be reached. But as the smooth device parts my lips and descends into the sticky darkness of my intimacy, I find my thoughts dispersing. 'Let the fear go, Missy,' she whispers. 'Ease your troubled mind, girl.' On it goes, widening me so I wince and make a noise that reverberates off the roof of my mouth. Back it slips to the tip, like it's attached to a man who knows just what I want. I need to feel that glorious entry again and again. Tearing the missing hymen with a sweet pain, Val stretches me, enters me, awakens delight, until I twist in my chains. 'Get anything from a man, that girl,' Hank once said, and I'm inclined to believe

135

the observation applies to girls as well; bad girls who even find pleasure in captivity. I'm a sinner. Maybe it's time I faced a Preacher man.

'Things are going to get crazy before they get straight, girl,' she says, fucking me into a high with her hand-held toy. 'You got to be ready for the Preacher. Maybe it won't make sense right away, but after all this is done with, you'll know the story of two men who once loved each other like brothers. And you'll know the reason why you are what you are.'

I hear her words over the rushing of the hot sea in my head. All my limbs stretch against the restraints so tight about my joints and I bite my bottom lip like it was toffee. Always liked to be held down and used up by some rogue or high-heel-stepping bitch, but now that I'm a real prisoner, with real cuffs I don't have the key for, my pleasure is blinding, deafening, obliterating.

'Like it, girl? All the pretty girls do.' Val whispers in my hair, as if my passion has produced a snapshot from her evil career for her to see and relive in her mind – some memory that thrills her too deeply. Pushing and pulling, rolling and rubbing, the slippery thing moves me around the bed like I'm a dog on a leash. Let me in, girl, I think. Let me see what you've done, bitch.

My climax begins to hum before it roars through me. 'Tell me.'

'Tell you what I did to sweet girls who had secrets and nasty stories that could break leaders of men? That what you want, my soft one?'

'Ugh.'

'Look.'

In my mind I see Val walking down a long white corridor. Behind her there are two big men in dark

suits who wear hats like Cary Grant. Between the
men is a pretty brunette with lavish eye make-up, held
by the elbows and marched down the corridor. She is
wearing a short dress. All hope has gone from her
face and her bottom lip is all trembly. She is led to a
room and left alone with Val. There is a bed in this
room, a metal sink, and a chair. Val gives the
frightened girl a bottle of soda pop and smiles at her,
strokes her hair, and puts her at ease. After the girl
has a little cry-baby, she starts to shake her head from
side to side and insist to Val that she doesn't know
something, or didn't do something. Val smiles and
nods. While she agrees with the girl she takes her
jacket off and rolls up the sleeves of her blouse. On
the captive's face is a mixture of bewilderment and
swiftly retreating security.

Val approaches the bed with her hands on her hips,
still smiling. Lashing out with her hands, Val seizes
the girl's shoulder with one hand and then slaps her
upside the head with the other hand. Side to side her
head is smacked silly and dizzy. The girl cringes back
on the bed and then throws a slap back at Val. Her
thin white wrist is snatched from the air and twisted
until the girl is writhing on her belly with her hand
up behind her back. Efficiently, Val pulls the girl's
dress up and then rips her shiny pantyhose and white
panties down to leave her botty all white and naked.
Hiking her black skirt up, Val places a shiny knee in
the small of the girl's back and begins to smack her
bottom. Screaming at the girl, Val's hair gets all
messy and her hand moves like a machine until the
captive's bottom cheeks are red. Crying and
squirming, the girl still maintains her innocence.

Suddenly, Val's mood changes and she climbs off
the girl and tidies her hair up. Cowering on the bed,
the captive watches Val make coffee. With her chair

drawn right up to the bed, Val then sits and crosses her legs. The heels and the points of the toes on her shoes look sharp and dramatic against the white linoleum floor. She snakes her front foot about, sips her coffee and talks at the girl who goes all red with what looks like embarrassment. Covering her face in the pillows, the girl hides from Val. This means she doesn't see Val pull a cream-coloured object from out of her jacket. It looks like the long bullet thing that Hank gave me as a paperweight – the things they shoot at planes with, he said. But this one is cream coloured and Val twists it in the middle to get the thing humming.

When Val holds it against the inside of the girl's thigh, their fighting breaks out again. Val retreats from the punching girl and stands off to one side. The captive's moment of victory lasts a few seconds. Val has only pulled back in order to unzip and then step out of her tight skirt. In blouse, nylons and heels, Val walks to the bed with confidence, swats the girl's puny slapping hands aside and then climbs on top of her. With her snarly face pressed close to the prisoner's red, tear-stained features, Val gets her hand working between them. I know this because her elbow is moving in quick little stabs. For a while the girl thrashes her head about and drums her fists on Val's back, but then her long legs suddenly stretch out so her toes are pointing at the ceiling. As she shouts something unpleasant, I notice her arms betraying her resolve, like the rest of her body seems ready to. These slender arms wrap around Val and then her bare legs circle Val's bottom. Shuffling, Val and the girl move up the bed, powered by the pumping of Val's elbow between the girl's thighs. They kiss and then the girl starts to move her hips to and fro to get more of that bullet in her. Soon, Val

138

sits up between her prisoner's thighs and just pumps away, real hard. Clenching up her eyes, the brown-haired girl makes the 'O' shape with her thick lips.

This is when Val starts to slow up with the prodding. The girl begs for speed and friction but Val won't relent until the girl opens up and says the right things. I guess this happens when Val angles her head towards the broken and hasty words that stagger from the girl's mouth. Then the fucking starts again and Val even strokes the girl's shin as deliverance is provided.

As the vision fades, I come, trying to cling on to the image of that brunette's screwed-up face. In the dream, the last thing I see is Val tidying her hair and retouching her lipstick by the sink, watched by the silent girl curled up on the bed. My head rears off the pillow and I cannot prevent the yelling I embark upon with that lovely bullet in me.

When I calm down, Val leaves the beautiful shape inside me and tucks the sheet under my chin like a serviette. 'Hungry?' she whispers, her voice taut with excitement.

'Mmm,' I say, melting into the pillow and mattress as the aftershocks of my climax leave me weak.

The darkness moves and shifts. Val leaves my bedside and I hear the bedroom door click open. When she returns, she is leading something on a chain. Something afraid but delighted by its own terror. I smell Denver. Traitor.

'Just a sip, girl. He's got to last you until those chains are off and you can run wild again.'

With Hank? I want to ask, but am unable to speak because of the sensation of a quick pulse so near my mouth. Dipping itself towards me, I curl my lips back to accept the given warmth.

Eight

Never heard Val and her Sweet Boy leave, but when I wake things have changed in my room. From the position of the sun that I can see through my open curtains, it must be midday and my hosts have wasted no time ushering the next stage of my captivity into this cell. While I've been inside a post-feed oblivion, sleeping the sleep of the drugged and lost, food has been brought to me along with water to wash in, a mirror, make-up and clothes. Unusual clothes.

Not until I am standing up do I realise that the manacles have gone from my limbs. Mystified, I look down at the faint pink ring around my ankles and wrists. What does the crazy Preacher have in mind?

Beneath my naked feet I feel vibrations made from raised voices. Falling to my knees I pull my hair to one side and put my ear to the floor. It is Val, shouting. The other voice is lower and fills in the gaps between her outbursts with a calm and even tone: Preacher.

Seems I've sent this ship off course.

The front door of the cabin slams shut. I race to my window and see Val scurrying across the yard, her head clothed by a scarf, her thin body wrapped in something long and black that brushes the dusty ground and shows a glimmer of patent heel beneath its hem. At the gate, she turns and looks at my window. Although her eyes are concealed by sunglasses, I know she sees my blonde head peering down. No smiles are exchanged; only a quick look of despair. I guess we are both trapped.

A key turns in the door to my room. I peer over my shoulder and see the door shake before it opens. Before they enter, I cast a final, pleading look down to Val at the gate. But she is gone. Vanished.

'Sleeps late, consorts with strange boys, and even takes girls to her bed. Hank lets this one run wild. Tries to nurture the same spirit she had.'

Tensing every muscle and tendon, I prepare to leap at the white-faced, black-suited freak who enters my room and closes the door behind him. In one gloved hand, he carries a leather attaché case.

'Relax, little lady. And please, put the robe on. I apologise for not knocking, but who knows what kind of surprise a firebrand might prepare for this old Preacher.' Preacher laughs and walks to the chair before the dresser where the clothes are neatly folded. He plucks the robe from the back of a chair and throws it to me. I cover my nakedness in a heartbeat.

'Don't worry about me, girl. Your virtue ain't at risk. I haven't had a date since '45.' He says this calmly and stretches his hand out, palm facing, towards the bed. Taking the hint, I sit on the edge of mattress, still tense, although curiosity has weakened my fear. 'This evening,' he continues, 'we must create an environment for truth. Taste of the venture is questionable, but there's no other way. At least I know you like my boys, which is just as well because they took some finding and some fine-tuning. Did you like the musical touch?' He laughs. 'Once you and Hank had to abandon a car in an awful hurry. If you'd left a forwarding address, I could have sent all your precious tapes on to you.' He laughs again, but I don't join in.

141

I am unable to grasp all he is saying, but there is an underlying implication that makes me swallow.

Preacher stands, at ease, no more than four feet away from me. In his smooth black suit and white shirt, which always seems unaffected by Texas dust, I see he is clean-shaven and his hair is stroked back into an immaculate, creamed quiff. I'm tempted to think he means me no harm. Even his eyes look kindly. 'Tonight you get a bedtime story, girl. There has been something I've been meaning to tell you for a long time, but you just keep running away.' He walks to the top of the bed by the pillows and places his case on the bedspread. Casually, he unclasps the case and opens it. For a moment something crosses his face. Looks like grief or remorse, but before I can get a fix on his eyes they change again. His gloved hands slowly pull several black undergarments from the case. As if holding a dangerous biological weapon that could spill over the brim of the beaker that holds it, the Preacher gently places the items on the bed: four flimsy items and then a pair of shoes, whose crushed velvet texture immediately catches my eye. What this craziness means is beyond me at present, but I can't help shivering from the intrigue of it all.

'Suggest you eat a good meal, girl. You're going to need strength of body and mind.'

'What do you want from me?' I blurt out.

'I want you to listen. To be patient until you understand.'

'You think I'm going to wear your crazy shit, psycho?'

Preacher winces and then looks hurt. Genuinely hurt. I almost feel guilty.

He looks me right in the eye and it's a struggle to endure that stare. 'Be careful with the clothes, Missy Lafeyette. They've been with me, unworn, for

142

nigh-on fifty years. Don't know what I'd do if something happened to them. They're real special to me. Like you, they're irreplaceable. And it's a terrible thing when precious items are lost. Don't you agree?'

Following his drift, I nod. He smiles and walks across to where I sit. From the inside of his pocket he withdraws a silver cigarette case and offers me a Marlboro. His smile broadens when I take a handful. 'You get dinner at six. Something light. Young Walt will prepare it. After that we start. Good day to you, girl.'

Without another word, the Preacher leaves the room and locks the door behind him.

Standing before my full-length mirror, I can see the hours I spent thinking and then the hours I spent preparing myself have paid off. Like Val, the Preacher has taken me back in time to the precious moment he was bonded. In the way I still favour the styles of the early sixties, my jailers are trapped in the forties. Even this room has nothing to remind me of the present.

The bra and French knickers are black and to my exact size, which makes me recall the Preacher's mutterings about Hank trying to recreate some other girl through me. Both items are sheer and tailored by a genius. Tiny labels with French writing on are attached near the hems, revealing the year of manufacture to be 1943. On my tummy, the fine material shines and makes my brown tum look more appealing than ever. They just don't make clothes like this any more. The bra makes a tight but not uncomfortable fit on my breasts, and in each cup my nips still appear pinkish. Wearing the brassière gives the sensation of a pair of woman's hands cupping my breasts. A wide garter belt went under the knickers

and then I put the nylons on. They are black with an
inflexible knit that has no Lycra in the fabric, and
coat my legs right up to the lips of my puss. On the
welt, a tiny white script in English gives the size as
Opera length, promises a run-proof resistance, and
tells me they are fifteen-denier stockings.

Over the slippery underthings I put the dress on. It
makes me feel dizzy with pleasure. Brushing the tops
of my feet, it rises up to my breasts where there is a
little V-shaped section cut into the middle to open my
cleavage. Two thin straps go over my shoulders and
my arms are left bare. Just below the place where the
silver clasps grip my stocking tops, a split in the left
side of the dress reaches its apex. This shows one of
my legs when I stand or both when I sit.

All of my nails have been lavished with the
gluey-smelling red polish that was left for me, and my
face is painted carefully. Somehow I feel different. I
feel dark inside and my lips are unwilling to smile.
There is a new power in me; rediscovered in captivity
when allowed finery. A fire builds in my belly; it's no
good for me to think of escape while dressed this way.
It makes me crave company. Prepared for anything,
I thrive on more mystery, need danger, demand
answers. I can be terrible. I am terrible. I will be
terrible.

It's like the Preacher has given me a loaded gun. I
think he needs to make a confession before I pull the
trigger. He seems without sex so I have been unable
to see inside his head. Such control and discipline
frighten but impress me. Who are these agency men
that love and chase me? I know nothing of what
made them, but tonight I aim to learn.

When I hear a procession of feet ascending the
stairs outside, I realise it must be six in the evening.
Everything has begun to go still outside and the air is

144

cool. I light my last cigarette and wait. When the Preacher enters the room, I am sitting on the bed, smoking. He stands still and stares. A lump moves in his throat. A tear shines across an eye and is blinked away. No words come from that mutterer's mouth. Standing to one side, he allows the two boys to enter the room. Their eyes are dipped but it is my turn to stare. Both boys have haircuts like they give in the services. Each limber body is clothed in a dark khaki suit – the uniform of an officer. They wear ties and shirts and there is a gold pin through each knot. Walt carries a tray of food and a bottle of Bourbon. Denver brings fresh flowers, chocolates, and Lucky Strike cigarettes. Outside, a crow issues a last forlorn cry and a shadow passes over the waning sun. I shudder.

When the boys come to me I embrace the designs they have for my body. This is how it must be. Resistance is unnecessary; compliance will bring truth. Each man follows the Preacher's script. They work like young actors, stiff at first before enthusiasm improves the role they play.

Sweet Boy Denver kneels before me. He smothers my crossed legs with hasty kisses and rubs his smooth cheeks on the tops of my equally smooth feet. They are shod in open-toes shoes, which have square heels and an ankle strap. Walt sits beside me and he is immediately drawn to the red and ivory snare of my mouth. Preacher is sitting by the window on a plain wooden chair, face obscured by shadow, legs apart, leaning forward with his leather-gloved hands clenched between his knees. He starts narrating the story:

1945 and the Nazis are all but beat. Me and Hank go into Berlin, like we did in Dresden, shutting our

*minds off, best we can, to the evil we see. Our brief:
locate pockets of resistance near the bunker. Watch
the Ruskies. Have the SS got a final hand to play?*

I hold Walt's face in my hands and move my head
back and forth, sucking his extended tongue. His eyes
are closed, but his hands go stumbly on my breasts;
squeezing, pressing, tweaking. I whisper calming
things in his ear like the woman who once owned the
dress would have done. Soon, his hands find a
rhythm; they stop trying to take all of my breasts like
a starving man clutching for bread, and begin to
stroke me, firmly.

*Everywhere there are old men with guns and kids
holding grenades, ready to run under tanks. Hank
gets hit; a deep shrapnel graze from one of our own
shells, so we take shelter in a bombed-out theatre,
but the basement is still holding. We go deep,
through the dark underground passages, climbing
over boxes, burnt props and singed costumes, down
stairs, around corners, down more stairs. I carry
Hank across my shoulders, holding one of his
dripping hands like he did for me at the Landings.
With only a Zippo for light, I move until my lungs
are fit to burst. Then, I see a light up ahead. Under
what must have been the stage someone has a light
burning. Gun drawn, I approach it. That's where we
find her.*

Opening my legs, I give Denver access to the shiny
valley of my inner thighs. My dress is pulled away
and off my legs. He can smell my heat under all this
museum finery that has its own faint scent of
camphor. Up his face goes; flushed, eyes wired open,
his hands following fingertips led by the seams on my

146

calves, up to the heart of me. Wider, I open my legs wider; slowly, tortuously, until he whimpers like a pup seeking a teat. Lapping for milky sustenance, his broad tongue brushes the beak of my sex, wetting the thin fabric, making it cling to brown lips, now sticky with their own juice.

It's like my heart stopped. Never seen such beauty. Never. Not before, not since. Looks like she's about to take the stage: pretty as an angel, blonde as desert sand at midday, dressed in that gown you're wearing, girl. She's an aristocrat. Anybody can see that. Speaks no English, only German. Or so she pretends. She has food, wine aplenty, and a steamer trunk full of real nice things all hoarded up. I hold a pistol on her but can't feel it in my hand. All my fingers go weak like they're not there. Saying nothing, she takes Hank from me and lays him on her bed. Dresses his wound while I stand there, like a dummy, wanting her. Don't care about what we're running from, or what we need to do next, I just want her.

Should have suspected something was wrong by the way her face hovers over the boy's flesh wound. Her eyes are green as the Pacific and deeper than the sky, but full of hunger. Long lashes are fluttering in panic over these jewels in her head. She can't wait to get that spirit and bandage on the graze to conceal temptation. Then she sits with the boy's head in her lap, stroking his hair, with this tear rolling down her cheek. I wanted to shoot her. Damn it, I felt so mad to see her touching him, I wanted to squeeze the trigger.

In time, though, she taught me how to share.

In so much ugliness, under broken things there ain't words for, she's hiding in the Berlin dark, waiting for salvation. Waiting to swap sides again.

147

Like she'd been doing since the French cut their king's head off. You see, she always backed the winners. A few days later, when it was too late for us, I followed a faint odour of something gone bad that had been troubling me. Deep inside that basement, I found three German officers. All dried out like the moths a spider's been at.

My teeth graze Walt's throat and he says, 'Yes, girl. Yes, girl, bite me. Bite me hard. Make me hurt.' I nip him and he whimpers.

'Take me, first,' I whisper through all the hot breath between our mouths that smell of lipstick and aftershave. Between my legs, Sweet Boy Denver has found a tiny fold in the knickers – a slit made by careful hands – that I never realised was there. Through the aperture his pointy tongue dips. My teat is found and suckled. Shivering and taking quick, frighted breaths, I lie back on the bed.

Squirming my body up the mattress to find the space I need, I watch two boys undressing around me. Denver still sucks as he strips, making my heels rake out and catch the bed linen with brass-tipped heel points. Broad chests and firm thighs are exposed. Clothes are peeled away from defined torsos and long cocks are unveiled from behind white shorts, already trembling at the tips to knife me. Hurriedly, I am rolled on to my front and the dress is peeled from my body, downward, over my hips, knees, feet, until my skin gooses from the evening air that bathes me and the inner need that flops my belly over.

Couldn't get out of that damn basement. You see, it was too tricky up above. And yet, I had no way of knowing it was more dangerous where we were. So me and Hank sat tight, like we had done in many of

148

our times overseas, comforted by the presence of each other, by the friendship we'd shared since school. The two of us and her ... Our prisoner and then our captor; this beautiful thing, so vulnerable, with her elegant walk and profile you'd just stare at until your mouth dried out and something ached inside you. Something there was no relief for.

At night, when we dimmed the lanterns to save paraffin, she would fold away into the dark. But sometimes, in a half-sleep, I knew she was close, blowing her sweet breath across my throat. You see, she was still waiting.

Hank slept in her bed, this big curtained thing covered in velvet, until he got his strength back, and I slept in a trunk full of muslin sheets. Don't know where she spent the night in the early days. Maybe she kept those smiling German officers company.

She made her move after the first week of our hiding out, and the war between Hank and me began. She must have been crazy for a fix. How long had she been waiting down there until those supplies dried out? Too scared to forage above with all the bombs dropping and shells exploding, she knew she had to bide her time until someone wandered into the lair.

I take a cock into my mouth. An anonymous cock. I don't know who it belongs to and I don't need to. She never did. She had appetite, she had needs, she was more deadly than any male, she started wars without ideology or greed for land. She was a god that mortals fought over.

The cock goes deep until I feel floss tickling my nose and I inhale the odour of well-hung, stiff maleness. Rinsing the soft skin with my saliva, I then create a suction that pulls my mouth flat and airtight around the muscle. Lightly furred balls rest on my

149

chin. Further down the bed, my legs are raised and stroked from ankle to thigh. Knees indent the mattress beside my buttocks and a few tense seconds pass before the swollen head of the second cock squeezes into me. Pulling the cock from my mouth, so I can concentrate on the beautiful agony of penetration, I hear myself panting and whispering bad things.

Fast strokes butt me up and down the bed, messing up my hair, making me feel rag-dollish. The second cock is forced back into my mouth. I am made to suck and suck and suck. This I do while forming a ring of finger and thumb to beat the base of the boy's pillar.

Told by a dry voice, the story goes on outside my head, and I want thick milk in my mouth as much as I want to hear the end of this tale.

It was the dancing that seduced us both. She'd play records on the gramophone, drowning out the sounds of killing and war above us. Besides the trickles of dust and plaster that would come down through the cracks after the boom of an explosion, we were lost to everything but the dancing. Waltzes with a silent princess. Slow cheek-to-cheek smooching with a countess on a brick floor. And from the dances she led us, one by one, to her bed. And then she took us together, so the brothers who had shared blood and pain could share love. Love that keeps you hurting for ever. You can't understand it unless an old one gives you the bond. There is something in their souls so corrupt and black and delicious . . .

Mauled breasts, bitten nipples, pounded puss and a wide jaw to take the heavy meat and its thick showers have me mindless the way she must have been. While

I suck the one, the other takes my puss. As they use me, I claw them and line their perfect young flesh with sharp talons. Changing positions, both greedy for the part the other takes, each of the boys shoots into my mouth first, which is good because while I swallow one, his comrade can continue pumping behind me or between my legs. Begging me for more, one of them even gets under my heels so I can stamp while his friend chokes himself on the breast he has sucked into his mouth.

From all fours I fall on to my side. With their first enthusiastic climaxes spent, I am in control and I want them both pressed in close. I want them inside me, right to the hilt, front and rear. Together, they raise my uppermost leg. 'Yes!' I cry out, knowing what is coming. Screwing up my eyes, my anus is opened by an insistent phallus. As it pushes and forces at the tight muscles in my rear, the second cock moves inside my sex. It's as if both fat heads are determined to meet somewhere deep inside me. Squashed like a pearl between two protective shells, I am moved about this bed by co-ordinated thrusts in my bottom and puss. When teeth sink into my shoulder from behind, I throw my head back to gasp but a tongue slips inside my open mouth. All plugged up, I climax, twitching in this embrace.

For weeks, we lay beneath her, gazing up at her, adoring her face and its strange, slight smiles. Stripped naked and clinging to her like she was an escape from all the horror, we threw off country, cause and duty. We just existed for her love and her mouth, desperate for the dark when her bite would go through our skin. First time in our lives that either of us lived solely for pleasure – a pleasure that would send us to sleep no sooner than she was done. There

151

was no sense of time passing, and the only consideration shown for the future were the plans she whispered to us about escape. She wanted the three of us to run away, recover her money from Zurich and then move to North Africa where she had interests. Opium, I think.

I believed she wanted us both, though sometimes I suspected her gaze would deliberately linger on Hank more than it did on me. Played the same game with him too. And so she teased us into loving her even harder than we were already. Either that or she was warning us about a choice we'd have to make. Some days, it was me who made her squeal, and it was me doing all those crazy things to her with the belt and rope. Other days, it was Hank taking the active role while I held her wrists like she told me. One to support her, one to indulge her.

Indigo evening passes to black night and our love continues. There have been two ejaculations in my mouth, three in my puss and one in my anus. Exhausted, the boys lie around me, dozing, only retaining enough strength to hold me between them. Preacher stares through me and then through the wall, his face the brightest thing in the moon-beamed room. I smoke and rest, regaining my strength, enjoying the tenderness in all the parts of me that have been so well used. Metering out my gluttony, it will be an hour or so before I will wake the boys for more. The beauty from Berlin wanted abuse from assertive hands. I will have it too.

Tied down; the roughness of their ropes burns around my wrists and ankles. Stretched like a star, my toes and knuckles point to the four bedposts. Damp from sweat, my underthings cling to my skin. Around my face they fold a scarf that still smells of her perfume; something musky and oldish. The silk scarf is the only sensation of softness on my body. My bonds are so tight, I am almost raised off the bed and can only move a fraction. How long can I stand this?

Tongues touch my skin, between my stockings and knickers, between knickers and brassière, between brassière and face. Roaming, dry and insistent, they venture into my clefts and crevices, rise over contours and then come back on themselves. Shivers pass through me. This is torture; not being able to bend into the mouths or shake away when they light too many fireworks in my softest parts. Strangled sounds leave my mouth which is all smudged now. Contracting the muscles in my thighs and biceps I hear the ancient bed frame creak and groan.

In our underground world, she would hang like you for hours, stretched open with curtain cords, blindfolded, and speaking quickly in German, French and then Italian. After tying her up like she wanted, we would go to her in turn, shocked and shaky on our feet. Never seen the likes of this before, or even known that such ladies existed, but we couldn't refuse her.

Soon as we were in her, something would possess us; jealousy, maybe, or lust so strong we'd be lost to everything save the look on her face and the thunderstorm in our heads. See, we knew she'd done this before. This was an act perfected over time with other lovers. Although we never understood much she said to us, in our minds we both saw her below deck on a ship. Once she had taken a journey across the seas by ship, and at night, on this journey, she would have the crew stretch her apart. Still painted like a lady, she let the men come to her while her husband

153

*wept upstairs. Nearly a dozen men loved her like
that, with their rough hands and bearded faces
mauling her whiteness. One after another they went
up to her in the vision – our first vision – crying out
as they emptied themselves inside her royal womb.
As she remembered and tried to relive the terrible
pleasures she took on that ship, Hank and me saw it
in our heads. We were bonded.*

At the moment when I can take no more of their
touch, purely of mouth, I am taken ruthlessly. My
thighs are clutched but my stockings prove slippery,
so the fingers of my captor dig in tighter. Welcoming
the second erection, I open my mouth wide, like she
did on that ship and in that bombed-out Berlin cellar.

I think of Hank. So much he has kept from me.
Partly from rage and partly from release, I encourage
my lovers to take me hard as they care to and as deep
as they can. Never have I given myself so freely just
to pleasure and be pleasured thoroughly. Both boys
pant away outside of my private darkness before
anointing my flesh and her relics with their seed.
Crying out, I climax, invigorated by the feeling of the
fluid warmth on my skin.

The seed of young men kept her alive for centuries.
In return she gave a select few a bond. Hank took the
bond and gave it to me. She is my ancestor. All this
time the woman has been inside me, guiding me,
whispering to me, seducing me.

*We were in too deep and it was too late. It's like me
and Hank stopped seeing each other. We existed to
pleasure her, to bathe in her wisdom and cruelty,
working together when she required it, alone if that
was her whim. And, yeah, she was cruel. Meanest
thing I ever knew. And so powerful. She only wanted*

the ropes and straps to understand what she'd done
to mortals. Changing the balance was a distraction
for her. A game.

Released from the ropes, the boys hold me and
whisper in my ears. Kissing my blonde hair and
stroking my pale skin, they tell me they love me. Will
I have them? Will I take them with me? They'll go
anywhere with me and protect me and worship me
until I've allowed them to follow me into every
shadow this world has to offer. In the darkness of the
room they cannot see my smile. And even if they
could they would not be able to read it. Preacher
must have seen the smile because he stops talking.

Near dawn I am able to revive the flaccid cock of the
poet. And this time I ride him as he moans in his
sleep.

Stained and crumpled, the queen's finery is now
scattered around the Preacher's feet. Revived by
whiskey and white chocolate, I grunt and root about
on the lovely thickness that ascends through me.
Flexing my claws, I leave tiny half-moons of pain on
the boy's smooth chest.

'Preacher,' I say, seeing him with his head bowed
in the corner. Grey light falls across his suit and
makes him look like an old photo of a minister, all
beat up by the heat and the privations of his faith.
'Hey, Preacher. Don't you know the bond must have
started with a woman? No man can make a girl's
heart ache the way yours does now. The bond in a
woman is a gift. Bonded men can't equal it.'

'Think you're right, girl,' he says, and raises his
head. Watching me rise and fall on the sleepy poet
makes something burn in his eyes. Just for him, to
remind him of her in me, and to make him come to

my bed so I can end his pain, I seize my breasts and pick up the pace of my pleasuring. 'Like this,' I cry out. 'She used to love you both like this while you slept, exhausted.' Gripping the poet's ribs with my thighs, I grind forward and backward, so my pip is squashed and rubbed on his bones. 'Don't you want this again?' I shout to him. 'One last time to fade that scar on your heart?' Squeezing my sex around the poet's thickness, which seems to grow even harder and longer inside me, I pummel his stomach until my face goes all screwy and I end up croaking in time with every wave of delight passing through me.

Reaching out a hand towards the Preacher, I offer an apology for whatever Hank did. He can come to me now – the enemy can take me and remember the feel of her.

Preacher covers his face with both hands. 'No,' is all he says.

Catching my breath, face down on the poet's chest, I see the Preacher dab his brow with a handkerchief.

Covered by the robe, I stand by the window and watch the fierce sun chase away the last wisps of cold night. Beside me, the Preacher sits and thinks in the same way my man does.

'So what did Hank do?' I ask, and pull on my cigarette.

'Don't you know yet?' His voice is low, sounding burnt out, like he can't stand another thought of her.

'Took her for himself?'

He nods. 'Two years after Berlin, he took her from me.'

'Took her away for years.'

'Yes.'

'Where did they go?'

'Don't know. Never laid eyes on her or spoke to

Hank since. They left me in Paris. Once I'd served her purpose, she beat it. After getting the right papers and so forth from the military and freeing some of her money through our intelligence connections, she and Hank split.'

'Is that when the search started?'

'No. I never bothered looking right away. No point. No one could find her 'less she wanted to be found. So I took the time that was coming to me and lived with the Franciscans in North Italy. It was there I began to understand what she really was and what she'd done. I tried to reverse it. I tried to free myself of her, but she'd changed me for good. I was bonded.'

'That where the Preacher bit comes in?'

He nods again. 'Went back to soldiering in '49 and to Berlin, hoping that she'd turn up. With a new war against the Russians there was always plenty of work for the likes of me. Plenty of access into places she might have been. Plenty of information too. And hate enough to keep it all rolling. Way it ends up, the search became all I had.'

'But she chose Hank and in time she'd tire of him too. And you were out of your mind about her. How can you blame Hank?'

'Because she tried to get me to leave him first, to take her away. Three was becoming a crowd. You see, we were always awful demanding –' Preacher smiles. 'You know how the boys must get around you.'

'Uh huh. Girls too.'

Preacher chuckles. 'Could not betray my friend, though, so I refused her. Hardest thing I've ever done.' He pauses to release a long sigh. 'In a moment of clarity, when we were away from her, I then told Hank we had to split or she'd be the end of us. He never did see the German officers in the theatre and the smiles on their parchment faces. But I did. She had used us, no doubt, even though she'd given a unique gift in return.' The Preacher's eyes lower. 'Now there was only room for one. We agreed it would never be right or fair for only one of us to be with her. We found her together and loved her together so we would leave her together. We shook on it and then we embraced, like it was a huge relief to have arrived at such a decision. One week later, they were gone.

'Being without her was more than pain. It's like being separated from everything you care about every minute of every day. Man could lose his mind being that way. This one did. And when he found it again, he knew he had some killing to do.'

'But she left Hank too.'

'Sure enough, Missy, and he went and found the next best thing near Austin, Texas. Am I right?'

Not sure I like the 'next best thing' implication, so I stay quiet.

'Which has kept him feeling fine all these years, just as long as he keeps clear of me. Am I right?'

'Could be.'

'But then she turns up again, and announces herself to each of us, not more than two weeks back. Sends a message to the corps we served in, which is forwarded to the agency and then on to us. If either of us is still alive, we can find her in Orleans. We both got the news on the anniversary of the day we first made her acquaintance in Berlin. Now what do you think of that, Missy Lafeyette?'

Feel sick and dizzy. Feel like the room is moving around my head way too fast. I feel just like you did in Paris, Mr Preacher. That's how I feel.

Nine

'Here,' I command. Denver rises to his feet and comes to me from where he has been sitting, cross-legged in just a pair of jeans, in the corner of my room. 'On the ground,' I say. Falling to his belly, every muscle tenses across his back and he closes his eyes, knowing a woman intends to use him. And from the look on my face, he knows Missy ain't messing around.

After the night of revelation they returned my clothes and things to me, bathed me, and only cuffed my wrists. Shocked by Hank's infidelity of mind and soul, I let them return me to this room and lock the door. After the initial shock passed, I found myself wanting my man dead from a jealousy that still frightens me.

Even food was left for me in the delectable shape of Sweet Boy Denver. This way he gets punished by both Val and me should I choose to hurt him. And I do. Dreadful things need to flood from my mouth and body. Hank betrayed his best friends – Val and the Preacher. Then he betrayed me – his lover for 32 years longer than he deserved. No wonder he says so little. Guilt must keep his tongue tied up lest he tell any more lies.

New Orleans was to be our end. The German bitch would take my Hank, who in turn would leave me with an old boyfriend; a man whom I once led astray only to lead myself astray. A musician who has never forgotten me. Someone my own age. But that's another story. Hank never paid me back for the indiscretion, but I always felt it was to his credit that he never raised the topic. Stupidly, I guessed it was on account of me going back that Hank forgave me for that one time in Orleans when my heart swayed just a little from his monopoly on my deep affection. Instead, our demise has been so neatly packaged: Missy gets taken care of and he disappears with the old one – the Berlin cellar bitch. Hank sure works things through to the last detail.

Crying has done me little good. More than anything I think slapping Hank's face would help me heal. But how can I mend after all this time, after all we shared, after everything he's shown me? Must the bond end in heartbreak? Is everything so temporary in the world and in our world? Will the Preacher's search and suffering become my own? Or am I destined to live underground and wait for juicy man-things to walk into my web like she did in the war? So many things whiz about my head. Doubts, anxieties, and horrible chesty, achy things have beat me up inside. Missy don't need this. No sir.

Least I have a heart, even if it's all in little pieces like a rare china antique dropped from a great height. You see, I won't let the Preacher hurt Hank. Like Val, I love him. Can't deny it and if I can do anything to stop Hank blundering into this trap, I will.

From what the Preacher told me before he vanished this morning, the agency people made Hank leave Val's farm on the first day of our visit after sending a decoy message to his laptop – an order for Hank to carry out a hit on the Preacher, who'd apparently become a liability over something he did

160

in someone else's country. And the job was all set up with the right security code from the agency, so Hank would run off to follow orders. Seems remorse over deserting his best friend in '45 has always kept him from doubling back and taking the Preacher down, but when the agency gives an order, Hank jumps. If need be, we can do anything we want in 50 states with immunity. Hank gets that plus a salary and the agency used his loyalty to make him take the job. That and his need to remove any of the Preacher's interference from his designs on the German woman in Orleans, I figure, would have been his motives for running off first day in Texas. But while Hank's been scratching around in another state, determined to end the Preacher's run ('To get us some peace of mind'), following loose ends and clever trickster ploys masterminded by the agency he served so well, I was captured. Stupid, trusting me. Seems another message was then sent to Hank, telling Hank the Preacher's been sighted heading toward Val's, so he's been speeding here ever since to save me. Racing right into a trap because he's so desperate to resume our journey to New Orleans without further delay, considering the delights awaiting him there. In addition, the thought of the Preacher getting to the prize first will increase his reckless ardour to return to Val's farm. Hank's going to take a fall; it seems inevitable. Even a star player can't take on a whole team. Stupid boy.

'Stupid boy,' I say, distracted.

'Yes, miss,' Sweet Boy whispers. His eyes are open again and he looks at my naked feet, all sculpted high and pretty in my high-heeled sandals. I just haven't had the energy to dress this morning. Never got further than the shoes which I need for the purpose I have in mind for this treacherous boy on his belly.

161

'Seems like every man is a snake.'

'Yes, miss.'

'We had a time, eh, boy?' I say. 'You had a good run with this girl?'

'Oh, yes, miss,' he agrees with a smile.

But the smile is short lived. I look at my nails and let my right foot descend until it can descend no further when it hits something soft on the floor. There is a cry from Sweet Boy's pretty lips, but I don't even bother to look down. Instead, I turn that heel with a little weight behind it. There is another cry followed by a quick panting sound, just like this salesman made in Idaho one time after getting too pushy trying to sell me a product I'd no use for. Made him crawl about my room too, pleading for help, then mercy, and finally more.

Removing my heel from the cushion it just sank into, I sit on the bed, cross my legs, and then light a smoke. 'Now suck the heel that hurt you, boy.' Denver crawls to me and takes the heel in his mouth. Suckling the spike with his pretty mouth, he holds my ankle, terrified the candy may be taken away.

I need to think. Wherever Hank is now – and he must be close because the Preacher left the cabin not more than an hour ago to take up his position – I have to get a message to him. Thought Val could be turned to my side, but I haven't seen her since the morning she left. Only method I have left is the bond. If Hank is close and I can get high and loved out of my mind, maybe I can transmit some image to him. Implanting a warning into his no-good head might give him an edge.

'That's it. You like that sharp thing in your mouth?'

Denver's answer is muffled, but sounds enthusiastic.

162

'It's more than you deserve.'

He nods.

'Whip those jeans and shorts off and hand me your belt.'

Denver's mouth retracts from the black spike he suckles. Looking paler, he swallows and then brushes his nose against the side of my naked foot. The contact makes me shiver.

Stiff as bone, the boy's morning wood is something I am not opposed to seeing despite the calamity of my heart. Beastly things growl inside me. I flick my cigarette butt at him and he flinches away, his face looking shaken. I stand up and feel the curves of my legs, hips and thighs swell once the heels take my weight. 'Seems like you have wronged this girl, Denver, so your keeper has handed you over to the proper authority. And where's your paymaster, boy? Tell me, where is the Preacher when you need him most?' I circle him, staying close but not touching, with my eyes lidded and teeth out from the meanness I feel for mankind. 'You could do with some divine intervention right about now, I reckon. What do you say, honey? Where's your priest, boy?'

'Stand still!' I shriek, when he tries to bend away from all ten of my claws moving so slow down his back. He makes a little huffing sound and moves his head back. Rotating my nose in his hair, I smell the pine loveliness of this sacrifice. Slowly, I dip a finger between his hard buttocks and scrape it up until his brown puckerage can feel a flick of nail before the insertion. 'Do anything I like to you. Did you know that, slut boy?'

'Yes, miss,' he says, shaking all over. Mind you, his cock has stayed hard and one of his hands makes a play to stroke the muscle. Whipping his belt from off my shoulder where it rests before the day's work, I double it over and then strap his knuckles. The punished hand withdraws, and with no warm pocket to dip the stricken paw into, he clutches it with his other hand.

Thoughts of my man's intended betrayal thicken up inside me, making me hot and swoony, making me choke on the bile of wretchedness. 'Get yourself on the bed!' I holler, and bring that strap across his butt with a mighty swing.

Denver yelps and flees to the bed where he cringes, shielding his cock between long thighs, all the time watching me with the dark mystery of eyes that ask for punishment.

'Lie flat. Go on! Flat,' I say.

Now it's like I'm swinging that leather at Hank, the Preacher, and then the poet, as I flail at Denver, two-handed because of the cuffs, making his body blush from the indignity. Sounds like a bad loser in a card game, slapping cards down on a table, the way my leather licks him good about the thigh and butt and back. But the boy just squirms and groans, rubbing himself on the bedclothes.

'On your front,' I gasp, when I'm worn out and feeling a little prickly about the nips and moist in the puss. It's an invigorating thing to flog a boy. Girls should try it, putting romancing and such distractions aside for the afternoon, and taking a sharp tongue and strap to a man, while dressed to tease.

Cautiously, Denver moves on to his tender back, wincing as his shoulders sink into the cool cotton sheets. Still hard, his manhood rises, vulnerable and alone. Before he has time to reckon on my next move, I'm on him, wild-eyed and tousle-headed. 'You want me to take this little old thing into my mouth?' I say, wetting my glossy lips no more than three inches from the tip of his penis.

'Yes, miss,' he answers, too scared and thrilled to say more.

'To suck it, taste it, maybe stroke it up too.' Beside his stiffness I form one of my hands around an imaginary cock and move the hand up and down, real slow.

'You can do anything to me, miss.'

'Damn right I can. Do what I choose to a piece of shit like you. That right?'

'It is, miss.'

'So when my mouth slips over this –' I touch the tip of his phallus with a painted nail '– you're going to do some talking. You're going to show me that a weak little pansy-ass has no loyalty.'

Denver seems to recoil into the crumpled bed. His eyes widen.

'That's right, honey,' I coo, giving him a smile. 'You are going to open up and tell me about what's waiting for my friend up at the farm. And while you talk the talk I'm going to have myself a good long suck. You hear? And then I might slide my pretty young body up and down your cock, once it's all moist 'n' ready with lipstick and high-school spit. Get my drift?'

Denver swallows. 'They left me out of things like that, miss. I swear. It was just my job –' Rising off the bed, with my top lip curling into a snarl and my eyes changing like something you might see looking through a window in a nightmare – something you're afraid of but in need of – I make Denver stop his lying. Beneath me, he pushes his buttocks off the bed, moving his wood upward.

I shake my head from side to side.

'Please, girl.'

'Yeah? Need my thighs around you? Want my heels strolling up and down your back?'

Denver rolls his eyes and dares to clutch for me. Grabbing a hand I stuff his fingers in my mouth and bite. He withdraws the smitten hand.

Sitting astride his thighs, I squeeze my legs together, closing his knees. Using my heels like spurs I scratch his skin, but at the same time I grip his cock with one hand. Knowing he has to confess, in order for my hand to begin work on his pride, Denver takes a breath. 'Preacher set a trap near the house.'

I lick the salty bulb poking through the ring I have formed with my finger and thumb.

'He has a rifle. The kind they use to shoot deer. I seen it in a case. And it has scopes along the top. Plus these two pistols in a shoulder harness.'

'That so,' I say, and let my lips pucker to kiss the tip of his phallus. There is a little pearl of moisture on the top and I wipe it away with the tip of my tongue. Taking my time, I slide my hands down to the base of his shaft and let my lips follow, their passage down his rigidity smoothed by lipstick. Groaning, Denver gently raises his buttocks from the mattress, pushing more of himself inside the warmth of my mouth. Breathing through my nose, as moisture wells under my tongue, I move my head up and down the morsel. As if he's made of ice and a footfall makes a thousand cracks appear on his surface, I hear Denver's sinews and joints stiffen and creak beneath me. 'Mmm,' I sound out, sucking him harder, making the inside of my cheeks hug the thickness that has entered my head.

'This morning, Preacher got a call to say your friend had passed the county line and would be at the farmhouse at a certain time.'

'Mmm,' I moan, moving my head faster. Thoughts quicken, my eyes become more alert. Between my thighs there is a craving for the sensation of something rigid to pass into me.

'Guess Val will meet him on the drive and then the Preacher's going to pull his trigger. Walt can shoot good too, so he's been put off to one side, pistol at his side, Winchester in his hand. That's all I know, girl. Val then sent me away to keep you company.'

My mouth leaves his shaft and I let it shine in the midday light that fills the bedroom. Moving my hips forward and rising to my knees, I let the lips of my puss brush against the cock I have just sucked. 'Bet you want to come, shitbird.'

Denver grasps my thighs and screws up his eyes. I hold his cock still and lean across his body so my nipples brush against his chest. 'Look at me.'

His eyes open and he sees my face. Slowly, I rotate my hands so the cuff chain tickles his groin and then his balls. 'Sure that's all you have to tell me?'

'I swear, miss. That's all I know and now I'm done for. Preacher's gonna finish me if you let on about how much I told you.'

'That's right,' I say with a smile. There is a flicker of panic on his face replaced by relief when I slip around his manhood. Arching my back, opening my mouth wide to let this big sigh seep out, I let Denver push through me, right to the back wall. I look towards the window that flashes so bright with white sunlight and with my mind I seek Hank.

Thinking of the Preacher, I rise and fall on Denver. He holds my hips and starts to push me upward and then pull me down to the flat land of his tummy. 'Yeah,' I say. 'That's good, boy. Real good.' And it is. For a while I can let the pain dim in my heart and seek a special kind of medicine with my puss. In my head, I picture the black crow Preacher, perched on Val's shingle roof, shouldering his rifle the way Hank did before all those jobs back in the sixties, when he had to prepare long and hard out in the desert.

Hoping this image reaches him, I sharpen the focus as I ride this boy beneath me. Clenching the muscles around my puss, I do him slow at first. Then I speed up my rhythm, tweaking my nips with my fingers. Soon I'm pounding on and off Sweet Boy Denver, loving every inch of the veiny girth where it stretches me and the ridge around his fat head that brushes my sides, right in the deeps.

Holding my hips and craning his head forward, he stares intently at my mouth and eyes and all the passion in my features. His own face is a dark crimson in colour and he grits his teeth. Looking fierce, I know he wants me beneath him so he can just throw himself into me. Idea appeals to me too.

'You on top, now,' I order. 'And you better fuck me good.'

Effortlessly, his strong arms manage to swing me beneath the weight of his body without his cock pulling free. Locked together, he places his hands on my shoulders and presses me into the mattress. Raising my parted legs, I place them around his buttocks and pull him into me. No encouragement is needed; Denver smacks his groin against my floss, thrusting wildly and crying out that he loves me, is sorry, and will follow me anywhere.

'No, boy,' I whisper. 'I need a stronger man with a bigger cock than you.'

This makes him go so fast I become incapable of saying more than two words: 'Don't come.' Thinking of Hank, and flashing up the image of the Preacher and his gun, I say it over and over again, hoping Hank will hear my words and carry on driving past Val's farm.

Unable to stop the way my arousal steers me, I see myself in ropes like the German woman on the ship with Hank and the Preacher attending to my needs.

Can't stop the thought and I pretend that Denver isn't riding me this hard and fast, but it's those two old friends instead; one in my puss, one in my rear. I can almost feel the ropes I pull against, and hear the breathing of two determined men, who kiss my face and throat.

'Don't come!' I shriek, as I climax.

'Oh, oh, oh, oh. Sorry, miss.' Denver says, and his body loses its tensile nature. Inside me, his pipe contracts, rears up, and then shakes itself down, repeatedly. Deep inside, there is a gush of warmth.

'We need to get out,' I say, treading Denver's back with the grace of the girls I've seen on TV, who walk those catwalks in strange frocks. My heels leave tiny indentations on his muscular back. White spots are left in his deeply tanned skin which then go pink and finally red. Even following such vigorous loving, I can't be sure my warning has carried to Hank. And the thought of waiting in this room until gunfire cracks across the horizon is more than I can bear. If anyone puts the hurt on Hank, it should be me.

'No way, miss,' he says, in the way a servant would talk to a rich man's daughter, with his voice tempered and slowed down for the sake of politeness. 'Put the lock on myself. It's a deadbolt and will hold up against a tornado.'

I move down to his lower back on the toes of my shoes, but then sink my weight into the sides of his waist. 'Then you better start thinking, boy, because my patience with captivity is worn through.'

Denver hisses and then does a lot of panting. There are lots of nerve endings where my heels have settled. 'Maybe we can use the window, but it's a mighty drop,' he says.

'Damn right it's a drop. How's a girl supposed to

keep her legs straight after falling from there?'
Another turn of my heels makes his body deflate, like
I've punctured him.

'Bed sheets,' he says, the calm gone from his voice.
'If I can tie the bottom and top sheets together, I can
lower you down so you could drop to the porch roof
and then shimmy down a pole.'

Hating heights has always put me off that course of
action and as there is nothing in the room you could
tie a rope to it's never been an option. But will the
sheets hold my weight? And can Denver be trusted
not to drop me?

'Right,' I say, before doubts dissolve my resolve.
'Do it.'

I step off his back, skip across to the window, slap
the latch off, and heave the window pane up its
runners to the top of the frame. Just the sight of the
hard, dusty ground so far below with the porch off at
an angle makes me feel dizzy and sick. 'You'll have
to do it. I'm strong so I can take your weight, and
then you can run up the stairs and unlock the door.'

'I can't,' he says.

'You a chicken, boy?'

'Preacher's got the key, miss.'

Sitting on the bed that Denver has just stripped, I
realise there is no other way of escape besides me
going down a home-made rope like some bum in an
old movie who hasn't paid the rent. Hank, what have
you done to me?

Look up, they say. Never look down. That much I've
managed, but all the strength seems to have gone
from my arms and all the grip from my fingers as I
hang no more than two feet below the window.
Letting go of the window ledge took twenty minutes,
while Denver gave me advice, like he was some

adventure camp instructor. And now I don't like the look of strain on his pretty face as he holds my weight. Sweat is dripping off his chin and I never realised my legs were so heavy, swinging down below.

'Go on, miss. Need to be quick about it,' he says, leaning further out of the window than I care to see.

Slowly, with a squeal accompanying every inch I sag down, I manage another few feet and reach the knot. 'Will it hold?' I say, with a voice on the edge of tears.

'Sure,' he says, but talking to me is a distraction from his holding me up, so I decide to keep my mouth shut. 'Porch is a few feet to your left, miss. You should hook a leg on the sill and then step on.'

'Hook a leg!' I cry. 'How can I hook a leg I can't feel, boy?' By the time I'm on the second sheet, the knot in the middle has gone all tiny and I believe there could be slippage too. Unable to prevent myself, I look down. Big mistake, and it's all I can do to keep from crying. It doesn't seem as if I've even moved from the window; everything is still so far away, like I'm looking at it through a beer bottle. Seeing the porch so far off to my left makes things worse. There is no way a person could just step off and put a foot on that rusty gutter and my cowboy boots don't have any grip.

No doubt, that knot is slipping.

'Now, miss! Do it now! It's going –'

The panic of having the wind knocked from my body and thinking I was about to suffocate were the first things I had to deal with. Then the inability to move a muscle, in case the agony of broken parts started to kick in, was the next hurdle I had to overcome. But, joint by joint, watched constantly by Denver's concerned face up at that window, I was able to

171

twitch fingers, toes, arms and then legs, before realising that nothing was broken or dislocated. A few bruises and one palmful of splinters from slapping my hand down the tiles as I fell, screaming, to what I thought was death, is all I have to show for my stunt. Actually, from the ground the window doesn't seem too far off. Why is that?

When I finally stand up, I cry and laugh at the same time. Denver smiles.

Doubting whether I can take any more of this excitement, I have to force myself to walk from the cabin yard and into the trees to find the path that leads to Val's house. It's a good ten-minute walk and after wasting so much time hanging from a bed sheet, I jog towards my objective, pulling straw from my hair and wincing from the pains that shoot from both ankles.

When I can see the chimney stack above a row of saplings I slow down and move off the path into the undergrowth. With no clear idea of what I can do, let alone the fear I'm experiencing by imagining the Preacher's cross hairs targeted on my body from above, I come to a standstill about 30 feet from the back porch.

Deserted. Besides the net curtains that waft through the open window of Val's room, nothing moves. Seems like time has stopped and the earth has paused in its mad rotation around the sun. Everything feels unnatural. Crouching down under a bush, smelling the dry clay and woody smells, I start to worry about snakes too. I need a plan. Need to do something, and hiding under a bush, maybe no more than two feet from some black snake, is no tactic. Edging around the rear of the house I come across a woodpile left from the previous winter, and grab a log with a tapered end that I can grip like a club.

Feeling better with timber in my fist, I crawl closer to the perimeter of the back yard which is shielded by a natural barrier of bushes and small trees before a ranch-style fence runs around the property.

Everything seizes up in my naked chest and my scalp goes prickly when I spot the poet crouching no more than ten feet to my right. Has he seen me? Although I've come up on him from the side, half of his face is turned in my direction. Casually cradled between both hands, with the barrel pointed at the dirt, is a Winchester rifle. Stuck in the waistband of his jeans is the mahogany grip of a pistol. Two guns versus a stick.

Guns make me feel weak and the sight of those two killers about the treacherous poet's lean body make me feel as small as an insect and about as useful as one too. Scared of moving, I stay in my huddle, hoping the sound of my beating heart doesn't carry through this quiet air to the waiting assassin.

If Walt is hanging around the back then I guess the Preacher will be up front, covering the drive and access road with his scopes. If the Preacher is up high he'll be able to see the sides of the property where the foliage is lighter, so it's a relief that I chose the back door for my approach.

The distant sound of a car makes Walt drop to his knees with his back to me. His fast hands shoulder the rifle, which he points at the house, and the silver breech glints under the sun as if the gun itself is excited by the prospect of a shoot-out.

One soft palm after another, I pad towards him, moving my legs like they're made from glass with only the toes of my boots touching the earth. When he lifts his head up and listens to the sound of a door slamming, with an ear cocked towards the house, his chiselled profile comes into view again. For such a handsome man, I never thought I'd want to see the back of his head so much.

Any movement at the periphery of his vision will surely give me up. A rivulet of sweat tickles my neck and my right ankle starts to shake uncontrollably. Biting down on the aches and scratches all over my body, which suddenly yield a chorus of attacks on my rigid posture, I hold my breath.

Slowly, he turns his face towards the house.

Lining myself up behind him, I creep forward another few feet. Over his shoulder I can see a natural tunnel through the shubbery which opens up a view of the whole rear side of Val's farmhouse. Through the gap, in the distance, I see the silhouette of a man. That's a walk I'd recognise if I were looking down from the moon. It's Hank, strolling across the back porch of Val's house as if he were without a care in the world.

Walt tenses, rises to his knees and takes aim. Three feet remain between him and me. With a whimper I cannot suppress, I struggle to my feet, rush him and swing the timber.

There is a big coconutting sound like something hollow has been struck hard and it makes me feel sick to my boots. Then a wave of vibrations runs up my arms after my weapon has come to a perfect standstill on the top of Walt's head. Slowly, he turns his head and faces me. For a moment I think I'm done for, that I haven't hit him hard enough, but when I see his eyes there's nothing inside them. His neck goes slack and his head lolls forward and then whumps against the earth. Some stupid, nervous part of me starts grinning, while another bit of me wants to ask if he's all right, apologise and then get busy with ice. While I hover, struck dumb by what I've just done, I see Hank walk out of sight after pausing at the sound of

174

my weapon hitting Walt's head. Looks like he's carried on, though, around the side of the house and back towards the front of the property.

From Walt's rubbery fingers I pull the rifle free. It feels cold and is much heavier than I imagined. Disarming him, I take the pistol from his waist, which is damp with sweat, and then throw it into the bushes behind me. Maybe I'd be better off with a pistol, but the last time Hank let me fire one I hurt my wrist, and as my daddy showed me how to shoot a rabbit gun not long after I started to walk, I decide the rifle is my best bet in a firefight. The thought of squeezing the trigger, while pointing it a man, sends another wave of sicky thrills through my gut.

Still, my blood is up after taking Walt out so neatly. This leaves two of them against two of us: Val and the Preacher against me and Hank, and they don't know I'm in the picture so we have an advantage.

Sneaking forward, I reach the wooden fence that runs around the yard and strain my eyes to see every detail in the terrain ahead of me. No Preacher on the roof, or in the trees, and I don't see any faces at the windows. After poking the rifle through first, I start to climb the fence and make hard work of it because of the cuffs.

Two shots crack the air, cleave the earth and blow my tense thoughts to pieces. They came from the front of the house and are quickly followed by a cry of pain. It's Hank. I fall from where I'm straddling the top rung of the fence, hit the lawn with my face, and start to cry. Can't help it. I'm too late and Hank's been hit. It felt like an electric shock had passed through me the moment I heard those shots, so I know Hank's been hit.

Staggering in big circles, and feeling like the rifle is

weighing me down, I move up the back lawn, seeing everything through a blur of tears. I pass the rear porch and the side of the house, driven by grief and rage like they're rocket fuel, before running straight into the front yard.

Hank's down. Curled up, like he's in a deep sleep, he's lying between our car and the steps that creak and groan up to the front porch. Across one of his shoulders I can see a bright red blossom soaking through his white shirt. Standing on the porch, and looking down at Hank's body, is the Preacher. In one black hand he holds a pistol, still pointing it at my man's fallen body.

Running fast on numb legs is hard, especially while screaming like an hysteric. And when your head is bobbing around, the chances of you even getting a shot off, especially against a man who kills for a living, are slim. This I know but I tear into the yard and hike the gun up towards the house.

The Preacher turns to face my charge. With his arm flying up so quickly, I soon see the tiny black hole at the end of his barrel pointing at my eyes. When he sees me, the meanness seems to evaporate right off his face, and I even think his jaw twitches with remorse on account of him having to shoot me dead. So I take my split-second advantage and I fire my gun from the hip while still running across the grass.

The rifle bucks in my hands and roars down my ears until all I can hear is a buzzing. Smoke shoots up my nose until I can only smell an acrid cordite vapour. With the noise of streak-lightning and rolling thunder, my weapon discharges. It feels like I'm holding a cannon and not a rifle. The whole house seems to jump a few feet in the air and I hear glass shatter. Smoke pours across the porch, and the

Preacher flips over and flies down those stairs to the very ground where he put my man.

Think I've taken a round too. Even though I never saw the Preacher's muzzle flash, and I never felt anything hit me, I guess he's capped off a round because I heard a second shot follow mine and now I'm going down to slam the earth with my head.

No blood and I'm still breathing hard. No sense of a bullet impacting into me either. Suddenly, relief relaxes me. I realise all I have done is trip over my own excitement and my boot heels to fall flat on my face, bruising my hip where I landed on the rifle stock. My whole body seems to deflate and although I reckon I could faint, the fall brings me to my senses. At least for a while. Too scared to open my eyes or lift my head just in case I do see a hole in my body, which carries right on through me and then out my back, I stay where I have fallen, chewing grass.

Only when I hear a woman's voice, low and serious, over by the porch, do I dare to look up. It is Val, saying, 'Karl, honey, you're done for. I'm sorry, Karl. I couldn't let you do it. Forgive me, Karl.'

The mention of a man named Karl adds more unwelcome confusion to my already messy head. But then I realise she's talking to the Preacher, who is lying all sprawled about the lawn, like he's fallen off a high building. Val has shot the Preacher. She's shot him in the back, scared he might pull the trigger on me before he finished Hank off. That accounts for the shot I heard and the smoke on the porch.

The realisation hits me: it's over.

Now I'm driving and crying. Alone in our car, I head south, blowing bubbles from off my bottom lip and feeling raw in the throat and stingy about the eyes. You'd think Hank was dead, the way I've been

177

carrying on for the last two hours, but then I guess he is to me. Our split is like a bereavement because I'll never have him again. Probably never see him again. He may as well be dead to me and perhaps that's the best way to view it, else I could end up like the Preacher.

It took me a while to comprehend that Hank didn't die at the farm, though. Looks like he's only acquired another scar to place against all the others like a trophy. Preacher shot him from close range, in the gun arm, shattering his shoulder and knocking the wind out of him, but Hank survived.

According to what Val told me before I left the farm, it seems it was hard for the Preacher to pull the trigger on Hank, having already failed to squeeze off a round when Hank first stepped out the car and wandered around the house as if he were only looking for somewhere to put a newspaper. And Hank had no intention of drawing a gun until he had an opportunity to speak to the Preacher. But when Hank came back around the front of the house after I'd clubbed Walt, the Preacher was standing on the porch with his gun drawn. Hank stood still and looked the Preacher straight in the eye. They exchanged some words that Val never heard and then Hank drew on the Preacher and got himself all shot up.

Apparently the Preacher wanted to talk before he ended the feud. There were things he wanted to whisper to Hank before he finished their friendship, so he made sure his first shot wasn't fatal. Seems my sudden and unexpected entrance then forced Val to intervene in the boys' fight.

Despite all the pain in Hank's shoulder, and the pain the Preacher must have felt between the shoulders where the slug dug in, I think it is Val who has suffered most. Having to shoot an old friend in the back was more than she bargained for on this fine day in Texas, and even on our clock I'll wager it's something she'll never forget.

At first, after regaining my feet, I stood like a dummy on the front lawn and watched Hank pull himself to his knees and then to his feet. He never even looked at me; he just kept staring down at the Preacher, whose white face had been cradled in Val's lap. Never felt so alone as at that moment. This scene had little to do with me. Even though I'd gatecrashed the party, there was never a part for me to play. It was between them; between the Preacher's madness, Val's broken heart and Hank's sorrow.

I went back behind the house and found some shade. When the judders and shudders had finished going through me, and the sobs had dried until they were heavy and hurt my throat, I went into the house and packed up the last of my things. Then I went down to where Denver was locked up to get my other belongings, stepping over the poet's unconscious body on the way. Ignoring Denver's pleading about being released – ungrateful, I know, but I had other things on my mind – I made him throw my bags down from the window. After returning to the farm to pack everything into Hank's car, I went looking for Val.

When she took time away from Hank's shoulder, she was in a daze and hardly able to stand up. We hugged in the hallway and I thanked her for saving the two of us who'd brought more grief to her doorway than she ever deserved. I then asked if I could help.

'Not unless you're a surgeon,' she said. 'Hank will live but he needs a hospital, and he'll be out of action for some time.' She looked at the crimson stains on her fingers. 'Seems like the worst part of the old

179

times, that I never wanted back, are here again. You want to see him, girl?'

'No, we're through. Never want to see him again. He can find another car when he's up and about. Then he can go to the German woman who gave him the bond. Tell him so. Missy knows the score. Tell him that too.'

When I walked out to the car, I looked down at the Preacher still lying in the sun. Don't know why, but I leant over and gave him a kiss on his cool, smooth cheek. Maybe it was a thank you for his not gunning me down. Strange thing is, that's the first time I ever touched him. All the time I'd been his prisoner – even offering to love him in her clothes – he never touched me once. Not on the wrists or ankles when he cuffed me. Not behind the ear where he tucked a lock of hair. Not even on the fingers when he offered me a cigarette.

But one thing gave me comfort – it seemed the Preacher had found peace at last. His face and body were relaxed, like he'd been delivered of a huge weight from off his shoulders. On his pale forearm, where his shirt was all ruffled up, I saw a hundred purple spots. Needle marks. I understood how he fed without love.

Before I climbed in the car, I turned to Val, who stood watching me from the porch. 'Poet's behind the garden fence with a bump on his head. Denver's hollering down in the cabin, locked in the upstairs room. And I'm sorry about the window.' We both looked at the gaping hole that was once the sitting-room window, where my Winchester bullet had passed with no patience for glass. 'Don't know when it'll be, Val, but when I come back this way, I'll call in and make everything up to you. I promise.'

She smiled and said, 'So long.'

I started the car. Then I started all this cryin'.

Part Three
Cheating at Solitaire

Ten

There were things he liked me to wear and there were things he liked me to do. Complying was easy back then and some things are just like riding a pony.

I find myself near Jackson Square, New Orleans, in Arnaud's new apartment. Walls are black. Ceiling is black. Bed is covered in black silk and black velvet drapes hang from the canopy. Incense burns inside black crystal glasses. Black tallow candles glow from an onyx candelabra. As if this is not black enough, we are dressed in black. There is nothing for the mirrors to reflect besides the flashes of our exposed white parts, moving like predators beneath dark water.

Screwing my fingers into his locks, which droop like a waterfall in hell to his waist, I pull his perfect head to my sex and let him inhale near the front of my leather shorts. 'Remember my heat?' I ask. Shadows flicker and lick about his cheekbones. In the middle of the darkness that moves around him, I can see his pallid face is full of a yearning and a fear of himself more than a fear of me.

'Yes,' he says, sounding like a lost spirit.

Gripping a larger handful of his shiny hair, I move his nose and lips against the hide that shields my puss. Although she is caged behind leather shorts, tight enough to cling to the cleft of my buttocks, with laces taut as harp strings against my hips, my puss thickens with warmth at the prospect of his skilled mouth.

'Remind you of the old times?'

He smiles and I never imagined such an angelic face could transform into something full of so much appetite.

'Never found quite the same things, have you? The sweet hurt of what we had?'

'Not since you quit me.'

'But still you look.'

He nods.

'I liked your album. It was about me, wasn't it?'

'Can you blame me? You ruined me.'

'For that I'm sorry, but you made a lot of money.'

'Shame you weren't for sale.'

Throwing my head back, I laugh like the reckless and dangerous thing I have become after all that driving and crying since Texas.

'To the bed, honey child,' I say, unthreading my claws from the black silk he was blessed with instead of hair. 'Missy's going to make up for lost time.'

Arnaud falls upon his bed, disappearing into the dark so all I can see is his face and slender torso, where the hair, leather trousers and swirly tattoos have let him remain pale. He languishes against the pillows and avoids my eyes. 'Are you here to stay?'

I don't answer because I don't know the answer.

'Don't know if I could go through it again, Missy. You did something to me. It scares me now.'

'Makes you want to take something from your girlfriends when they're beneath you.' The truth in my words freezes the expression on his face. 'Want to drink from them and drink from all the pretty girls who lean over the stage and chase you through the Quarter?'

My breasts swing free from behind the tiny leather waistcoat I unzip, as I sit astride him, making sure my long legs, so shiny in black stockings, crush against his ribs.

'Don't make me love you again, Missy,' he says, with a face that both implores and recoils from me. It's as if he's pleading for more of the torment he can filter into his eerie songs, while also dreading more of the hopeless hours a lover leaves behind.

'I'm through with love,' I say. 'You know I belonged to someone before. I told you. But even though that has changed –' I swallow the lump that tries to form in my throat '– this girl has a good memory and she has to eat. She doesn't want to hurt you again and would rather die than make you feel what she has lying so heavy in her heart. But maybe she can give you something to savour for your second record.' I pluck the leather police cap off my head and throw it into the darkness. The chain around the peak makes a little jingly sound when it hits the floor, finding space among all the bottles. Down, down, down my red lips go, seeking the cushion of his boy-man mouth, leading me away from thoughts of the past.

Kissing Arnaud electrifies a girl all the way down her back to her tailbone. Sucking his purple tongue into my mouth and tasting all the wine on his breath starts the purring in me. Because I haven't fed in a week, this boy won't sleep until dawn breaks above the cathedral steeple.

His hands, strong but careful, sculpt my waist, ribs and breasts. Breaking away from the kiss, I gasp and then screw up my nose from his touch. He rolls my breasts under the bones of his hands, squashes them against my chest and then lifts them on to his face. Biting my nips with little piranha pinches, he gets me

185

moaning from a pleasure which makes me press my milky chest against his face. 'That's it. Be hard there.' Then I shriek as he obeys, his memory unfolding the map of my parts.

Slipping my hands down his body, I unlatch and open his leather jeans. No underwear. I smile. Just like the last time. Cradling the white cock, I flick its pinky head around my leather crotch. 'I want to be fucked,' I whisper to him, as he lathers my nips with saliva and chastises them with sharp teeth. He doesn't answer and I know the game has begun in earnest. So as his hunger reaches a peak, I take the titty candy away from him. He snarls but I leap off the bed, ignoring him.

Yanking his jeans and boots off, I make his whole body lift off the mattress. Then I strip his chest bare, except for the coloured beads and leather thongs that hang around his neck. Now he's smiling again; pleased and a little arrogant with this display of a woman's desire for him. I know Arnaud has to be careful or girls will tear him apart. Inside his head, when the dark mists break and let me in, I can see that hundreds of girls have been in this bed since I left; writhing, twisting and thrashing themselves against him. This man was made for the bond and I nearly passed it to him last time, three years back when I strayed from Hank. Never have I felt such an appetite for the dark in another, or seen such beauty in a man with the potential of finding it in a woman, anywhere.

'Greedy boy,' I say, as he sits up and slides his fingers around me, preparing to grasp handfuls. I am pulled back to him and again my breasts fall under the spell of his fingers. So do the tickly parts at the side of my waist, followed by the tops of my thighs where he spreads and slides his palms over my stockings, making them whisper.

'Take these off,' he says, and touches my shorts, raising his square jaw and pouting his lips close to my chin. 'Please, girl. Slip out of them. I want to eat you up.'

I slap my hands against his cheeks and pinch the skin of his face but he only smiles at the shape of my eyes and the nasty stare the hunger can bring out in them. Taking two of my fingers into his mouth he introduces them to the velvet of his tongue, softening my aggression. The moment I relapse from wanting to slap him silly, both his hands collaborate to give my breasts a squeeze that makes me wince. 'You do it,' I say with difficulty.

Nimble fingers unthread laces and release my hips from the leather corsetry. Sitting between his thighs, I watch him slide the shorts down my legs. Holding my ankles tight enough to hurt me, he proceeds to lick the dirty soles of my shoes. Then he takes my shoes off and licks the warm soles of my feet so his tongue tickles my instep. My red toenails, hazy beneath nylon, are taken inside his mouth and made wet. From my toes his mouth moves to my ankles and he pinches the ankle chain off my skin with his incisors. From my ankles, the sculpture that is his face moves to my knees, licks behind them, and then rubs its cheeks down my inner thighs to the kitten in my lap. From his nostrils his breath streams and then breaks against my sex.

Lying back with my toes pointing towards the top of the bed, so my head hangs over the end, I feel the canopy drift against my face. Arnaud will make me wait for the quick and hard penetration I want to dull the edge of my delicious suffering. He'll make me wait until I'm ready to claw his black eyes from his face. But the delay will be worth every tortuous second.

Under my shorts there was no room for panties, no

187

matter how thin, so my puss is exposed to the warm air and his warmer breath. Parting my lips with deft fingers, he goes straight to the tiny tendon that brings so much pleasure and ruin to this girl. He wets an index finger and I watch his eyes narrow in concentration. The finger is placed on my spot and starts to circle. As the pressure gets firmer and the motion faster, a spirit takes control of my body; it forces me to arch my back off the bed and to kick out with my legs. Two more of his evil fingers slip inside me and go deep. The pressure of his rubbing is maintained without pause until I'm chewing bed linen and snatching at his face, which he quickly moves from the harm red claws can do when they plough. I try and trap him between my legs, but he slips his body free, still managing to keep those fingers in place.

Now I'm raking my claws against the mattress and I feel my head and shoulders slide further over the end of the bed when his mouth engulfs my sex. Made hard, as if cartilage runs through it, his tongue skates on top of my spot, whipping me into a frenzy of bad mouthing and hip jerking until red flashes fill my skull and my muscles turn to liquid.

Two hours later and my nip at his shoulder, for a taste of the good stuff, has left me dreamy. Giggling like the girl I was when I stole pear wine and drank it in the woods with my friends, I find myself staggering around the bed upon which Arnaud lies, face down. I put nine thin tails of a flail to use against his feminine back, hitting him with lazy but heavy strokes. Thrilled by his moans and quick breaths, I watch the tiny red lines appear on his skin as his hands fist into the pillows.

After he had eased me a little, with his fingers, from

a need that had begun to make me irritable, he asked me to mark him. No matter how hard I then sucked his length, or clawed his belly, he demanded the touch of whip before he dealt with my yearning for a consistent and lengthy penetration. This is why he whips me into a frenzy with his mouth and hands, so I in turn will whip him into a red mess. It's a formula he introduced me to long ago; the way this spoilt boy can get his own way. It makes me want to beat him and fuck him. And we can last all night and probably will, driven by a need to reduce, empty, destroy and then revive each other. Just like the last time when he took me out of small towns, stucco-walled motels and wise-guy bars, replacing my life on the endless road with his world of cellar clubs, cemetery dances and tight restraints. We are rediscovering a lost passion – a love we shared while Hank worked overseas, having left me in the French Quarter when Arnaud was only eighteen but going on 50 inside, just like me. Back then I needed to forget Hank for a while and he always encouraged me to find distractions so I could both hurt and thrill him with my stories when he came home. And the moment I saw Arnaud playing rock'n'roll in a leather club, standing before three emaciated waifs who backed his vocal melodies with their crunching guitar and drum power, I wanted the boy to be my distraction. Just as for every other girl in the club, the heat of need made my cheeks ruddy and my eyes green. Little did I know then that Arnaud would take a piece of my heart and keep it.

Just as I beat him before – taking leather, cedar and hot wax to his angel body – I perform the curious ritual of our love again. Only this time things have changed: I belong to no one.

He grunts as my lathering of his flesh with leather increases in power and velocity. Angry, red thoughts mist my reason, like they did in Baton Rouge last week when I took the cycle cop into the lair of my back seat, or in Natchez the week before that, when I stole a girl from her date in a picture house and made the nervous beau watch her suck me in the dark. Missy leaves her mind in these hot moments – she takes and hurts and thrills. Maybe I'm hiding from confusion and escaping from the magnitude of my loss. Perhaps this is where the love of my man Hank has delivered me, to twisted and dark places where you lose all sense of what you are or feel in daylight, like the twisted road that poor Preacher walked, or the moonless night of Val's attic. Maybe this is what Hank does to those who love him and this is what life becomes without him.

'Good? Harder?' I say, throwing my arm back and then forward, battering the slender youth into his own sheets, so soiled with the honey extracted from curious girl-things who follow him home from shows. He never hollers or shrieks; he just contains the energy of pain and pumps his butt until I whip it still.

Casting the lasher aside, I rush to the bed, suddenly intent on appeasing my own needs with this beautiful creature. Curling my fingers across his scalp, I twist his hair and his body follows. Mouth gaping for air, eyes startled like a rabbit who sees a black-eyed stoat slipping into his burrow, Arnaud watches my mouth creep forward to his own soft lips. I suck the sweat from around his mouth and then slip my thighs around his ears. Still clutching his hair, I guide his mouth into the honey and salt.

Never will I lose my heart to another, I say to myself while pulling at my nips with my own sharp nails, increasing the fervour of the power I feel inside me. Love imprisons; its crime is its temporary nature, but its damage is a life sentence. So I will sail oceans alone, read mountains of books, look for wisdom in every famous painting and poem, acquire every skill, ride a thousand cocks, adore a thousand throats, caress a thousand breasts. The German bitch is strong in me; her memory and influence have broken all impediments from me until I have become her. This is the destiny of the bond. Hank was just the thing that changes without being changed: the messenger, the catalyst. And she is close – the precursor, the origin of it all. I can feel her.

Arnaud laps at my sex, which I hover above his lips and occasionally dip on to his mouth. He slips a finger in my anus while preparing my hollow with his tongue – readying it for his rock. 'Now, baby. I want you now,' I beg shamelessly. His hands guide my dizzy head and greedy body to the sheets and pillows. My legs are raised and placed so the back of my knees are spiked by his shoulder bones. I watch his pretty-boy face above me. Beyond his head, almost invisible against the black ceiling, I can see my feet; toes already curling in anticipation of the thrust and jab.

His thickness will remain firm and long for hours. I am to be used and exhausted, attached to him until dawn, diffused and then made to explode by the changing rhythms of his efforts, each of us seeking a crescendo. Like the moment when the melody and power in one of his songs sends an audience into a frenzy that curiously moves as one, we find our old harmony. Drilling himself into me, jack-hammer fast, we bounce off the bed and spit insults at each other. Suddenly maddened and renewed by this corrupt love, I shout, 'Harder, you fucking bastard!'

'Slut,' he says with a sneer. 'You live for this. Don't you?'

I stay quiet.

191

'Don't you?' he repeats, and stops the fucking when the head of his cock is just within my lips.

'Yes. Yes. Yes,' I cry.

'Dress for it, you hunt for it, you destroy for it.'

'Yes.'

'So what about me?'

I smile. 'Fuck you.'

Grinding into each other, so our floss and softness gives way to bone pushing against bone, he sends himself deeper and launches me further from control.

'Gonna put you on your tummy, girl,' he whispers. 'Gonna fuck you properly.'

'You're too fat. It hurts.'

He smiles and withdraws from my puss, making me moan as the length retracts. Slapping my bottom hard he gets me to turn over and then he smacks me into position, so my knees and elbows take my weight and my bottom pokes upward. Holding my shoulders with a tight grip while positioning his legs on either side of mine, he lifts his hips so his cock juts out below him, poised and taking aim at my purple flower with its gnarled red bud, waiting to be stung.

And I want to be hurt, to be rifled and thrust into, to be mounted like a timid creature in a black forest, rutted under a red moon by something dark and ferocious and starving from a long winter without me. Biting the sheets and pushing the top of my head into the mattress, I muffle my scream as Arnaud descends through me, splitting me from pussy to coccyx, moving pelvis and muscle to one side, impaling me through to the stomach. Can't open my eyes for the pain. The sweet pain of my surrender.

He eases in and out of me until the desire for speed grips him and I begin to whirlpool my clit with the fingertip of the hand I have slipped between my thighs. He pants, fighting to hold his seed back as the

192

scarlet ribs of muscle in my anus grip and strangle his white cock. Uttering whistling sounds with my pursed lips, I feel like I'm hanging on to a ledge with fingertips, about to drop into a climax to anaesthetise my torment.

We come together; shuddering, sobbing, falling. Along my damp back, I feel his smooth chest and, inside it, the mighty breaths that wrack his bones and wheeze through his pipes. Inside my depths his warmth spills.

We kiss for a while and then break apart to rest in silence and smoke. Gradually we shuffle across the sheets to be closer to one another's warmth, never dropping eye contact. What we have said and done to each other goes beyond explanation, so we just leave it as something that is mad and happens whenever we meet. I accept his craziness and he accepts mine.

When he rolls on to his front, he reaches for my hand and squeezes it. I pick a candle off the bedside cabinet and drip the wax down his shoulders and back. As it lands it splashes into little opaque droplets which immediately go hard and darken. Arnaud closes his eyes. Along his spine every muscle tightens as he bottles the sting inside himself.

'I'm going to fuck you again,' he says, opening his eyes. 'I want to see your face in the mirror as you come. I want to record the memory of it.'

First he pulls the sheets off me, then he takes my smoke away. He yanks my body around in a 180-degree arc so my head is facing the base of the bed. From the hip, I am raised and entered without preliminary. It makes me gasp but my puss is far from exhausted; she wants that fat white thing stuffed into her a second time. As he pumps into me, he skilfully moves my upside-down body off the bed and across the floor towards a large mirror that can spin around within its ebony frame. Black wax cracks off his back from where I poured it to revive him from weariness. With my chin pointing at the ceiling and my hands reaching behind my head so my bent arms take my weight through the palms I have spread on the rugs, I perform like a gymnast to squeeze my fill out of this man. With one hand placed in the small of my back, he supports my body, and moves in and out of my sex, using his quivering thighs and iron calves to rock his love through me. With legs wrapped over his hips and my ankles crossed behind, I inch backward with every thrust, one hand at a time until I reach the mirror. Staring into the oval glass pool, I see my reflection: teeth bared, perspiration running with cosmetics over cheeks and chin, eyes wild, tongue hot. I think of Hank fucking Barbara.

Before the mirror we come together. Our exhalations and groans are delivered in unison and our eyes open at the same time. Our faces are full of the same shock and delight at what we have done to each other through this long night in a dark room. Slipping on to my shoulders, I ease the aches in the joints that have been stretched. I am a delicious mess; scratched in places, my stockings torn by his black fingernails, my skin smeared with red wine and his wine and my wine. And he is worn out too. His eyes are full of fatigue, his sack hangs flat and depleted against his thigh, his skin stings from the many abrasions that have resulted from our needs.

We catch our breath and laugh together, saying nothing, but feeling grateful for having this empathy that allows and revels in such shameful things. He takes me to the bathroom. It is lit with red candles and has a marble bath in the middle, supported on little clawed feet. From the old steel shower-head he runs a thick rope of water into the tub which turns to steam when it hits the stone. Holding his hand I step into the wide tub and hang against him while the hot water smashes against me and saps the last of my strength away. Through all the blinding heat and cloud, I feel him push his throat against my lips. Is it the sound of the water or is it his whispering voice asking me to bite? Purring loudly, so my vibrations run through his body, I scrape my needles against his pale skin. Pink rivulets streak his chest.

With the curtains closed, there is no way of telling the time in his chambers but I know we have been awake through the night, from the show where I met him until our shower at sun break. Arnaud sleeps beside me but I stay awake and am content to view his beautiful profile until the real darkness swells inside me again. Last night distracted me, but I wonder just how long it will take until I can lose these horrid blues. Where is my light? Did Hank steal all my fire? Who can teach me to live without it?

It is rage as much as lust that motivates me. Perhaps that is why I have been so hard on Arnaud's snowy complexion all night, and made such demands on this man after suddenly reappearing in his life yesterday. Hank is behind this. No matter how wantonly I lose myself with the flesh of others inside me, I cannot forget my time with him. These are early days, I know, but it is the moments when I am least active – driving the Buick, idling along sidewalks, slowly drinking coffee surrounded by the colour of these streets – that I am most at risk and unable to stop my recall. I feel there is no one man or woman who can heal me, including Arnaud, who I sometimes think is a crazy mixture of each. But at least he takes the pain away for a while. And he was all I had. There was nowhere else for me to go.

Besides Hank, I have never spent so much time with one man. Nor have I found such empathy. In this city, our friendship like our love was once subject to sudden impulses. There was a time when we took each other with haste under balconies and in cemeteries, or in gardens and clubs, and always after he had stared into my eyes for too long. One time, he even managed to insert himself inside me as we were part of a jostling crowd who watched a parade, going into me through the slit in my skirt. But there were quiet times too, when we stroked each other, giggling under sheets, or sitting opposite each other in street cafes, our eyes vacant from the strong drink we used to live on while our hands moved beneath the tables. With so much love, I was unable to stop myself feeding like a glutton right up to the critical moment I have already spoken of. There came a time when I had to make a choice: to break him or bond with him. So when Hank came back from overseas and was ready to carry on the killing he'd conducted across the oceans when he found Arnaud and me in love, I left my raven-haired rocker and broke the poor boy.

And now, something is building up in me that I don't recognise or understand, and it frightens me. No, it goes beyond fright; it is like terror mixed with exhilaration at the very moment when you jump off something high and wonder how hard the water, so far below, will feel against your feet.

Maybe I thought I was in Orleans for revenge too, to betray Hank again with Arnaud. Even if Hank wanted to palm me off with Arnaud in compensation for his being reunited with the German bitch, I know a renewal of my love with Arnaud would hurt him a little. But then maybe I kidded myself that I am here for the 24-hour buffet and the oceans of drink that I have begun to lap at, sitting on the shore and looking out at oblivion. It is only now, though, that I accept my presence in this city is for another reason. The spices this town offers are merely flowers on the surface of a murky pond. I am here for her. And she is near. I can feel her. I hate her but I want to know her. I need to see the woman who stole my man and I am part of the long story that extends from her mouth. I will destroy the old one or be destroyed by her. This is my will.

Arnaud stirs beside me. Without opening his eyes, he trails an arm around my waist and kisses the side of my head. 'I've been dreaming about you, girl,' he says. 'And you're grown. You've changed in the same way you made me change. You're all busted up inside. I can hear all the little pieces rattling around inside you.'

Turning my head to the side, I cannot stop my mouth and then my face from wrinkling up with the upset of being so lost.

'Can I heal you, girl?'

I swallow to get my words firm and when I speak I feel like I'm holding my breath. 'I came here to forget a man, not to collect another. I'm sorry.'

There is a long silence, then he speaks. 'The floor dropped out from under me last night when I saw you walk into the club. And the walls an' all started to swivel about my head. I felt real sick too. You don't know how much I wanted to see you again, Missy. You have no idea how much I wanted you to just reappear. But your colours have changed, girl. If the truth be known, you kind of scared me. Thought you'd kill me with that whip last night. I ain't complaining, but how come you're so bitter-sweet?'

'Throw me out if I'm so old,' I say.

'Spoken like the teenager I fell in love with,' he says, and musses up my hair.

197

'I'm no girl. You have no idea how old I am.'

'Reckon I know more than you think.'

I turn to look at him. 'That so?'

He smiles and somehow I understand that we are more equal than I feel comfortable with. He can hold back on what I want just as easily as I can hold back on him. Gave him too much of a taste of the bond last time and he's clung on to it. This I can see.

'I want this gift you have, Missy. You let me take the wrapping paper off, but I want to open the box and take what's inside it too. You left something in me. You know it. You didn't mean to, but you got carried away and now I have this appetite you spoke of last night. And the dreams. And the energy I can't contain. It tries to eat through me sometimes from the inside out. Last year in Japan, where we played some shows, I just took this woman. I could have got in real trouble, but I didn't care. I wanted her so bad because she looked kinda like you. So I just swooped on her, like an animal. I was lucky she wanted to party that way in the bathroom of a bar and then again in my room at the hotel. Even though she was important and stuff and worked for the record company, I was lucky she wanted steel on her skin.

'But I know I don't have the whole of the thing in you. So I want it. I want it all. You could give it to me. You owe me.'

'I know,' I say, closing my eyes and wishing I could take away all the confusion I've stirred in this boy. Could I give him the years, though? The future, and the bond to me he'd never outlive? The very thing that ruined Hank, Preacher, Val and me? After he's loved a legion of girls all over the world, released a dozen albums about a mysterious girl who once kissed him too deeply, what then for pretty boy Arnaud? Do I want his lean shadow crossing mine whenever I stop to rest under the sun I match, day for day, life for life?

'I don't hate you for the hurt,' he says. 'I need it. My music needs it and I love my music and the life it gives me. Love it more than I could love anyone. I'm bad, girl. Real bad. You know it and it makes me right for the thing you have. And besides, you know I just can't let myself get any older.'

'We'll see,' is all I can say.

'You think on it, baby. One way or the other you gotta help me out of what you did before.'

'I know. Later. We'll talk about it later.'

'OK. But don't you go running out on me again before we do.'

'I won't. I promise I'll make things right somehow.'

'Good.' I can hear the relief and hope in his voice. 'And you should come to the show tonight. We're rehearsing for Europe and I want you to see how good we are now. We're playing the Laissez Les Bons Temps Rouler. It's back aways from Bourbon Street.'

It's beautiful the way he says the French name. 'The name, what does it mean?'

He kisses my ear. 'Let the good times roll.'

Eleven

She's here, she's near. I cannot see her through all this dry ice, heat, body mass and noise, but I don't need to. The bond is all I need to tremble and rejoice at being so near the beginning and the end of this story.

Up on the stage in the club, Near Dark are playing; three songs into a set that can last until the musicians drop from heat exhaustion. Below them their most devoted audience churns in waves of slick leather and unkempt hair. Hands punch the smoky air and purple light ripples across heads that rock forward and backward on slender white necks ready to snap. From the large speakers, hung by chains from the roof, blues chords, punk attitude and country heartbreak gush their strange blend across the sea of people. The crowd smashes itself against the rocks of the wet black walls, only to reel back into one another before breaking apart to start the waves all over. This is a furnace; airless, too hot, too dark for inhibition, too secret for intrusion. There is no escape from the energy Arnaud's music creates. Gripping a microphone and teetering on the edge of the stage, Arnaud stretches and then crouches into strange postures, using his body as a conductor for his voice. From his mouth drift angel songs; fallen angel sounds from the long drop into hell. He is stripped down to leather trousers; the marks left by my heat are visible on his pallid flesh.

Opposite the stage, at the far end of the club, stand two large iron doors now closed for the night. Before the gates, I lean into shadow and drink from a long glass, watching the mêlée over the mixing desk. My lips seek the crushed ice that vanishes too quickly into the syrupy whiskey and coke; my mind seeks the spin and judder of drink; my skin grows anxious for someone's touch. Anyone's touch, as long as it is firm and able to shape me, pull me apart and reveal my appetite to her. I want her to see the power and hunger of her legacy in me.

As the frenzied crowd is lulled and slowed down by a slide guitar, I start moving to the far edge of the bar, towering above men and women in the boots that stretch up my thighs. Despite the temperature inside the club, I wear a long leather coat that belongs to Arnaud. It is belted tight to contain my recent purchases. With some of the money Hank left in the car with his other things, I have bought the patent boots with spike heels and a black basque without frills or pattern, just sheer panels to tint my ivory skin on the tummy and the sides of my waist. Peeking over the tops of the boots are the dark tops of my stockings that are attached to gold suspender clips. My panties are tiny, my garter belt thin, my bra transparent. All black, all trapped under leather, all designed for sharing. Maybe I need to recreate myself. Go through a change. Escape the clothes that Hank liked me to wear. It is all part of revenge and healing.

In the moving mass I cut into, moving through the heart of the incinerator, a hand seizes my arm. I turn so quickly the felon is surprised. Looking into the rough male face, I can see cruelty. Not the cruelty that goes with love but another kind. The type of disregard for feeling and delight in pain that I once saw in Kentucky when a man kicked a stray dog who was only looking for food in the street. When I left that man under a bush on wasteground, he wasn't moving. Then I bought the dog a big steak and Hank and me had to clear out of town real quick, before Johnny Law found the red mess I left under a lime tree. The dog was happy to come with us until we found him a sanctuary. I have no patience for this cruelty.

Something snaps in my head and I punch a fist into the rough face of the man who has taken my arm. Cartilage and gristle snap under my knuckles and his hand releases my arm. People move back. Someone says, 'Whoa!' Another cries, 'Easy girl!' and the grabbing man falls like a big tree. Giving up what little space they have, the crowd parts and I walk on to the bar where I shout for service. A barkeep with a pony-tail starts to look nervous. He wastes no time and pours me a drink. Then I move off, swaying my hips and my head to the rhythms of Near Dark, rolling on the outside of my boot soles, slinking through the tight package of drunks, pretty chicks, leather boys and Gothy people with whited faces.

Suddenly, in the middle of the club, I feel the sweat freeze on my body as if the barrel of a gun has just been pressed into my back. She is closer now; her eyes are fixed on me. Keeping my composure, not daring to look about, I move towards two men who watch every aspect of my approach to their side of the dance floor. After earmarking them earlier for a possible tryst, I move towards their rangy slouching. There are three girls near them who suddenly look all pissy and aggressive when they see me nearing the object of their own hunt. Staring the dark-eyed rock chickadees down, I pass in front of the two pretty men. From the corner of my eye I see one of the men swallow while his friend tosses his hair back off his face. Blood thickens a part of them against the leather of their trousers. I can feel their need – the stomachs turning over, the prickling of the napes of their necks, the opening of their mouths, the posturing of their limbs and bodies to appear broader and taller to me. These boys will do, I decide. So calm down, sluts, I think. We can dispense with the rituals. I tell them all this with a flash of my eyes and move on to the door marked FIRE EXIT with glowing red letters.

Behind me, I can sense the hesitation. They are looking at each other, gesticulating, wanting to know which of them I want. But soon both of them move after me; each determined to succeed despite their friendship. As I look over my shoulder and smile at each of them, I see one of the chickadees snatch a hand out at the two pretty boys. Too late. They are gone. Lost to a pursuit of me.

Before the door I turn and face my prey. Lured into the hunt for a predator they cannot understand, they stop walking and then ease themselves closer to me. Our eyes are level on account of my high, high heels and I can see they are unable to look past the face of a pretty seventeen-year-old blonde all dressed up for rocking and rolling on a back seat, against a wall, or on a hard floor. Reaching out, I touch one of the men's big golden earrings and giggle. He blushes. Before his friend can shift around any more with disappointment I poke his bare midriff and then trace my nail across his firm brown tummy. Now they are both smiling and asking my name, asking me where I live, if I'm new in town, telling me they are in a band, pouting their lips, narrowing their eyes, and easing back on to their hips to look cool. Staying quiet, but smiling, I weather this torrent. From an inside pocket of his leather jacket one of the men removes a silver flask and unscrews the tiny lid. He offers it to me. I take it and empty it. The other offers a packet of smokes. After I take one and put it on my lips, pursing them as if to suck on something bigger, he strikes his Zippo down his leather leg and brings the bluey-yellow flame up to the shorn tip of my smoke. I nod in thanks.

Suddenly between their shoulders I see another face – white, beautiful, bright eyed, gone. The men turn their heads and follow the intensity of my stare. But she has vanished. I smile, take their hands and draw the boys to me. Leaning towards me from either side, they seek the blue of my eyes and a closer look at the gloss on my lips. I put an end to their chit-chat by kissing each in turn. With an arm around their waists, I then pull them tight against me so they form a corral, defending the sight of me from her. Let the German bitch wait. She'll see me soon enough. In the meantime she can see how wicked her prodigy can be.

Taking it in turn I kiss each man open-mouthed. While I take the press of a stubbly mouth and hard jaw against my slippery lips, the other kisses my neck. This I like and I am encouraged to close my eyes. Hands move over my leather-coated body; over my bottom, across my breasts, around my waist. They are gentle, their hands tremble, they are self-conscious. Leaning against the wall, I tuck a finger inside their waistbands and encourage them to squash their hard maleness against me. Two cocks touch my hips. Fat, hard cocks full of foam that I need to take a slug from. So while they kiss and inhale me, I unbutton my coat. They finger the lapels and then accept my invitation by slowly pulling the coat open.

Now they can't blink or stop this heavy panting breath that comes in hot plumes over my throat and face. With my shoulders pressed into the wall behind me, I open my legs and plant my heels wide apart. Over the boys' shoulders I can see a few people peeking and trying to work out what they're doing to me.

The band plays on; Arnaud's voice becomes full of tremolos and whispery pain. As I listen to the result of the love aches I put into his heart, which in turn gave shape to his wonderful music, I feel the strangers' hands touching my unveiled body. Each of them goes for my breasts first and they squash those ladies against my sternum before rubbing the palms of their hands against the gossamer covering the warm skin. Nips are tweaked, which makes me sigh, and knuckles brush against my tum before a finger is inserted under my garter belt. I am being inspected and fingered and fondled. Tugged forward to their lips and teeth, I close my eyes and let my body go limp. Despite the heat I can feel a steel belt buckle cold against my navel and two hands exploring my lower back. It is not long before a hand rubs my puss through the fine panty material that clings to her. A finger slides across my beanie and I gasp. The finger returns to that spot and begins to work in a circle. Sighing with delight, I realise that hand has administered such a pleasure before. Now one of my breasts is fondled from the other side. She is cupped and the nip is brushed with a thumb before the whole soft mass is squeezed hard enough to make me squeak like a mousey caught in a trap and about to show her long teeth.

Yes, boys. Come on, boys. Get me started. Touch me. Feel me. Tug and pull me between you.

Their mouths are all over my hot face; even my

205

eyes are kissed and my cheeks are nibbled. Rotating his hips, the boy on my left starts to rub his wood against my thigh and soon his friend places my hand on his leather-covered pipe, with some insistence. Nearly time.

Beyond the red velvet of my closed eyes and through the wet misty heat of the club I can feel her circling us. Her heckles are rising at the thought of a feed; her pretty nose is wrinkling, her eyes must be lovelorn and half-closed. Somewhere in the reek of spilled beer, petunia oil, wet leather and cigarette smoke, I can detect her fragrance: not sweet or sour, but sharp and ancient like the scent in the clothes I wore for the Preacher.

Another moment longer under the ministrations of these hands and I feel my desire for a cock overwhelm me. It's as if my puss is becoming a pair of wet lips, protruding and tingling as if brought out by a poultice and now pleading for the stretching pain of entry. Throwing my head back, I smile into the swirling dark inside my head and inside the club. Draping two slender arms across their shoulders, I push against them and move against the thick cock meat they press into me. Viciously, I bite at a mouth and then lick a stubbly cheek on the other side of my face, tasting salt. Losing control, losing the strength in my legs, becoming weightless and wanting to be hung between them before the skewering begins, I fall against them so they are forced to hold me up. Deep, ruthless stabbing from their groins is what I crave before I rip into them.

Yes, it is time. They and I have waited long enough for the consummation of this lust between the minds and bodies of strangers. With my hands I reach behind me and knock the metal bar of the fire exit down. Immediately, I feel the cold and refreshing night air engulf us. Slowly, I teeter backward and out into the night, followed by the blind and groping boys.

The door is pulled to with a bang and the violence of Arnaud's music is reduced to a far-off rumble; muted as if dropped into deep water. As the fire door closes I have a sense that something else has followed us out into this alleyway, twisting and then dropping straight into the dark, like a long and slender stray cat that bends its spine to slip through a hole to find food.

Amongst the metal garbage cans and on the slippery brick wall the two blond men take me. Pushed down to my knees, my coat is pulled up to my waist. Expectantly, my buttocks rise and my mouth breaks into a smile that makes the men yank at their belts and button flies. I laugh at what I have turned them into and my voice is soon lost in the noise of the party that engulfs the city and carries on for miles around us. I can hear water splashing on the tiles near me, and in the street beyond this alley a horn sounds from a car, discordant against the swing-band music that spills its brassy sounds on to the sidewalk from a gloomy club doorway, out there in the neon-blurred distance.

'Take this,' the man before me says. I look up, so sweetly, and open my mouth. 'All of it, girl. Suck it.'

This desperate pleading sends the other man, who stands behind me, into a similar frenzy. His fingers seize my buttocks and I feel his untrimmed nails dig into my doughy flesh. The downy peach half of my puss is located and nudged against by his cock. The other penis is shoved into my mouth while its owner entwines his fingers into the hair at the back of my head. Both my head and hips are held tight and then fucked into. Take this, Hank, I think, as I accept the stiffness into my throat and pussy. Rutted back and forth like a soft deer caught between hungry wolves, I am thrust at both front and rear. Save for the heavy breathing of my lovers I am deafened to everything by the sound of the hard flesh packing itself into me. Let her watch, Hank. Let your German bitch see your cast-off girl love like a demon before feeding like a devil. Let her run and tell you about what you left behind. I feel victorious, libidinous, free.

Thighs slap against my buttocks and a wet cock squelches between my cheeks. Veins stand out on their engorged faces and their hands clench on my pale body. With a palm against the stomach before my face, I push my mouth off the cock long enough to say, 'In my ass,' before the rigidity is shoved back between my teeth. Boots scrape the bricks behind me and the thickness is withdrawn from my milky puss. When the rounded head of the stranger's cock presses against the tightness of my pinkish bottom ring, I am forced to release the other cock from my mouth again. Wary of biting down on it, I beat the wet muscle with my hand instead. Its thick counterpart breaks the seal in my ass. Yelping like a pup whose tail has been stepped upon, my mind closes itself off to everything but the electric shock of pain in my bottom. On and on the meat seems to go, forcing itself into a space where there is no space. All the air leaves my body and just the thought of such a savage violation in the open makes me come. I am not alone in orgasm. Almost immediately, a hot flood breaks through my bottom and runs to the heart of me. 'Fuck it into me,' I say, and the man buried in my back passage makes a big 'urgh' sound as if he's been pulled apart at the seams. His thrusts become savage before his rigidity wanes and every drop in him is rinsed into me. At the sight of this sin, the cock I have been sucking so thoroughly is suddenly beaten by the owner's hand until it too opens to shoot a white lather at my smudged mouth. I manage to get two loops of his phlegmy goo on my tongue, but the rest is lost somewhere in my hair.

Nearby, she starts to purr at a frequency too low for the boys to hear. Pungent male scents have carried to her pert nose in the shadows and I know how the rich odour must be affecting her.

As I rest against a wall, catching my breath, one of the boys comes back to me. Widening my eyes and grinning, I welcome him. This time his hands are more confident and even rougher in their treatment of my compliant body. He twists the skin on my arms as he pulls me on to his mouth and unsheathed cock. Savage kisses bruise my mouth and now his hands don't know which part of me to squeeze. Making his choice, he falls to his knees and pushes his mouth at my wet puss. Lapping at the folds of brown velvet that he and his friend have already drenched, his breath speeds up until it sounds like he's hyperventilating. I fling a leg over his shoulder and push my sex on to his mouth from an angle. 'There,' I say. 'Suck me right there.' He complies and runs his hands up and down my boots – so stiff around my ankles, tight calves and zippered inner thighs. Fingers find the zips and open the patent skins of my boots to reveal another skin – a nylon-smooth skin that is warm and fragrant. As if his face is burning and thrust under a stream of cool water for comfort, he rubs his cheeks against my stockings and I can see that he is inhaling the smell of my sex and my hot legs until he overdoses on the leather and meaty odour. I know this scent of mine has shut down his other senses, so the one remaining can concentrate on my rare perfume. I know I smell like that down there because Hank told me and that particular scent would drive him even wilder than the smell of my hair.

'I'm going to fuck you again, girl,' he tells me. The desperation in his voice sends a little thrill up my back and my anticipatory pleasure is doubled by the fact that his second erection will last longer than the first.

'One at a time,' I say. 'You can fuck me all night, but now I want you one at a time.' The second man, who watches his friend smother me, goes pale and swallows hard, unable to suspend his disbelief that this pretty girl with crazy fifties hair and thick eye make-up could be so reckless. I smile. If only they knew how this night will change the rest of their lives.

My boots are wrinkled around my ankles now and even though my panties are slit for access, front and back, the man between my legs pulls them down so they stretch into a thin black string around my open knees. As he rises to his feet, licking my body all the way so the tickling brings out my drunken giggle, his cock ascends with him and thuds into my puss. Standing on my tippy-toes and raised another few inches off the ground by the strength in his shoulders, I stretch to a suitable height. 'Get it in me. Shove it in,' I say, and no longer care about the frantic delivery of my words. 'Come on, that's it. Let me –' I assist with one hand and pull the sticky shaft up at an angle so the fat head can find the opening to me. 'Yes. Right there.'

As it starts to go through me, my body slumps down and my weight forces it in so quick and deep. I gasp and then whinny. Using his knees, he throws it in me, chucks it in hard and I clasp my legs around his buttocks. One of my boots falls off and my eyes roll up into my head from the pleasure of this.

Shunted up and down the wooden panels of the club wall, I feel the friction, from where my lips cling around his cock, increase with the tempo of our rutting. The other man goes hard as he watches. There is movement behind him.

I blink the tears from my eyes but it is still hard to see what has followed us from the club, especially now my head is bobbing up and down like I'm running backward to catch a softball on a dusk-shadowed field. But there she is. A long silhouette is visible; stretching up the wall, faceless, impossibly thin, crowned with blonde hair, and trembling when so near food. Her victim is distracted by my being fucked so furiously against the wall. I start to choke and grunt and my claws draw blood on the man's back but he just goes at me even harder.

It's as if a shadow envelops the other man who took my ass before. He is pulled backward and off his feet to where all the cardboard boxes are stacked against the wall.

Suddenly, a firework screams above the street that runs adjacent to the alley. Its red tail of sparks casts a momentary illumination into our cove. In that split second of reddish light, I see her long white fingers with the blood-clot nails stretching up his face as she seizes his chin, I see her latex suit highlighted and made to look like oil under artificial light, and I catch a glimpse of her cruel heels digging into the ground. Then the firework dies and all I am left with are the sounds; his whimpering, the sound of her hand beating his erect cock, and the noise of her mouth suckling.

I come at the sight of her feeding. Never have I seen something so quick and terrible. Practised in many centuries, I know now that her arts could take any man as slowly and seductively as she chose, or in the space between the beats of his unsuspecting heart. Hank and the Preacher never had a chance. Even this night around me has changed as if she brings black magic with her. The air seems thinner and anything living is suddenly made aware of its weakness inside the icy radius of her presence. Curiously, I do not care what happens to me. I let my upper body fall back from the stranger's body so he is forced to hold my waist in order to stay inside me. I bare my throat to the danger that is near. Part of me wants her teeth and the pain they promise. I come again. My lover throws his final, hurried strokes into me before collapsing to his knees, taking me down with him. His body shakes and a stream of hot seed is squeezed inside my womb.

My feet touch the ground and the man falls against me, breathing like he's run a marathon in the sun. Pulling myself up against the wall, I catch my breath and try to clear my head. My lover clutches my waist and rests his head on my tummy. I peer down at his long blond hair and where it parts, looking for the tenderest bit of him. Bending down to him, I start to moan through my nose and keep on moaning until my kitten needles have sunk deep and found a home. Bourbon rich, bacon salted, cigarette tarred – he has such a delicious night-time taste. 'Ahh,' he says. 'Yesss,' he says. Then he goes quiet and I have to hold this dish under the arms to support it.

Between the slit eyes of contentment, I watch her go to work. It seems she has unzipped her suit at the crotch to make these quick rubbing motions on the penis of her man. In her excitement, which makes me think she hasn't fed for a long time, she slaps his face and giggles to herself in between her kisses, leaving scratches on his face. Then her rubbing crotch starts to speed up and she dips her blonde head between her shoulders. His booted feet stretch out between her legs and start to twitch and then kick. Little spasms make her body jolt. A high-pitched whining sound comes from her and then she goes 'Oh, oh, oh' as each bolt of his cream is delivered up in her. Her back arches and the tight latex around her spine glistens in the thin light. With one hand, she shoves his face down into the cardboard boxes and I can see that his body has gone all limp now.

I push my man away and he slumps to the floor, smiling to himself, and occasionally saying a random word. Opposite me, she springs to her feet. I can see her teeth and wet mouth but nothing more. 'You didn't have to,' she says. Her voice reminds me of an actress in an old black and white movie. It seems sad and thick with an accent that I think is both German and French at the same time. Something inside me pulls towards her. She backs away and all but vanishes into the shadows on the other side of the alley.

'It was a gift,' I say, imploring her to stay.

'Thank you . . . Missy,' she whispers, and is almost gone.

'Wait.'

'Come and see me. In a few days I will be ready for you.'

'Where? Tell me. When?' I cry out, and my voice sounds so distant because of these head spins I have. But she is gone. At the mouth of the alley I see her flit into the street light and then she disappears, riding the back of a shadow into the rest of the night.

Twelve

'And the heel. That's it; take it in your mouth. Oh, yes. Swallow it, boy. All of it. Take it deep. Now, ain't that good? Not my foot. I never said you could touch my foot with your lips. Just the shoe. Kiss the shiny leather all down the sides to the toe. That's right, but if you leave any marks you're going to clean them off with a rag. You hear? Fuck the time. You ask me about the time again and I'm going to lose my head, Arnaud, and you won't be doing shit for a week. Now take my shoes off. Slowly. Ease them off. They're so tight.

'Mmm, that's good. Not your hands. I don't want your hands on my feet. They're not fit to stroke my toes. Just your mouth; I want something soft on them. They're tired and achy. I wore these heels to show you what a wussy you are, so the least you can do is ease my tender skin. That's nice. And under. Stop! Don't tickle. I'm telling you, Arnaud, you do this right and you take your time. I don't give two hoots about your meeting. You see I'm right first, then I might let you go. So slow down.'

Now I start to laugh at how silly he looks, crawling on his belly all trussed up in the harness. His shoulders stiffen when he hears my laugh and I tighten my grip on the chain that runs down to his collar. For a moment, through the eye sockets of his hood, he looks at me. I can tell he's frowning because he never expected me to keep him down for so long this afternoon. The boy thought I'd play with him and then let him get fixed up for his meeting with the record company. They're putting a lot of money into Near Dark's upcoming tour and they expect him to show his face down at some swanky hotel in under an hour.

I glance at my watch and then put a hand to my mouth as if I hadn't realised the correct time. Arnaud rises to his knees, his eyes now wide with panic. 'Down, punk!' I yell, and thrust my hand to the floor. As there isn't much slack in his leash, his face plummets to the rug. If he wants to be my little doggy, then he will obey and not get all uppity because his schedule doesn't fit in with mine. This crawling worm has got me riled with his fretting and clock watching. 'On your back.' Arnaud twists on to his back and I plunge my feet straight on to his face, covering the holes for his nose and the slit for his mouth. He goes still. Between the leather straps that run around his waist and crotch, I see his cock reach maximum rigidity. Pressing my feet down harder, I hear him snuffling for air. I lean forward in my comfy chair and flick his cock with the leather loop at the end of my crop. His legs kick out and he raises his hands as if he's about to grip my ankles. 'Don't you dare,' I say, surprised at my own tone of voice and how deep it goes. But at least he quits messing with me and his hands drop back to the floor, limp and useless. I flick the bulby head of his cock again, making sure my feet are clamped fast to his face. Now he needs air and is forced to breathe in my hot feet. He snuffles and wheezes; I hear his breathing speed up as I tickle the sides of his shaft and then the bulgy head with the leather loop.

'Want some fresh air?'

He grunts.

'Then you promise not to think about your meeting. Even though we're getting close to the time you should be leaving, and we haven't called a cab or anything?'

He stays quiet; petrified into being still.

'Can't hear you?'

His hands rise from the floor a second time and then drop. He grunts agreement.

'OK,' I say and lift my feet from his face. 'Now where is that strappy leather thing I cuff you with?'

Arnaud sighs, but knows better than to query my intentions. Through the doorway that leads from the lounge to his bedroom, I see the cuffs on the bed. 'Go fetch them from the bed and turn the air conditioning up. I'm getting hot in this dress.'

While he trots off to perform these simple requests, I light up a Salem Menthol and wonder how long the German bitch is going to keep me waiting. It's been three days since she followed me to the club where I treated her to dinner. She knows my name from the rat that is Hank, and must have found out I'm staying with Arnaud, so why is she making me wait? If she wants me alone that's fine; I've been walking the streets ever since that night to quell these jittery things in my tum, and Arnaud was out most of yesterday for his rehearsals, so she has had ample time to call on me.

I'm scared but I'm ready. Slipping the Preacher and easing Val from my enemy to my friend has given me confidence. Now, I know this cellar woman is a different animal, but in Austin, Texas, we breed tough. But it's just the waiting isn't doing this girl any good and that's why I'm so down on Arnaud today.

'Good boy,' I say and take the cuffs from my

216

puppy. 'Turn around.' He obeys. I know he loves this part. 'What other things you got stashed here?'

'They're in the bedroom, but . . .'

'But what?'

Arnaud stays quiet.

'You about to mention the time?'

'No.' I don't like the defiant tone of his voice.

I'm off the bed real quick. I fling my arm back behind my head. Arnaud hears the whooshing sound as the crop cuts the air. By the time his head is half-turned towards me, wood has connected with bare buttock. He makes a grunty sound like a little piggy and staggers forward clutching his cheeks. Slipping back into my shoes, because this rubber dress don't look so hot without high-heel leverage, I rise and strut across to where he moves from foot to foot on the rug. Grasping the leash, I shorten it to a smaller loop, suitable for walking a naughty dog who leaps and pulls at pedestrians. 'Take me to your toy box. I want to see what you got in there.'

With the memory of my crop work still hot in his thoughts, Arnaud drops to his knees and leads me to the bedroom. It's cooler in here with the conditioner on full, and I enjoy the cold air on my back, where it's naked between the laces that criss-cross over my naked skin. Arnaud bought me the dress. The shiny rubber is so soft and I love the way it hugs my curves; the feel of it on my skin makes me shiver too. Shame I can't wear it out, because the laces run from between my shoulders down to the hemline, so you can see all of me from behind. And even when I'm real hungry I don't like showing the tops of my stockings beyond a quick peeky when I cross my legs under a table, but in this dress you can see all of my nylons and even my bare bottom.

Feeling all compact and rubbery, with my knees

217

pulled together and my heels forcing shorter steps still, I walk my doggy to the toy box. It would be nice to walk him in the street like this, especially with me wearing my sunglasses and my pill-box hat too. What a pair we would make, but outside of the clubs Arnaud took me to last time I was here, it creates too much fuss.

It's not a box I am led to, but a drawer in his big ebony dresser. The one with the lock that I couldn't open yesterday when I went mooching. From a key on a chain around his neck, Arnaud unlocks the drawer. For some reason he has kept all of this from me, which has stimulated my curiosity further. Girlfriends don't like the secrets of boyfriends. But I guess his fears for missing the meeting have encouraged him to open this up without more of his whining and dithering that could waste more time than he has to play with.

He pulls the door open a fraction and puts his hand inside. 'It's just stuff,' he says, afraid to look up at me. So that's his game. Does he think I'll be satisfied with only select items, pulled out and shown to me?

'Come out of there, puppy,' I say, and haul him away from the drawer by his leash. He resists me and then tries to shut the drawer but I'm too quick. I slap his sore butt cheeks and then wrestle his hands behind his back where I cuff him tight with shiny leather straps.

'No, Missy. Leave it be. It's mine,' he says.

I backhand his leathery face. Arnaud goes quiet and sits back on his knees with his hands behind his back.

'That's enough from you,' I say, short of breath, but I mean it. 'You just stay at heel, pup. I don't want to hear another word or I'll go at you with this crop and then leave you out in the swamp for them nasty gators. You know I'll do it, boy. Even if it's your place, I have no mind to be messed with.'

Boy, has his cock gone hard. It's beginning to pulse like he could come without even touching it. That's good, because I'd like something rich on my tongue real soon.

I open the drawer so the light from the bedside lamps adds some definition to the shadows in there. My tummy does a little rumba; I love to peek where I shouldn't. First thing I lift out is a pretty cigar box, inlaid with silver. There is a tiny catch which I flick down. There are photographs inside – a neat stack of them, like the baseball cards a high-school flame of mine used to keep in his drawers, which I also went sneaking through. These have been taken on an instamatic because they have a wide white border and the colours of the pictures are dim and greeny. As I go through them, I hold my breath. 'Japan?' I finally say. There is a squeak of hood beside me as Arnaud nods his head. They must have been taken on tour. Once again, I make a note to look up these girls in Asia. He has pictures of their wide mouths sucking his cock and leaving long smears of Tokyo paint on his skin. There are pictures of them taking his length in their little pink bottoms while they wear nothing but white ankle socks. On others, he has set the timer on the camera to take pictures of himself fucking two of these groupie girls in his hotel bed. One of them has big dark eyes and a big appetite to match. 'Nice shoes,' I say, and then flash the picture at Arnaud. She wears high heels with a clumpy sole and black spike heel. 'You liked her,' I say, finding another dozen or so of this bad girl in a blue nursey outfit made from rubber. The Japan collection goes back into the drawer. 'You can put them back in order later,' I tell Arnaud.

'What's this, sick boy?' From the corner of my eye, I see my rock star flinch as I lift a stringy mass of lingerie from one corner of the drawer. 'Souvenirs?'

Arnaud coughs.

'These are mine,' I say, and pull a pair of black nylons from the tangle. 'Fifteen denier, harmony points from London. You laddered them with a broken nail. And these –' I tug a pair of panties free. 'I thought I lost them at the party after the Faster Pussycat show. Looks like my sick puppy had them all along.' Thinking of the Preacher and his stash in the attaché case, I hold the mass of flimsies up to the light. 'Whose are the rest?'

'Just girls I met when looking for you inside of strangers.'

Something gives way inside my stony heart and I look away from him, making sure he doesn't see the little movements around my mouth. I put the underwear back. My sifting fingers cross a ball gag and some hoods before finding the tinkle of chain. From what I can see of the shiny knot of metal I'm fingering, this is a suit that is attached to his body by dozens of little clamps. They have angry steel teeth but I reckon they must look nice on white skin that marks easy. There is a mask too with a mouthpiece that goes from a mouth to a crotch. That I don't like and I don't want to hear what he does with it either, so I leave it be. When I find a long black rubbery cock-thing on a belt, though, my curiosity peaks. 'What's this?'

'Just a thing,' he says too quick.

'This been inside you?'

'No.'

'Then why you got it?'

'There's a girlfriend who likes girls and she wears it with her lovers.'

'I like her already.'

Arnaud's breath comes quick. 'You can meet her.'

'Maybe, but why is it in here?'

'She gave it to me.'

'I see. For when she comes over, maybe?'

'That sort of thing,' he answers, just praying that I'll put it back. No such luck, puppy, I think, and wriggle my dress up into a ruffle around my waist. Then I strap the cock around my waist so it protrudes out in front of me. Now I have a cock and I feel all funny. I touch its veiny surface. Then I walk about in it and check myself out in the mirror. I don't wear panties under the dress with no back, so it looks like I'm a white-skinned girl with a dark erection. I giggle.

'Stop it,' he says.

'Beg your pardon, sir,' I say, and turn to stare at his rubber face.

'It's not for fun. It's special.'

'Oh, I'm sorry, Arnaud. Well, I guess I better treat it and you with a little more respect.' He swallows: I approach. Looking from his mouth slit to the rubber cock, I start to feel all crazy inside. Suddenly I think of the men who have stuffed my pretty lips with their desperate organs, and I think on how I would like to do that to a girl sometimes. Just to be sucked by soft lips all covered in glossy lipstick. Men are real lucky on that account.

Arnaud never has a chance to flee. I step to him and seize his pony-tail that hangs in a girlish spout from out of the back of his hood. He cries out but I'm stuffing the rubber cock at his lips. 'Suck it.'

'No. Quit fooling, Missy.'

'I ain't fooling. Suck it, rock star. Suck my penis.'

'Missy, I said –' But suddenly, he can't speak with his mouth so full of rubber. 'This is what she does. Your girlfriend makes you suck her toy. I knew it,' I say, pumping his mouth. His hands struggle in the cuffs and his cock twitches between his legs. I unzip his hood because I want to see his sensual lips on the rubber. Me and Hank never did anything like this and never wanted to – we had other games – but the beauty of Arnaud is the flexibility of the boy. He just never stops surprising me. With the bond, he'd be something else. Especially with all those pretty Asian girls on tour. The thought gets me hot. I pull the cock free from his mouth so I can whip the hood off his face, and then up and over his pony-tail before throwing the deflated thing on the floor. Then I reach for his cuffs, getting even more excited by the sound of his speedy breathing and the size of his pupils. Unbuckling him, I speak quickly. 'You're going to suck this. You hear? Then you're going to let me suck yours. I'm in a sucking mood, Arnaud. I'm going crazy in this city, so don't start quibbling. If you want to get to this meeting, you do as I say.'

He nods, watching me with big eyes full of fear and excitement. With his wrists untied, his greedy paws go straight for my legs. Stroking them aggressively is his style and he always manages to ladder my hose, but this afternoon I don't care. Opening his mouth wide with closed eyes, Arnaud accepts my veiny shaft again. Gently, I push it in and out of his mouth and am pleased to see him sucking with passion. 'Next time you think you're hot shit and start strutting around like some rock star, just remember that a good ol' girl made you suck cock. That's right; the girl whose record collection you laughed at.'

Arnaud smiles over his mouthpiece and I cannot stop giggling. Suddenly I think of how fond of him I am and I promise myself to do something real nice for him. Since I blew into town there have been so many of my tantrums and wicked caprices. Love too, and laughs, but mainly my darkness and shooting heart pains have dictated the script. He's a dirty boy, I know, but there are few men I have met as generous as this pretty thing with Cheyenne hair.

'My turn,' I say, and fall to my knees so I'm facing him. We kiss hard and then flick our tongues together. It makes me think of how he likes to hold his whiskey and coke in his mouth before siphoning it between my lips when we kiss in bars. Stroking his cheeks, I whisper, 'Lie on your back. You've been such a good doggy.'

Smiling, Arnaud slips into position on the rug. I unbuckle the toy from around my waist and throw it aside. Frowning, he makes a little moaning noise when I push my dress down for comfort, so I pull it back up to my garter belt, remembering that he likes to look at my legs and pussy when I suck him. Now he's grinning again.

Right away, I take him deep inside my head and push my face right down to his dark thatch. With my long nails I tickle his balls that have a soft golden down on them. 'Mmm,' I sound through my nose, enjoying the salty taste of his meat. I never told Hank but Arnaud tastes so good; I reckon mother nature gave him this fragrance down here for the purpose of moistening the mouths of girls and ladies. I want to get his balls in my mouth too, but his stem is too long and I'd choke if I tried. So I just lather his firm contours and sup at all the little grey beads that seep from the top, which incites my need for a special kind of sustenance. Slowly, I withdraw the tight seal of my lips up his shaft and then off the purple tulip of his phallus. 'Please come in my mouth, sweetheart,' I say. My tone of voice has lost the cold and demanding edge it had when he was just a doggy. I use my tender voice now; the same one I use to coax him into doing unusual things to me in public. A voice I know he cannot resist.

'Maybe,' he says.

'Please, baby,' I say, because he likes a girl to plead for his cream. 'Please, honey. Let me have it in my mouth.'

'You sure? There's a lot of it today.'

'Mmm,' I moan through my nose. He thinks I'm pretending. That my wanting his brine down my throat is a big act to turn him on. He doesn't know that when I beg for his cream, I am actually desperate for it. His not knowing is the best part of it and that is my secret. 'Come on, baby,' I beg, and beat his cock with my hand. As Arnaud watches my greedy mouth paused for collection, and the action of my red nails on his pale cock-skin, his brow goes wrinkly between his eyes. He starts to gasp like someone dropped an ice cube down the back of his shirt and I know I'm nearly there. I mouth the words, 'Go on,' to him and flutter my eyelids a little. 'Let me taste you,' I whisper. His body goes all stiff and then it goes all soft. Out it comes. I can feel the muscles pumping in the palm of my hand. By holding my mouth wide open, an inch from the tip of his cock, I am able to catch every hot drop. Then I tilt my head back a fraction so it all stays inside my mouth, in a creamy pool around my teeth and gums and under my tongue. When my lips close, I savour the mouthful with shut eyes. Then it's all gone, into my tum.

As he catches his breath, I clean the rest from his phallus with a little suckling sound. 'Thank you, baby,' I say, and then unbuckle the harness from around his waist. 'You better get moving, Arnaud. You'll be a little late but that's what rockers do. They keep the suits waiting. If they start bitchin', tell them Missy was hungry.'

Arnaud kisses my mouth and then my forehead. 'You're crazy, girl,' he says, and it makes me go all warm to see the true affection in his eyes.

Arnaud had been gone about ten minutes, leaving me with my indecision about his right to the bond, when I heard the doorbell chime. I answered the door, opening it only a fraction so the caller would be unable to see my dress. Astonished, I saw a young man dressed in an old-fashioned bell-boy outfit, with a round hat on his handsome head and a blue uniform on his slender body. The uniform had gold braid on the sleeves and epaulets on the shoulders.

'Message for Miss Missy Lafeyette,' he said, and although he was smiling I detected a little anxiety in his general demeanour.

'Yes,' I said, still stunned.

He handed me a small card in a pale blue envelope. As I opened it, I felt my head go swoony and my tum get all fizzed up. It had her scent on the paper; the perfume in the Preacher's clothes. On the card was an address in the part of the square lining St Peter Street and St Anne Street. Below the printed address, she had written 'Come to me tomorrow morning' in a beautiful script that, strangely, made me more frightened than anything else, like it was indicating that the author was far smarter than me.

'Thanks,' I said to the courier, still shaken.

He didn't move.

'Sorry, a tip. I forgot.'

'No, miss. I don't take tips. My orders were to wait should you want anything else.'

'Anything else?' I queried.

He swallowed. 'Anything else from me, that is, miss.'

Now I understood. I opened the door wider and

225

watched his eyes just eat me up. Entering the spirit of my introduction, it seems the German was returning a favour. As Arnaud had made me so hot and was too distracted to service me properly, I decided to accept the gift. I held out my hand to the youth. 'Well, I guess you should come in, then.'

Thirteen

Across the street from her apartment, I wait in shadow and take a long draw on my third Salem 100 since leaving Nola's restaurant where I ate two portions of coconut cream pie with cinnamon ice-cream. Nerves keep getting the better of me. No matter how hard I try and concentrate on staying calm and not getting all clumsy and jittery, thoughts of her slinking through that alley will just go and tip a big table over inside me and send all of my hard bits crashing to the floor. Even the sight of her apartment frightens me. Her bankroll must be fat because she's staying in the French Quarter and her apartment is in one of the Pontalba buildings. Pastel-stucco fronts have suddenly given way to weathered brickwork when I find her place. There are no baskets of coloured flowers on her balcony either; the filigree is empty and dark.

After a big huffy breath, I stomp out my cigarette and then teeter across the road. To get to her apartment, I walk past an ironwork gallery and then duck into an entry that leads to a courtyard. Orange blossoms explode from the greenery and I take my sunglasses off for a second just to be dazzled by the garden at the rear of her apartment.

When I'm outside the lobby, I realise I need to press a buzzer for her to let me in. Now I'm going to

227

pieces. It's the thought of Hank being there that upsets me most. Why am I here? I suddenly think with more clarity than I did when blubbing down so many highways in his car to Louisiana. If he's with her then I'll just have to suffer another rejection. They won't believe that I'm just tracing my roots back to the precursor of my bond; curious about a bite in Berlin that carried on to a grooming of a seventeen-year-old girl in Texas, so many years later. Because Hank bonded with me, all three of us know what that means and they'll presume I'm just hanging around unable to breathe without the man who swore he'd love me for keeps. The indignity would kill me. How dare he leave me for an older woman? I think, in a burst of immodesty. Magazines always say it's the other way around. Fear and pain get me all dizzy again and I have a little cry, which annoys me further because my eye make-up could run.

We've made contact and I have to see her; no amount of scaredies can change that. It has to happen. Where is my evil? I ask myself. My desire to destroy her for taking what is mine? A score should be settled. No Lafeyette is good with grudges. I had two cousins in the state pen before they were 21 and they say my great-grandfather was pushed out of a tree with a rope around his neck. We're bad. I'm bad. Yes, sir.

I stand back from the reception door and check on my outfit in a reflection. All the traffic and rushing of people has failed to muss up my hair which has good Jackie O weight on top and a pretty curl on my shoulders. This pleases me. And the sight of my dress – Hank's favourite – all simple, black and sleeveless, like the one Audrey used to wear, gives me a spurt of strength. 'Girl, you're looking fine,' I mutter, and twist my leg around so I can check on my seams.

Straight as a preacher and longer than a memory, as the song goes; right up to where my hem goes tight an inch above my knees, which are shiny in coffee-coloured nylon. I'm ready.

She's on the second floor in number 3. I press the buzzer and feel one of my eyelashes go into a twitchy spasm. There is no sound of the buzzer working and because I'm wearing white gloves I wonder if I pushed it hard enough. I depress it again. Before I can stand back and try to dampen the sparks in my tum, there is a loud crackle from the rusty speaker panel. I jump and say, 'Oh, my,' which I hate to say on account of its mumsy nature which I am without.

'Hello, Missy,' she says in her European voice, like she's looking right at me.

I think of flight, then I panic and say, 'I'm come,' when I meant to say, 'I'm here.' I feel my face go hot and red and I curse myself for such silliness. There is no answer from her, so I say, 'It's Missy. I'm downstairs.'

'Yes,' she says in a distant way, like she's thinking of something else. I curse myself for introducing myself as Missy because she already knows that, and swear it's the last of my imbecile ways. Maybe I should be silent. That could freak her.

There is a click somewhere inside the lock. I pull the door open and walk into the lobby. All the stone on the floors and walls makes the air cool. I take my gum out, stick it under the old banister, and start climbing the stairs.

Silence seems to suck me up into the building. There is just the solemn clack of my slingback heels on the marble stairs but nothing else. Even the street sounds are gone. There are two other doors on the way up and I wonder who lives there. This place has a mystery that makes me quiver, but it suits her; I can feel this. The old French put these up way before the civil war and maybe even Napoleon once owned it, as Jefferson had to buy the town off him for a cool fifteen million. Was she here back then? There are so many years in her; I am overwhelmed by the thought of it.

Walking up to her front door is hard. I cannot feel my legs, and when I see that the door is already open, I am afraid she may come through it, grinning for me.

She doesn't and I peer into the gloom of her hallway. There is majesty here. Through the darkness, because she must have all the blinds closed, I can smell old, expensive things. 'Hello,' I call. A far-off voice says something that I don't catch. I creep further into the hallway and peer over the top of my shades to see where I am walking.

'Come,' a voice says from nearby. Sucking in all my breath in one go, I clamp a hand to my bosom. Looking about on all sides, frantically, I try and see her in the murk. How could she get so close? I think. Then I hear her again in the distance. There is no one near me then. Could it have been my imagination?

'Don't be afraid, child,' she says, and there is pleasure in her tone. Somewhere in this place, I know she is smiling.

I walk on with my back straight, concentrating on the placement of one foot before the other. It's all shadowy too in the dining room but I can still see the oil paintings on the walls in fancy frames. There are no lamps but big crystal chandeliers instead, hanging above my head. Behind all the shiny glass doors in the cabinets, I can see lots of treasure and in the middle of the dining table is a silver tea set. I feel all delicate inside and the air in this room feels heavy and seems to be pushing down on the top of my head.

'Come through, girl. Let me see you.' Her voice

comes from the side and I spin to face her, but all I can see is a dark doorway that leads to another room. I approach it, crossing red rugs with woven patterns that make me feel guilty for walking on them.

'My, aren't you a pretty one,' she says. I walk into the room, my skin all icy under the dress and my tummy threatening to make sounds. Squinting through the shadows, I see a large bed with a canopy – the largest bed I have ever seen. There are two small lamps behind me, by a drinks cabinet, but their light doesn't stretch much further than the pedestals they are mounted upon. Her smell is strong in here but all I can see is her shape on the bed. It is long and robed in black, stretching from where she is propped up among the big tasselled cushions.

'I apologise for the poor light,' she says. 'I'm resting my eyes. But your presence is soothing. The benefits of your visit are immediate.'

I smile and feel like I should curtsey, but all I do is tighten my hands over my little handbag and say, 'Thank you.'

'Pour yourself a drink. There is Bourbon and Scotch behind you. I imagine you drink whiskey. It's in your voice. Gin is my drink. Will you get one for me?'

'Sure,' I say, and walk to the cabinet, so conscious of her eyes on me. I fix her a gin – a big one – and pour myself a double Bourbon. I put a slice of fresh lime in hers from a little silver dish, using teensy tongs that I realise are probably for ice once I've finished the manoeuvre. The shot of Bourbon will help me relax and I can only hope gin will soften her. Last time I drank gin, though, I put a barstool upside a man's head.

With the drinks I walk back to the bed. She directs me to a chair beside her cushions by extending a pale

231

arm. 'Please,' is all she says, and I can't stop staring at her hands. They have the alabaster tint like Hank's skin. I imagine her fingers on the keys of a grand piano.

By the time I am beside the bed my eyes are more accustomed to the dim room. Black satin covers her eyes. So how did she see me while wearing a sleeping mask? I go all freezy as I sit in the chair. Usually I cross my legs the moment I sit down, and the whisper turns every man's head within earshot, but her spookiness makes me keep my knees and ankles locked together.

She wears a black silk gown over a floor-length slip. There is a trim of fine lace around the hem of the slip, just before her nylon-covered feet slide into thin-heeled slippers. Through the sheer sleeves of the robe, I can see the deathly pale skin on her slender, hairless arms.

'Relax. You are with friends,' she says. This makes me think there are people hiding in the room and I can't resist a quick peek behind me.

She raises her sleeping mask and leans towards me to take the drink. Everything slows to a standstill in me. She is beautiful. Never have I seen such a thin but perfect nose or a mouth that could make any pair of lips feel unworthy after their touch. But it is her eyes that drop me. It's like my face is lit up by them. They are jewels; large green jewels. 'Please,' she whispers, holding her dainty hand out for the heavy crystal glass I hold with a shaky grip.

'Sorry,' I squeak, and let her take the drink from my hand. She makes me think of Grace Kelly and I just want to stare at the perfection of her. When she took the bond I guess she was 25.

'Twenty-six,' she says and puts the glass to her red lips.

I look all shocked about the eyes; I know it and I can't stop it.

'We hear things,' she says, and reclines back to her cushions.

'Thoughts?' My voice is lost.

'You will too.'

'I will?'

'In time. In so much time.' She sounds sad. 'But don't be frightened of time. You can be immune to loss, also.' Now she is smiling again. 'We have so much to tell each other, and I am pleased you never came here with a pistol in your garter.' She laughs in a way to crush me all flat inside, and I panic that she can know my intentions to destroy her.

'I have caused you pain. Made you melancholy. I apologise,' she says and looks into my eyes, 'but it was unavoidable. It is history.'

I can think of nothing to say. She is inside me. I can feel her cold in my head.

'What spirit you have. How have you kept your warmth, I wonder. Maybe a strong man protected you, my angel.'

I swallow. 'Where is he?'

'Not here.' Concerning the rat, that is all she seems prepared to say. A long silence follows when we look at each other and I manage to keep my eyes level with hers. Reaching across to me with one hand, she strokes my cheek. 'And so much love in you, angel.' I give her regrets. I can feel this. 'Yes,' she says, smiling. 'I feel jaded next to you.'

I try and disagree because I feel an urge to please her, to make her keep smiling at me, but she speaks first. 'You want answers?'

'Yes,' I say, not knowing what I want any more.

'Sit beside me and hold my hands, pretty Missy.' I do as she bids. 'There, take them both and close your

233

eyes.' Her porcelain fingers grasp my hands and I sink into the cushions beside her. Sleepiness and a sense of well-being fill me up from her touch. All I can think of is whether I should put my shoes on the bed. 'Don't worry about them,' she whispers. 'Relax. Let me inside you. I want you to understand.'

It was like a long dream in the deepest sleep. So many of her memories were nothing but fragments. Many were in black and white. Others had fading tones. But those at the end were bright and vividly coloured.

Never had I seen so many lovers. Just the dreamy experience of them all left me exhausted. I struggled to comprehend the passing of so much time, was drained by the thought of so many broken hearts and saddened at the sight of so many wandering souls, still looking for her, who, in turn, were followed by other fresher souls, pining for their own masters or mistresses – their own branches of the bond.

It is a miracle her beauty survived the ravages of so many hands, mouths, teeth, ropes and chains. Sometimes I blush hot when remembering some of the things I have done in the cause of my love and freedom, but I forgave myself when made to consider the strength of her appetite.

In time I stirred to being half-awake. From this world of visions I suddenly found myself under the whims of her passing fascination with me. After she had shown me a dream where she was tutored by a handsome man in Vienna – a man who never smiled as he stretched her legs apart, and wrapped her arms to her body in strange corsets and with thin strips of leather – I had a notion that I was being undressed.

Down went my dress and I was eased on to my back. Without invitation, her slender fingers explored every tingly part of my skin between bra and sheer knickers, and between stocking tops and buttocks. Soft lips brushed my neck and ears. Claws ran along my sides and under me, from my shoulders and down my back. A thin tongue traced the V of my groin, sending ripples of loveliness to my puss. Tasted, inhaled, explored; she then opened my hot mouth in order to put her own upon it.

From these sensual arts she applied to my powerless and trusting body, it was not long before her will moved to more forceful applications.

As I saw her in my mind, dressed up in a corset, black nylons and the highest heels, with her arms strapped to a wooden pole that ran down the middle of her spine, my ankles and wrists were circled with rope, pulled apart and tied off so tightly my feet and hands went numb. Something slipped between my teeth and pulled the sides of my lips into an insane grin. The bitter taste of rubber filled my mouth. Just like her thin neck, so closely bound into position by the leather collar the man in the dream had put on her, I felt my own chin being raised to bare my throat.

Shivers passed all over my body. I found myself unable to move any limb or joint. I hung, suspended in the gloom of her hidden life, opened and splayed and readied.

Although I remember bracing myself for something sharp, and beginning to feel the first icy touch of fear that you can smell coming out of your pores, the touch of her lips between my legs was heavenly. Replacing her tongue at the exact moment I wanted a firmer touch on my pip, her long fingers slipped through the damp folds of my sex to rub me, hard. They entered me too and opened like scissors to stretch me. Not long after, I recall a moment when the lightning in my body threatened to extinguish my mind.

I was unable to writhe or shout. Besides the trembles in my muscles and the sheen of sweat that seeped across my flesh, I was forced to remain still, to contain the exquisite torture – the storm of delight and discomfort within my body. And this was a glimpse of her taste; her flirtation with submission, her craving for tight bonds, a tightrope walk above a shadowy world of dangerous passion. She liked to give herself to men. To relinquish her power for a while; a strength they would never comprehend. I understood that it was the gamble she enjoyed, the risk, the danger, the extremes she would experience. We were not dissimilar.

While she worked on me, driving me out of my mind, more visions were flashed into my head. I watched her hunt and trap. Confused in a ballgown, lost in dark streets, feigning sorrow in steamships, trains and then airports, she lit beacons with her vulnerability to summon food. Taken into alleyways, and inside the shadowy rear seats of long cars, ushered into hotel rooms and penthouse apartments, she was invited across thresholds by the poor and the mighty, the sadistic and the love-struck. I watched her mouth slide up and down the cocks of these helpful strangers, these protectors. I saw them bend her over or twist her into positions where her movement was strictly confined in their dim or glorious bedrooms, where they would use nylon cord or jewelled leather to bind her, and rough hands or crafted flails to beat her. And once they had brought tears to her eyes, and that smile to her wide and rapacious mouth, she took their hurried and desperate loving between her legs. She let them release reservoirs of lust inside her and over her beauty, and allowed them to adore and imprison her, but her smile never waned. It just changed when the fury of her feeding commenced. When she became master.

Something moved inside my sex as I remained stretched like a starfish. Something thick and ruthless was pushed into me. At first it teased my pip, circled it, nudged it, but when it squeezed through me I nearly bit through the strap between my teeth.

Filled and pummelled for what felt like hours – hour after hour of continuous, undimming, concentrated penetration to the very pit of me – I lost myself in climax after climax. She had been inside my head and learnt something of my own tastes – my love of the hunt, my delight in restraint, my crafty acts of playing the victim and little girl lost in the woods in order to gather good food – and then she showed me how this was merely an apprenticeship on my way to mastering the craft. Her craft. Were we the same?

When I briefly surfaced from the comatosing effects of her dreams and the peaks she constantly rubbed and fucked me towards, she was waiting with other stimulants.

The restraints were removed from my wrists and ankles, and her hands, now so kind, rotated my upper arms to soothe my shoulder joints, so recently punished from the stretching. My sleepy body was comforted and packaged within soft pillows. A strange oil, which made me tingle, was soothed into my sore parts. Kissed deeply, I felt the gag slip from my mouth as if the magic of her lips made it vanish.

Falling back under her spell, I experienced a curious half-sleep enlivened with more of her history.

She favoured men in uniform. Preferred the powerful. In a dozen countries, I saw these giants of war and finance and politics on their knees in her presence. I watched her ride them and feed from them until they tumbled at the hands of other giants, who were only too ready to take her along with the other spoils of invasion and conquest. Only she remained unconquered, always the victor, always adapting and surviving through civil wars, coups and conflict. There was so much suffering and so much pain all around her, but never did she succumb, even up to the moment when she became trapped in a city on fire and bombed from the sky. A ruined city in which she hid, as she had hidden so many times, until the moment was right for her to surface and begin again, overseas and on the winning side. The city was Berlin; her hiding place was a theatre.

I would have thrashed and fought to escape her enchantment, to evade my helplessness before this final story, but I found myself bound again – stuck fast, with my body bent over and my wrists tied to my ankles. Taken from the bed and positioned like a mannequin, she hooded me. Another layer had been added, so I could not escape the power of this final tale.

Crack! My buttocks were struck with a sting and heat so powerful my hood was filled with tears and the condensation of wet, panting breath.

Crack! The pain exploded across my flesh and ran its spikes through me. Even though my thighs were closed fast, I squeezed them together harder until my knees passed across each other like the ropes in a slip knot.

Crack! Falling forward, a hand then seized my garter belt and hauled me back into position. Honey seeped from me.

In the vision, I saw Hank and the Preacher, weary but still lithe despite the privations their battles had caused. On their knees in the cellar, they worshipped her. Hourglass in shape, she was redefined by a satin corset, and contoured by the elevation of Cuban-heeled shoes. Indifferent but mesmerising, it was as if her face had been painted with the brushstrokes of fine artists.

Inviting, slender, slippery, perfumed, she slid into bed and offered herself to the beasts. Suddenly spluttering, her hair in disarray, her skin marked, they thrust into her mouth and sex, through her hands and inside her anus. Engulfed by them, strapped by them, tied down by them, she was made to climax again and again until her lovers were exhausted. Then she fed.

Covering them in the dark, wrestling their hands away from her mouth, tugging their stiff cocks back inside her, she prepared them. And then bit them – sinking her ancient needles into unblemished American skin.

I groaned inside my hood at the sight of Hank's thick cock oozing inside her pinky folds. She showed me the close-up of his mouth tearing at hers, of his hands desperately squashing her breasts into bruises, and his nose rifling through her hair.

He took his belt to her in the way he threw that thin snake, with its delicious bite, at my bottom. He held her wrists and pushed them into the pillows behind her blonde head, restraining her so she was still and compliant for the hardest of his muscles; the one he loves to plunge into the most sacred softness in a woman. The softness that he craved most of all in me. This was the way he loved me; so ruthless, so thorough, so deep. Her hair is the same colour as mine. Our lips have been forged by the same mould. Our length and legs and breasts were sculpted to be similar. My eye make-up is the same, my heels just as high as hers, my nylons just as sheer, my brassières as fine as those she wore for him, my French knickers slit in the same way. No, I wanted to say. Even the sharp and the square bits of our faces could be matched. No, I tried to cry.

Crack! The stingy thing hit my thighs. My claws came out. I wanted her throat. Let this kitten free.

Crack! She showed me the years of their love and the fire in my man's eyes every time he looked at her. No!

Crack!

No!

Crack!

No!

Crack!

Eventually, my fire smouldered out. Dozing to the sleepy warmth of defeat, I knew my fight had slipped away. My eyes grew heavy and my mind began to shut itself off to her film. With my arms and legs wrapped together, and my body strapped up, and my head hooded but made to watch these scenes, I was beaten by her evil. But despite this storm, this electric weather she poured over me, I was still aroused. Dampened by her blows and made sticky from the restraints, I wanted more of her. To be shown my man loving her, and then to realise it was her he sought in me, and only her, I loathed her but desired her. It was madness; an animal madness that made me sacrificial in a way that shocks me now. But there is no other way with this one. She is too strong and could break any marriage or promise made between lovers, just to investigate and revel in the results. Evil like her should never have been given such beauty; it only breaks things.

Perhaps she was trying to send me beyond jealousy. To her, my love for Hank was a twisted thing that stifled and retarded my freedom and my will. Invulnerable to deeper attachments, she has remained free. This in itself has become her addiction. Her bond is to liberty which has always allowed her to leave the lover when another fine body whets her appetite. Maybe this is the only way to survive so much time.

Younger and fresher and more innocent than the man I loved, she finally showed me Hank's despair and devotion by turns. The madness in him. She showed me her departure from his lean body and defined features into the arms of another man; someone willing to transport her into yet another life.

As I looked at the broken thing that Hank became with his drink and slumpy shoulders – the ruin she fled and left without hope or joy – I felt something warm and long slip inside me from behind. She made it feel like a man was taking me from behind, but it was her. I could feel her nails on my waist and her thighs rubbing against my damp stockings. Another implement, then. Another instrument to take me away from the longing for Hank and to turn my passion towards the torment and delights she offered, crafted over so many years and with so many lovers. She pleasured me in heartbreak to show me that a bonded girl must never fall into wretchedness or routine. There were always fresher delights. It was a tempting philosophy.

And so she pushed herself inside me and rubbed me with skill, until she was thrusting at me with the strength of any man. I came; I fainted.

I had been selected as her new companion. When I came to, I could tell this by the way she kissed me. After finally freeing me from her ropes and cords, she had taken me between her sheets to love me. Pressing her thin but soft body against me, she kissed me, took my breasts in her mouth, nuzzled her head into mine, purred down my ears, and squeezed me so tightly it was like she never wanted to let me go. Never had I been kissed so passionately or bitten so finely. Never had I begged for more of that sharpness and surrendered so much – not even when I was in high school and used to sneak out of the house at night to see Uncle Hank across town, dreaming of the strength in his jaws.

How long did I sleep for? Exhausted by pain that became delight and overwhelmed by the caresses that were gifts from a goddess, I remembered nothing more until I awoke, still beside her, in that ancient room. Dressed and refreshed, it was like nothing had ever happened to me. We were in the same position as before I took her hand. Only the refilled glasses beside the bed suggested that she had moved since I had been under her spell. And beside me, she was smiling.

I watched her beautiful fingers move a cigarette holder to her lips. It was embraced by those dark lures and sucked upon before a long stream of fragrant smoke was blown from her mouth towards the ceiling.

'Why did you come back?' I asked.

'It was time to return from exile.'

'From where?'

'A place I had been for many years.'

I frowned at her, but my face softened the moment she hypnotised me again with her elegant smoking. 'There is a special place I go to from time to time. A convent. A place I founded for bonded women. It has such peace.' She closed her eyes. 'And there are a devoted few who serve our needs.' She smiled and then exhaled her fragrant smoke. 'We cannot always be on the move. Sometimes we need to pause, to recover, to look back on experience and then turn it to wisdom. But the world keeps changing while you are away.'

'But why come here?'

'To learn from my most recent converts. To have them show me the new world and all of its glory. Also, I had a special fondness for those boys.'

'They were trying to kill each other.'

She sighed. 'Sometimes this happens. Even the numbers of our own race must be kept in check.'

This made me swallow.

'Why not be my new guide, Missy.'

I stiffened.

'Trust me and show me this world. In return I will tutor you. Cultivate you. Polish you. And share pleasure. Show you things that will keep you in harmony with time. With so much time.'

'What about Hank? I thought you came back for him.'

'I made an offer. He declined.'

Something like a heartbeat seemed to start thudding behind my face. I went dizzy.

'Yes, princess,' she said. 'He chose you – the only woman I have been overlooked for. Ever. So are you surprised I had to meet you, angel? A girl who saved a man from his original bond. This I have never known. So it was you I needed. Not him.'

'Where did he go?' I asked, unable to see much of her any more because of the salty springs that wet my eyes.

'Away to the places men usually go to forget women that have possessed them. You should be proud of him. It was hard for him to say no to me. But there was a part of me he could never accept. Something that developed in time. Something I once thought was ugly. That is, until I accepted its pleasures.'

I was unable to speak. With frost powdering my skin, I watched her long fingers part the gown in her lap. Resting against her pale thigh, beneath the gossamer of her French knickers, was a small penis. Half-hidden by the golden floss on her groin, it rested; a strange twin to her other sex. Suddenly, I was reminded of that strange length she plied inside me from behind.

'There is something in those legends of mermaids,' she said, and then laughed.

Shock kept me silent. This I did not expect. But it was not without beauty, seeing it framed by fine fabrics, above stocking tops and beneath the gauze-sheer mound of her small tummy. I was glad I had felt it inside me.

'You really want me?' I finally said.

'I wanted to give you a choice. A future with me or one without me. We could both benefit. I need someone to help me hunt, Missy. Like we did the other night, at the club. It was so fine. Have you ever felt so alive?'

Her hand rested against my cheek. 'Go now and think of my offer.'

Somehow I managed to leave the beautiful and enchanted creature on her big bed and find my way to the door and the last of the sunlight outside. As I walked to Arnaud's place, capable of seeing nothing around me, I made my decision.

Fourteen

'I am disappointed with your decision,' she says, the moment I am standing in her vast dining room. I haven't even spoken yet, but with her you don't need to.

Without turning her head to look at me, she cradles a cigarette and gazes down at the street below her window. A haze of smoke adds another filter to her beauty that is already veiled by a fine net, hanging over the top half of her face from the little hat perched on the front of her head. Dressed in black, her outfit has all the elegance that the simplicity of a single colour and fine cut can give. I know she has always possessed and will always maintain this forlorn grace about her – the sad beauty that puts an ache in the heart of any hapless and sensitive soul that dares to look upon her. So fragile, so perfect, so deadly.

Her thin eyebrows rise and, at last, she turns to me. 'Disappointed, but not broken. Never broken.'

'Others have been.'

She smiles. 'By me? Yes. By you also, I think. Broken by all of us with the bond, but they have been given an obsession they would never be without. A craving to outlast all their other secrets. A glimpse of our bond is a gift. Those we have loved see through the eyes of gods, Missy. Do you know how many

245

artists I gave immortality to? Not in the life that you and I walk through, but in the work they left behind.'

I would like to hear about them all, spend years listening to her stories, but I'm afraid to stay for too long. If I do then I may change my mind from a decision I know to be right.

I think of the Preacher lying in the dust. 'I meant that some with the bond are broken too.'

Her smile stiffens and she looks icy. 'I know what you mean, girl. But we can never be entirely sure how individual spirits will adapt. That is why we must be careful with our choices.'

I nod, knowing all too well about that. 'You know I can't go with you, even though a big part of me wants to. It's just that I feel I'd have to lose what's left of my heart. I know I'm bad and all, but some say I have a big heart and whatever they see in me I want to keep hold of.'

She looks at me like I'm a child who's said something foolish but amusing on account of its innocence.

'But there is something I must ask,' I say. 'There is one man I was careless with. He is stuck halfway between. Maybe I'm out of line, but this man needs your help. I just can't bond with him even though he's so right for it. And right for all of you, ma'am. If you know what I'm implying. Well, I was thinking he could show you the world you want to see. And every corner of it too through his line of work. He's a rock . . . a musician.'

She stays quiet, but I can see she's thinking on my proposal.

'If you can't help, I'll understand.'

She looks over my shoulder at the front door. 'Come in, boy.'

I stand aside and wait for Arnaud to appear. Clad

in soft leather trousers, so tight around his slender hips and bottom, and a black silk shirt, open to his belt, he walks into the room. Sensing her significance, he bows his head, keeping his eyes on his boots.

She points her cigarette at a seat beside the dining table. I go and sit down. When I'm seated, I realise I'm hurting myself by digging my nails into the palms of my hands. And with my corset so tight too, all the pressure starts to make me feel dizzy. She just has to take Arnaud from me. Otherwise, I have no idea what I can do with him.

As he stands before her, I can see him shivering. Smiling, she places a long red fingernail under his chin and raises his face. There is no communication between them. Not the kind I can hear, anyway. They just stand staring at each other as she goes through him with her other sense.

'Terrible,' she mutters.

No! I want to cry out, before telling her about his loveliness.

'Dissolute. Undisciplined. A drunk. A whore. Garbage that blows through the streets of night. An urchin,' she adds, showing me her stern face.

She walks away from him and takes another cigarette from a box on a polished table beside the window. 'Undress.'

Arnaud looks at me, confused and afraid.

'Take your eyes from her and do as I ask,' she says, concentrating on lighting her cigarette.

It's hard for me, but I lower my eyes and leave the boy all alone on the rug before her. Slowly, he sheds his shirt and the dim light shines on his lean body and all the intricate designs on his skin. By placing toes to ankles he levers each biker boot off his feet. When his leather trousers are discarded, only his long hair remains to clothe him.

Disinterested and aloof, as if inspecting furniture, she walks around him, close but not touching. 'Open your mouth,' she asks.

Tilting his head back, Arnaud opens his mouth. She looks inside and then nods. 'Go through the door to my chambers,' she says, and points in the direction of her room. Naked and without pride, Arnaud moves through the doors to her bedroom. She follows, pausing as she draws level with me. 'I make no promises. And it would take time for me to be sure. Although this is not how it works, girl, I feel I owe you something in return for all the things I have broken. You are fortunate I have experience with slaves.'

'I couldn't ask for anything more, ma'am. Just that you would look him over.'

She nods and then walks into the room.

A long silence follows. I sit still, straining my ears and occasionally peering over my shoulder at the doorway. Just when I am prepared to take a peek, desperate to know how Arnaud is faring, I hear him cry out.

Trembling, I rise from my chair and tiptoe towards the door. Her teeth must be clenched because I can hear her snarling. There is something swishing through the air and then there are the wet sounds of hard slaps. From one side of the doorway, I peek into the gloom. All I am able to see are flashes of white skin and her blonde hair. I blink and let my eyes adjust to the dark.

Her white face shakes with rage but not a hair has fallen from place among those pins beneath her hat. Still dressed in her elegant suit and hat, she has Arnaud on the floor. Legs sprawled, he tries to get to his knees, but the leash she has him fastened to is short, and where her gloved hand moves his body is dragged with it. Across his back and bottom and thighs, she goes at him with a little whip. This is necessary for him to realise, right away, that no liberties could ever be taken.

Hissing, she drags him to the bed and makes him scrabble on to the mattress. As he turns and falls on his back, I see his long cock is rigid. Good boy, I think, and nod in approval. Grasping his pretty hair, she yanks his head forward and makes him stare at his own lap. While he looks at his betrayal, she whispers things into his ears that make his face change through so many expressions of torment until a state of bliss fills his big eyes.

Whatever hopes he entertained about the bed are dashed when he is suddenly plunged to the floor. On the thick rug at her bedside, he squirms on his back, as she makes herself comfortable, slowly crossing her longs legs above his face. I wince and then look away when her sharp heels go down on him. Although I hide my eyes I can hear more whispering from her and groaning from him.

Unable to control my habit of sinful peeking, I look again, terrified of what I may see. Brought to heel and in no doubt of her power, temper or strength, Arnaud's face is being rolled about on the floor with her foot. The cruel shoes have been removed. With the long toes of one of her feet hooked around his nose, she shoves his head about; with the other slender foot, she inspects his cock. If his hands rise from his sides, she cracks her whip across the bony parts of them. They only rise once in all the time I am looking.

Good, good boy.

Without a murmur, he is kicked on to his front and allows cuffs to be attached to his hands. No sound comes from him either when a rubber hood is yanked tight over his face. In her stockinged feet, she then walks to her dressing table. Slowly, she unclips her earrings and removes items of sharp jewellery which are placed in boxes. From her table, she crosses the room to a dressing screen, and removes her suit. Each item of clothing – jacket, skirt, slip, scarf, nylons, gloves, garter belt, French knickers – is carefully folded and placed along the top of the screen she shields herself behind. Arnaud's wait is agonising, but he does not even twitch on the floor where she left him, blind and cuffed.

Held by the leash, he is then pulled to the bed where he cringes in the middle of the vast mattress. Naked, with her blonde hair swaying about her chin and throat, she goes to him. Flushing hot under my clothes, I see her position him lengthways. With a little shudder, I watch her head fall to his lap. Arnaud's body tenses when all of his length is consumed. Like that of a sword swallower I once saw at a carny, her face then withdraws right to the tip of his cock before releasing it. She stares at the ceiling with her eyes closed and moves her tongue around her mouth, examining his taste. I know it to be good and she does too. There is a flicker of a smile on her china face, before it descends to suckle once more.

Oiled and shiny, his meat is now prepared and extends into the air. Grinning in a way that unsettles me, she tousles her hair and then falls upon his cock so quickly, I hardly see her move or spread her legs. But the ripe organ is now inside her. Digging her claws into his smooth skin around his nipples, she rises and falls, slowly at first, but then with a vigour that makes me long for the removal of my own skirt.

Slapping her sex on to his groin, she spits and murmurs things in foreign words. Arnaud forgets himself and reaches for her breasts with cuffed hands. A mistake. The fingers are bitten.

On and on she drives herself, whipping his cock into her sex, banging her spot against his bones, forcing his bulbous head to the top of her velvet pocket. And Arnaud holds on. In his stifling darkness, with smitten hands that have been refused a touch of her royal softness, he moans in a desperation to touch her intimacy with his cream. Not yet, boy, she warns, by slapping his face and lining his stomach with red welts. She'll take his seed when she requires it and not before.

For an age she pounds against him, writhing and plunging and squashing herself into a frenzy until, finally, she starts to moan. Her noises are like the groans of the bereaved – long and full of anguish. When her pale back arches and she sinks her nails into his forearms, this eternal widow climaxes. Only then, at this moment of finality, does Arnaud dare to contribute. As she trembles in his lap, he thrusts his buttocks upward and turns her moans into little yelps. The slave is rewarded; he is allowed to fill her with the essence of his labours. Not a drop is spilled. What is not taken inside her womb is supped like a spicy gravy from his pale meat.

She cleans her lips and begins to laugh. I return to my chair. It would be unwise to watch the beauty of her feeding or to stare at the erect surprise between her thighs that still awaits Arnaud. I clasp my hands over my ears to shut out the music of her teeth.

With shaking fingers, I then light a cigarette. I am not kept waiting for long. Invigorated, she glides from the room, wrapped in a green kimono. Her make-up is perfect, her long feet left bare, her shiny hair rearranged – as if she has done nothing more than left the bathroom, untouched by a lower breed. In her eyes, though, there is a wildness that makes me envious. When she speaks, her words are slightly slurred too. 'Wonderful. I must compliment your taste. I would offer him to you, but perhaps it is best he is made to forget the touch of your sweet lips.'

A lump forms in my throat. With this, she means Arnaud is now lost to me, for ever. I should feel relief, but I can't. I allow her to torment me a little with her smiling glee; it is only right after I refused her offer.

She pours herself a drink and lights another cigarette. 'You have regrets?'

'No. I am pleased he may have a future with you.'

'That remains to be seen. I may, however, go to Europe with him. A little earlier than I anticipated, but I will try him for your sake.'

'Thank you.'

'You're welcome.'

I walk to the door of her bed chamber and look at the shape in her bed, still hooded and bound. 'Bye, baby,' I call out, but my voice goes all quivery and I turn away.

I jump backward. She has crossed the room and is now standing right behind me – guarding her meal. I move to step around her but my elbow is held. She leans forward and kisses me on the lips, the nose, and then the forehead. 'Go to your rogue, angel. Make him forget me and be content.'

Unable to speak, I close my eyes and feel her slip around my body. When I open my eyes she is gone – vanished into the dark of her room. In my hand is a card with the convent's address upon it. At my feet is the emerald gown made from silk.

Fifteen

'The man who put this song on the jukebox, where is he?' I ask the barkeep.

'Girl, if you can get him to leave, you drink for free all day.'

I raise an eyebrow at the podgy man who polishes glasses behind the long bar.

'Don't get me wrong, I like Hank Williams as much as the next man. Jeez, I was raised on Hank Senior, but this guy's been feeding quarters into that machine to the value of ten bucks a time just to play the same song, over and over. Yesterday, I went to unplug the damn thing, but the look he gave me changed my mind. He's a good customer, but I got other customers too and I just can't take no more of this song.' The barkeep nods his head towards the back. 'He's over there.'

I smile. 'I'll see what I can do.' Walking through the empty bar, I struggle to keep my mind all in one piece. Hank is in here drinking hard and playing his favourite song, 'I'm So Lonesome I Could Cry', performed by his namesake, Hank Williams. After leaving the German, it didn't take me long to find him in Orleans; I followed my ears and the tingle in my tum.

I approach him from behind. He's bent over the table in a booth, facing the wall. An ashtray is full of Marlboro butts and there is a bottle of Wild Turkey with the label half peeled away beside his Zippo lighter. With the collars of his coat turned up, Hank's face is concealed from me.

'Hey now,' I say, and come to a standstill beside him. He turns his head towards me but I can't see his eyes on account of him wearing his shades. One arm is tucked under his coat and I guess he's wearing a sling. He clenches his jaw.

'They say you shouldn't drink and take painkillers.'

A faint smile appears on his lips and I go all shivery. 'They be right,' he says. 'You have a choice, the bottle or the pill. I made mine.'

With his one good hand he waves me towards the bench on the other side of his booth. Then he goes to stand up because I'm a lady and some men in the South still follow a code.

'Don't get up,' I say. His face goes a bit shaky and I hear his teeth grind together; locked on the moan he wants to let out on account of recently having a bullet tugged from his shoulder.

I sit down and cross my legs under the table. Out of habit, he listens for the whisper and then he looks at the table top. 'Drink?'

'Sure,' I say. I splash whiskey in a tumbler.

Nobody says anything for a while. So much has happened and I'm not sure who should apologise or where we stand with each other any more. We just smoke and drink the whiskey and look at our hands on the table.

'I met her,' I venture, because with this man we could be still here when all the stools are put on the tables with no word having passed between us. Sometimes it makes a girl crazy.

Hank doesn't even twitch. 'I figured.'

'She asked me to go along with her.'

He stays quiet but I hear him swallow. I wait,

254

keeping silent myself. Hank drains his glass and then dips his head. He picks up his Zippo and I can see his thumb all white on the inscription, from all the pressure he's applying to the tarnished metal. Guess he's had enough.

'She's an interesting woman.'

He nods but keeps his face down.

'But not everybody's taste. Not mine.'

Slowly, he raises his face to me. There is a shiny trickle coming from under his glasses. He clutches one of my hands and I close my other hand on top of it. Rare I see this man break down. Seen him with fevers and delirium and pain, but hardly ever what you would call an expression of strong emotion. But this man is crying softly to himself.

'Guess you told her the same thing too,' I say, but my voice has gone all cry-baby too.

He nods. He sniffs. He says, 'God damn it,' and then shakes his head a bit. 'Guess we ain't through like some thought,' he adds in a whispery voice he's trying to get together again.

I swallow. 'Maybe not. But for all the years we been going steady not so much has changed. In the past few weeks it could be said everything changed.'

'Could be, two people needed a shake-up,' he says, looking down again.

'My thoughts too. But I done some bad things while you were gone, Hank.'

He nods and takes his hand away to touch his heart. 'Felt it here.' Hank then puts his hand back in my warm palms.

'But a girl gets all confused when a man has secrets. Don't think she can be blamed too much.'

'She ain't blamed any.'

'Really?'

'Said so, didn't I?'

'Only I'm afraid I've changed some. After all that happened in Texas and what I learned from the Preacher and then the German cellar woman, I've gone all cold and empty inside. All this rotten jealousy over your bond and all has bust me up. Just like Preacher and Val and everyone else.'

Hank removes his glasses. The rims of his eyes are red. With his index finger, he dabs the side of my mouth and then waves the tip of his finger before my eyes. On the tip of his finger is a big crumb of the jelly donut I ate for breakfast. He starts to grin and then laugh in his wheezy, teasy way. I feel my face get all hot from rage on account of this belittling.

'No, girl,' he says, before I can go off like two barrels. 'You ain't like Val, or Preacher, or me. More than anything else, you're nothing like her. You're better than that.'

Unable to resist the smile in his stone-grey eyes, I end up giggling too. I recall what Val said about my quality and if Hank can still see it in a donut crumb then that's OK with me. Yessum.

He squeezes my fingers, gently. 'It's why I kept it from you, Missy – all the people and the history we had between us that could have put your fire out and hardened your heart. That's why there was no agency for you like there was for Val, and why there were so many secrets. Then there was my shame too, with everything I'd done. Especially to friends. I didn't want you to ever see that side of me.'

'But everybody has got to grow up.'

'There's a difference between growing up and giving up. Now, I came down here to settle things with Preacher and the woman who gave me the bond. In Orleans, I planned to tell you the whole story, and let you meet all the concerned parties. Had it all planned out, but some people at the agency just got in the way. Bit off more than I could chew, girl, to keep you out of it. But whatever you did to Val saved us. She came through because you came through, even though you thought I was going to split down here.'

'Always trusted you –' I snap, but Hank shushes me by holding his hand up and fixing me with his eye.

'Yes, you did. Put up with more than you deserve and I lied to you about the woman on the plane, which is why this all went crazy. So there's no blame coming your way.'

I go silent and swallow. There is something else I have to know. 'About the Preacher – about Karl, I mean. Did you get my warning, the vision?'

Hank rubs my thumb. 'Yes, I did.'

'So why did you just come sauntering up to the house and walk right into his trap?'

'Cus, by then, I knew he had you and that the agency had betrayed me. I wanted to meet him face to face. Owed it to him.'

'Val said you talked. What was said?'

'I told him the German was all his. That I wouldn't stand in his way. All I cared about he had, locked away. Preacher said no. That he was gonna teach me about pain. What it feels like to lose a lover and a brother in one swoop. Knowing the time for talking was up, and seeing something in his eyes that no words could fix, I drew on him.'

'He had a good side too. I saw it.'

'Yes, he did.' Never heard Hank sound so tired when he said that.

'So all this time you had no intention of going back with her?'

He nods. I feel foolish.

Hank strokes my cheek with the back of his hand. 'Don't you see, girl? Even all your nippin' at me and your going off at the drop of a hat like a wildcat, is part of the reason I love you. Why I couldn't love anyone else.' He nods and clears his throat. I am in shock. 'You got something to bring this boy to his knees. And you always have. You're a dream, girl, that I never want to wake from. There, I said it now.'

Hank's never said so many nice things to me in one go. Usually, I don't get words to go on, just changes on his face. I want to kiss him and I can feel water in my eyes, but I just got to hold off a moment longer.

'That right?' I say. 'Then you're through running for the agency. You want me back, they're not coming with you. That's my final thought on the matter. I want things simple.'

'Me too,' he says, agreeing straight away. This throws me off-guard. 'Me and Val fixed it so I'm dead. Time I thought about retirement, honey. About spending all these years showing my girl the world. Seems to me that we should do things right too. Might seem crazy with our lifestyle, but I got other plans too. That is if you'll have me. What do you say to making things permanent?'

Somehow I get to be sitting on his knee without hurting his poorly arm. Somehow we get to be making up for everything with this kiss I want to last for ever.

'Now you just lie there and keep that shoulder still. Let Missy take the strain. How's that?'

'Fine,' he says. 'Real fine.' He smiles from among all the cushions I've fashioned around him. Never thought we'd have such a sedate wedding night, but I can't say that I've ever been so happy. Even Val came down for the service and bought us our solitary wedding present – two tickets to Thailand. Our honeymoon.

'Guess it's been a while,' I say, and slip my man's beautiful cock inside me.

258

He groans but not from pain. 'Long time.'

I look him in the eye and give him the most wicked smile. 'Must be hard on a man. Me, I just can't go without.'

He gulps and I know his mouth has gone all dry. 'You don't say.'

'Oh, yeah, Missy needs her loving. That's for sure.'

He stays quiet, but I feel him trying to slip further inside me by pushing his buttocks off the big bed.

I start to squeeze my nips and feel my eyes go all sleepy from the feel of his thickness, welcomed back to its rightful home. 'Now that I'm an honest woman, though, I've been wondering on if I could be good. If it's possible, that is. You know, for a pretty girl like me with an older husband. They say it's hard.'

'They do.'

I speed up the rotations of my puss on his fat stem. 'She might have needs.'

He closes his eyes. 'I guess.'

'Extra-marital needs.'

His breathing goes all raspy. His one good hand slides up my thigh, whispering along the pretty white stockings I wore for the service.

'Girl's got to eat, baby,' I say.

'Uh-huh.'

'Yes,' I say. When his fingers find my sex, my neck goes loose on my shoulders. Never felt anything so good as those fingers picking at my puss again. 'As long as she's straight and tells the older guy about where she's been, it could work.'

Hank just can't hold back. Warmth floods inside me, collects, and then coats the parts of us that are bonded.

'But you know, she could only ever love one man,' I say.

His one good hand collects the back of my head and lowers my face to his mouth. We kiss.

NEW BOOKS

Coming up from Nexus, Sapphire and Black Lace

Devon Cream by Aishling Morgan
March 2000   £5.99   ISBN: 0 352 33488 6
Devon Cream traces the history of the innocent but wilful Octavia Challacombe as she is corrupted by the wicked Maray family. Along with the bouncy Polly Endicott and a group of other buxom Devon girls, she is cajoled and teased, first into providing her own breast milk for the Squire and then into increasingly perverse services. Her unabashed pleasure in her own sexual enjoyment lasts through spankings, bondage and ever more peculiar uses for her milk, until finally she takes her revenge. By the author of *The Rake*.

Police Ladies by Yolanda Celbridge
March 2000   £5.99   ISBN: 0 352 33489 4
Deep in the Scottish highlands a curious training academy teaches young women how to pound a beat. Restrictive uniforms, strict training and the special use of truncheons characterise the Glenlassie approach to police training – but the recruits are slowly being siphoned off by a neraby pony-girl training establishment and a unique medical clinic. By the author of *The Discipline of Nurse Riding*.

Conduct Unbecoming by Arabella Knight
March 2000   £5.99   ISBN: 0 352 33490 8
Deep in the English countryside, a group of patriotic young Wrens are doing their bit for the war effort, interrogating women who may or may not have slept with senior enemy officials. Some are willing to talk; others are not so forthcoming. And that's where Captain Cordelia Quidenham comes in. Together with her small, efficient and perfectly formed team, Cordelia applies every method of persuasion to wring information out of her quivering subjects – especially methods that involve the smack of leather on flesh. A Nexus Classic.

Plaything by **Penny Birch**
April 2000   £5.99   ISBN: 0 352 33493 2
The latest book in the Penny Birch series continues with bad girl Penny's dirtiest antics yet. After going a whole month without doing anything naughty, she is desparate to be even more filthy, despite her imminent departure to Brittany where she is instructed to set up a university field course. Once there, her academic responsibilities get pushed aside for the more deliciously rude indulgences in knicker-wetting, anal play and her old favourite, pony-girl carting. This time, however, she will encounter a French voyeur called Tom, whose penchant for dirty fun will shock even Penny and her playmates. By the author of *Bad Penny* and *Brat*.

Slave Sentence by **Lisette Ashton**
April 2000   £5.99   ISBN: 0 352 33494 0
Chained in his own dungeon, former master McGivern is at the mercy of punishments far crueller than any he ever devised. The torture he receives is perverse, degrading and always sexually humiliating. Determined to overthrow his gaolers he forms an uneasy relationship with the most sadistic of his female tormentors and agrees to all her demands in his bid to regain control of the castle. But his greatest fear is that he will come to enjoy his bondage before he can return to his dominant position. By the author of *The Slave Auction*.

Candy in Captivity by **Arabella Knight**
April 2000   £5.99   ISBN: 0 352 33495 9
Candy Brompton is a smart ambitious girl working her way up in the world of real estate. When she journeys to a remote Hebridean island to investigate the sale of a castle her life is set to change irrevocably. She stumbles upon an all-female community who adhere to a lifestyle of strict discipline, and who intend to make her one of their bond-maidens. Delightfully painful consequences await those who are disobedient, and Candy's independent streak guarantees that judicious use of the cane will be employed before she knows what's happening to her. Very soon, a sore bottom and injured pride will be a prelude to the exquisite joys of submissive games. A Nexus Classic.

SAPPHIRE

A new imprint of lesbian fiction

Getaway by Suzanne Blaylock
October 1999   Price £6.99   ISBN: 0 352 33443 6
Brilliantly talented Polly Sayers had made two big life shifts
concurrently. She's had her first affair with a woman, and she's also
stolen the code of an important new piece of software and made her
break, doing a runner all the way to a seemingly peaceful coastal
community. But things aren't as tranquil as they appear in the haven,
as Polly becomes immersed in an insular group of mysterious but
very attractive women.

No Angel by Marian Malone
November 1999   £6.99   ISBN 0 352 33462 2
Sally longs to test her limits and sample forbidden pleasures, yet she's
frightened by the depth of her yearnings. Her journey of self-
discovery begins in the fetish clubs of Brighton and ultimately leads
to an encounter with an enigmatic female stranger. And now that
she's tasted freedom, there's no way she's going back.

BLACK
lace

Fire and Ice by Laura Hamilton
March 2000   £5.99   ISBN: 0 352 33486 X

Nina, auditor extraordinaire, is known as the Ice Queen at work, where her frigid demeanour makes people think she's equally cold in bed. But what her colleagues don't know is that Nina spends her after-work hours locked into fiery games with her boyfriend Andrew, one in which she acts out her deepest fantasy – being a prostitute. Nina finds herself being drawn deeper and deeper into London's seedy underground, where everything is for sale and nothing is what it seems.

Wicked Words 2 ed. Kerri Sharp
March 2000   £5.99   ISBN: 0 352 33487 8

Black Lace anthologies have proved to be extremely popular. Following on from the success of the *Pandor's Box* and *Sugar and Spice* compilations, this second *Wicked Words* collection continues to push the erotic envelope. The accent is once again on contemporary settings with a transgressive feel – and the writing is fresh, upbeat in style and hot. This is an ideal introduction to the Black Lace series.

Gothic Blue by Portia Da Costa
March 2000   £5.99   ISBN: 0 352 33075 9

Stranded at a remote Gothic priory, Belinda Seward is suddenly prey to sexual forces she can neither understand nor control. She is drawn into a world of decadence and debauchery by the mysterious aristocrat André von Kastel. He has plans for Belinda which will take her into the realms of obsessive love and the erotic paranormal. This is a Black Lace special reprint.

Sauce for the Goose by Mary Rose Maxwell
April 2000   £5.99   ISBN: 0 352 33492 4

Sauce for the Goose is a collection of exceptionally filthy stories from the pen of a talented female author of erotic fiction. With fetishes and settings to suit all tastes, these lusty tales are guaranteed to amuse and arouse. From sleazy high jinx in the office to the dirty locker-room antics of the armed forces, a naughty sense of shame runs throughout.

Hard Corps by Claire Thompson

April 2000   £5.99   ISBN: 0 352 33491 6

The strong persona of army cadet Remy Harris belies a secret submissive, desperate to explore the realms of sadomasochism. Introduced to an elite secret society known as the Hard Corps, where slaves are bound and used for the pleasure of their masters and mistresses, Remy changes from virgin to slut, and learns to submit with grace and control. That is until one day a master goes too far and Remy fights back.

NEXUS BACKLIST

All books are priced £5.99 unless another price is given. If a date is supplied, the book in question will not be available until that month in 2000.

CONTEMPORARY EROTICA

THE ACADEMY	Arabella Knight		
BAD PENNY	Penny Birch		
THE BLACK MASQUE	Lisette Ashton		
THE BLACK WIDOW	Lisette Ashton		
THE BOND	Lindsay Gordon		
BRAT	Penny Birch		
DANCE OF SUBMISSION	Lisette Ashton		
DARK DESIRES	Maria del Rey		
DISCIPLES OF SHAME	Stephanie Calvin		
DISCIPLINE OF THE PRIVATE HOUSE	Esme Ombreux		
DISPLAYS OF EXPERIENCE	Lucy Golden		June
EMMA'S SECRET DOMINATION	Hilary James		
FAIRGROUND ATTRACTIONS	Lisette Ashton		
GISELLE	Jean Aveline		
HEART OF DESIRE	Maria del Rey		
HOUSE RULES	G.C. Scott		
IN FOR A PENNY	Penny Birch		
ONE WEEK IN THE PRIVATE HOUSE	Esme Ombreux		
THE BOND	Nadine Somers		
THE PALACE OF EROS	Delver Maddingley	£4.99	
PLAYTHING	Penny Birch		
THE PLEASURE CHAMBER	Brigitte Markham		
POLICE LADIES	Yolanda Celbridge		
THE RELUCTANT VIRGIN	Kendal Grahame		

RITES OF OBEDIENCE	Lindsay Gordon	
RUE MARQUIS DE SADE	Morgana Baron	
'S' – A JOURNEY INTO SERVITUDE	Philippa Masters	
SANDRA'S NEW SCHOOL	Yolanda Celbridge	
SKIN SLAVE	Yolanda Celbridge	June
THE SLAVE AUCTION	Lisette Ashton	
SLAVE GENESIS	Jennifer Jane Pope	May
SLAVE SENTENCE	Lisette Ashton	
THE SUBMISSION OF STELLA	Yolanda Celbridge	
THE SUBMISSION GALLERY	Lindsay Gordon	
TAKING PAINS TO PLEASE	Arabella Knight	
THE TEST	Nadine Somers	
THE TRAINING OF FALLEN ANGELS	Kendal Grahame	
THE YOUNG WIFE	Stephanie Calvin	May

ANCIENT & FANTASY SETTINGS

THE CASTLE OF MALDONA	Yolanda Celbridge	
NYMPHS OF DIONYSUS	Susan Tinoff	£4.99
MAIDEN	Aishling Morgan	
TIGER, TIGER	Aishling Morgan	
THE WARRIOR QUEEN	Kendal Grahame	

EDWARDIAN, VICTORIAN & OLDER EROTICA

BEATRICE	Anonymous
CONFESSION OF AN ENGLISH SLAVE	Yolanda Celbridge
DEVON CREAM	Aishling Morgan
THE GOVERNESS AT ST AGATHA'S	Yolanda Celbridge
THE RAKE	Aishling Morgan
THE TRAINING OF AN ENGLISH GENTLEMAN	Yolanda Celbridge

SAMPLERS & COLLECTIONS

NEW EROTICA 3	
A DOZEN STROKES	Various

NEXUS CLASSICS

A new imprint dedicated to putting the finest works of erotic fiction back in print

AGONY AUNT	G. C. Scott	
THE HANDMAIDENS	Aran Ashe	
OBSESSION	Maria del Rey	
HIS MASTER'S VOICE	G.C. Scott	
CITADEL OF SERVITUDE	Aran Ashe	
BOUND TO SERVE	Amanda Ware	
BOUND TO SUBMIT	Amanda Ware	
SISTERHOOD OF THE INSTITUTE	Maria del Rey	
A MATTER OF POSSESSION	G.C. Scott	
THE PLEASURE PRINCIPLE	Maria del Rey	
CONDUCT UNBECOMING	Arabella Knight	
CANDY IN CAPTIVITY	Arabella Knight	
THE SLAVE OF LIDIR	Aran Ashe	May
THE DUNGEONS OF LIDIR	Aran Ashe	June

Please send me the books I have ticked above.

Name   ....

Address   ....

               ....

               ....

               .... Post code........................

Send to: **Cash Sales, Nexus Books, Thames Wharf Studios, Rainville Road, London W6 9HT**

US customers: for prices and details of how to order books for delivery by mail, call 1-800-805-1083.

Please enclose a cheque or postal order, made payable to **Nexus Books**, to the value of the books you have ordered plus postage and packing costs as follows:

UK and BFPO – £1.00 for the first book, 50p for the second book and 30p for each subsequent book to a maximum of £3.00;

Overseas (including Republic of Ireland) – £2.00 for the first book, £1.00 for the second book and 50p for each subsequent book.

We accept all major credit cards, including VISA, ACCESS/ MASTERCARD, AMEX, DINERS CLUB, SWITCH, SOLO, and DELTA. Please write your card number and expiry date here:

....

Please allow up to 28 days for delivery.

Signature   ....